DENIAL'S ORPHAN

Warren DeVere Stephens

.

3rd Edition

Published by DeMore

ISBN 978-1-7376770-2-4

CHAPTER 1

INSTITUTION OF HIGHER LEARNING

Rock-n-roll, Brylcreem, bazoombas, poodle skirts, knuckle sandwich, Lay a patch, Peepers, daddy-o, cool, Blackboard Jungle, Aqua Velva, Elvis, butts, motorcycle jacket, Bill Haley and the Comets

October 11, 1955. Another Monday, another school day and high school Junior, sixteen year old Geraldine DeMore, Gerri for short, is walking slowly on Van Ness Street toward the entrance of Fresno Central High School. A car slows, nearly stops beside her and Gerri glances in the direction of the car. The sun obscures the passenger windows but the driver, a man, appears to be staring at her. It startles Gerri and she jerks her head back straight again, clutching her books in crossed arms across her chest as she walks. Why would anyone do that? Some weirdo. The car proceeds past her and pulls into the school parking lot. As the sidewalk crosses the parking lot entrance Gerri looks to see who's in the mysterious car.

Her heart does a flip and a flop!

It's Mr. Penn. It's handsome Mr. Penn. He gets out of his car, reaches in the backseat for his briefcase, turns toward the sidewalk, pauses, looks over the top of his sunglasses and half-waves in Gerri's direction. Gerri can't fathom why he'd wave at her. He's probably not waving at her and it must be her mistake. She feels her face flush as she resists waving back. Mr. Penn is a Prince Charming, in the flesh. He's also a

4

teacher, so he's older and way out of her league. After all, Gerri's dad is also a teacher so it's best to ignore what she may have thought happened. Obviously it was a case of mistaken identity on his part.

It's hard to imagine how a day can change so fast. When Gerri first got up and was preparing to leave for school she couldn't shake the thought that today will be typically boring, particularly until she is in language arts class with the fabulous Mr. Daniel Penn. But he's never paid any attention to her, at all. He's handsome and charming but Mr. Daniel Penn seems aloof, barely familiar in a friendly way with anyone in class. But what may have been a wave earlier is enough of a fantasy sprout to cause a pleasant start, a brighter day and she's motivated to entertain herself by daydreaming.

She's generally comfortable with how she's accepted at school, perhaps a bit self-conscious, a bit cautious around her friends, and always worried about her personal looks. Gerri is five feet- eight inches tall, taller than most of the girls and many of the boys. But she knows from her morning getting-ready-for-school ritual that her body is changing rapidly in all the right places. She may be tall and slender but she's filled out remarkably early in both the front and rear, compliments of her mom's genetics. In both these departments Gerri stands out from her peers and she's aware how her physical curves intimidate many boys into a momentary paralysis and intimidate some of her girlfriends into secret jealousy.

Gerri has long blonde hair that she wears in a ponytail. She has big brown eyes, high cheek bones and a cute nose and they all are accentuated when she practices in the mirror as if making unexpected eye contact, pause for a split second, and then let her nearly perfect white toothed smile captivate the looker.

Since the beginning of high school most girls her age have worn pleated plaid skirts and solid color blouses or sweaters. Last year in

Gerri's school the style changed and the long socks disappeared-that is, if one wants to be cool. Knee-length socks became white bobby socks worn with black and white saddle-oxford shoes. Toward the end of the last school year the rage changed to felt, full-circle skirts with a single image embroidered on the skirt. Most of the designs are of fluffy little poodles but there is the occasional custom skirt with an image of a hot rod. The need to fit in with the crowd is all important so the overwhelming preference is now a poodle design. This school year the poodles' images sometimes have a leash embroidered leading up to the waist line which is covered with an elastic belt nearly six inches wide. Many of the blouses have remained solid colored but with a poodle image on the blouse matching the one on the skirt. Gerri is keeping up with the fashions. At the first of this year she went through the motions and wore one of her two poodle skirts each week but for the last two months she's been on a renewed obsession to go shopping and collect the latest.

So today, Gerri's poodle skirt swishes through the hallway, propelled by her long legs capped on the bottom with bobby socks and saddle oxfords she smiles and takes a deep breath. Today, she feels attractive! Her confidence is bolstered by Mr Penn's wave, accidental or not and also by vivid fantasies involving the parties she's attended lately. At the parties, boys gravitate toward her, seeking attention and the distant hope of pairing-off in a dark corner. Though Gerri's actual experience of cuddly interaction with the opposite sex is limited, it's safe to say the teenage fissionable hormonal material and the awakening fascination about sex is alive and well. Ever since last weekend she feels like her brain is swollen and all she can do to relieve the pressure is to fantasize about the next kisses …and touches. Touching that's getting closer and closer to the main topic of speculation, a few dares and way more fantasies than reality.

Students begin arriving in the classroom for first hour Government and Citizenship class and it begins with a couple of greetings, books

6.

dumped on desks, the overwhelming mix of Coty Accomplice perfume on the young ladies and a hearty lathering in Old Spice after shave with a dab of Brylcreem on many of the boys. As the student voices gather, each trying to be heard over the other, the crescendo of noise builds and the room quickly becomes a bedlam of sound trying to stuff in every comment possible before the bell brings it all to silence. This scene is repeated six times a day and is fueled by the participants hormones jumping about like water molecules in a boiling tea kettle. The bell sounds for the class to begin and a few students look sleep deprived but for most the entire reason for being at school is to have fun and it may as well begin right now!

Gerri's doodles are harmless enough, horses, nurses, women in long gowns, a soldier, and she repetitiously letters "DP". She's still enjoying the early morning thrill of the remote possibility that Mr. Penn may have actually noticed her and maybe, just maybe he even waved to her. At least Gerri would like to think he waved at her but she explores more likely reality that he was waving to someone else or maybe it wasn't even a wave at all. But for sure next year she's going to try to get into his class once again, maybe earlier in the day so she can be reminded of his handsome face for the rest of each day instead of this year where she sees him last hour and that provides no daydream fodder for the beginning of the day.

But at the moment Gerri's daring and entertainment skills are the center of attention for a dozen or so students around her.

"Go ahead…now. Now." Phyllis Mckenzie's whispering to Gerri, and Phyllis' eyes are locked on the teacher, Miss Henderson, at the blackboard, her back to the class as she outlines a stimulating flowchart of the legislative process.

Gerri moves her hand cautiously forward, holding a cough drop between her thumb and index finger. Her target is in the desk right in front of her, the hunched over frame of Billy Boyd, greatly overweight and at the moment head down on his arms catching some needed rest. With his body leaning forward, arms on the desk, Levi's stressed downward, he's exposing a fine specimen of "plumbers' butt". With giggling anticipation of students around her and with her skill and precision Gerri drops the cough drop down the dark crevice where it falls somewhere into parts of Billy that are unknown except to him.

Billy jerks his head up in surprise and quickly realizes he's the brunt of a practical joke. He looks around at Gerri who shrugs her shoulders as if she is clueless as to why he'd look her way. Many around him are laughing and whispering and all the while Miss Henderson continues writing on the blackboard, lost in her own world of what she thinks is teaching. Students continue to snicker and Miss Henderson turns to find Gerri holding her index finger to her lips as if to shush those laughing around her.

Miss Henderson pushes her glasses to the tip of her nose, "Geraldine, what are you doing?"

"Nothing Miss Hennnn-derson."

The class erupts in laughter because the teacher's nickname is "Old Hen" so Gerri is obviously trying to entertain.

"All right then, class! You'd rather listen to the rude antics of Geraldine so why don't we do this for more entertainment? Turn your text to page one-hundred twenty-four and take a look. There are ten essay review questions. That's your assignment. You write a minimum of one-hundred words for any three of the questions by class time tomorrow. If your homework is incomplete or unacceptable you will get a big fat "F". "

Groans and moans around the class.

"You can start working on it right now for the rest of the fifteen minutes or so of this period. You didn't want to listen to me today anyhow so good luck with the assignment and after class why don't you all thank each other for this assignment and particularly Geraldine. Now you can get to work."

Miss Henderson sits down at her desk and smiles a satirical smile in Gerri's direction.

Later leaving class, "Heck, Gerri it was worth it. I think Billy even woke up. Want to bet what Billy's looking for right now?"

"Yeah, there's probably a whole load of buried treasure in those big drawers of his."

Another chimes in, "Or a load of something. I don't think treasure."

Everybody continues laughing as they exit the classroom. None of the students apparently take Miss Henderson's attempt at maintaining discipline seriously.

"Gutsy, Gerri, real gutsy!" sounds off one enabler.

Gerri smirks and responds, "Who cares? Whooo cares?"

Phyllis laughs, "Gerri, why do you say things like that? You make yourself out to be a hopeless rebel. You never used to do anything to risk being in trouble and I think most teachers are shocked with some of your actions lately. You've always been Miss Goody-Goody-Two-Shoes."

"Ya know Phyllis. It's sort of strange. I used to worry about getting in trouble in class but I don't anymore. I guess I used to worry about what my mom or dad would say but lately I just really, really don't care."

"Yeah, but I bet I know what you do care about. How about Ronny Owens? Huh? Huh? Yeah, Just the mention and you ought to see your face. All flustered. Him you care about."

"So? He's cute. That's all."

"C'mon, Gerri. Can't fool me. You guys looked like a couple of octopuses in heat last weekend at Julie's. And the slurping. Licky-face."

"We did? So what? And I'm surprised you'd have noticed. And so tell me where Rich had his hands on you, little innocent Phyllis? Did Rich get to the promised land? Huh, Phyl?"

"Shoot. There's the warning bell but listen, I heard a bunch of kids are gonna get together at the drive-in or out at Riverside Park this weekend so get ready, get set…woo hoo."

" I don't know...mmm...have to see about that. Gotta go. See you, Phyl."

"Yep. See ya, Gerri."

Gerri passes a couple of friends but no one going her direction so she hurries down the hallway. As she reaches the last intersection of hallways before her next class she comes face-to-face with Mr. Penn. He looks as though he's surprised but he looks directly at her and smiles. "Hi, Gerri. I have next hour off so I'll walk a ways with you. By the way, I hope I didn't startle you when I waved at you walking to school this morning."

"Oh no. I wasn't really thinking while I was walking and I didn't recognize the car."

"Oh, well that's good then. Wouldn't want to have frightened you…Oops, gotta go this way so I guess here's where I leave you.
10

Hope your day is a good one and I'll see you later today in class, Gerri. Okay?"

"Sure."

Gerri is shocked. He knows who she is. The entire thing was no mistake. He even called her by name. In class he always refers to his roster to even recognize students, even Gerri. Gerri is floating the rest of the way to her class.

This is so different than most days at school. She suddenly feels strangely motivated. Just a little nice comment by a nice, handsome teacher and she really feels a thousand percent better. Why can't her own father be more like Mr. Penn?

Gerri hurries away from her locker and down the hall toward her least favorite class, third hour History.

"Hi Gerri."

Gerri snaps out of her thoughts and sees Betsy Alder probably the most popular girl in the entire school.

"Hi ya, Betsy."

"Hey Gerri, I've got something for you but I left it in my locker. I'll see if I can get it now without being late. If not I'll see ya later or even after school."

"Sure, Betsy. See ya."

Minutes later Gerri is settling into her desk staring at the ceiling in anti-academic preparation to suffer through another hour of history.

Plop!

Just as the final bell rings for third hour an envelope lands on Gerri's desk and her head and shoulders jerk from the sudden surprise. Her eyes are wide and body upright. A few of her classmates turn in their seats to see what happened and Gerri can feel her face blushing. It's partly from the surprise of the envelope hitting her desk and also from the embarrassment of being caught daydreaming waiting for class to begin.

"Betsy, I…"

"Shhh. Quick, Gerrie, stick it under a book and read it later. Don't let "Moldy" see it."

What in the world? She quickly sticks the envelope among pages inside her history book and strikes a pose as if she's being ever so attentive and ready for class. What's in the envelope? Gerri can't wait until class is over to see. Besides, Miss Morris' history class is so boring and that's earned her the nickname of "Moldy" Morris. She's another of Gerri's high school old maid teachers and Moldy dresses like a convent refugee. Gerri's not sure what really happens in a convent but whatever it is Miss Moldy Morris would likely fit right in.

The class is assigned to read a chapter nearly every night but it doesn't matter. Miss Morris starts the class with a mini-lecture of what is in the assigned reading and writes an outline on the blackboard as she lectures. So, even though boring, this class requires little participation. Just sit and try not to go to sleep or worse, get caught looking like you're not paying attention. Gerri watches for an opportunity to open the envelope as she tries to imagine the contents. Finally, "Moldy Morris" predictably turns her back to the class, writing on the blackboard and droning on and on about the War of 1812. This is Gerri's chance. She nonchalantly opens her textbook, never taking her eyes off the teacher. She blindly feels for the envelope, finds the edge, pinches it and carefully, slowly tears it open, withdrawing the card while looking straight ahead, fearful of being seen. She sneaks a glance at it. "To: Gerri DeMore".

It's a party this Friday night. And this will be a *really* cool party! Gerri's heard of Betsy's parties but never been invited to one. Now here's her chance. All the coolest girls and guys go to Betsy's parties. The stories of what's happened at some of Betsy's parties make Gerri's head spin with excitement. And Gerri's invited! Her eyes are glued to the invitation and she's drifting a million miles from the class. Growing up in high school is so strange. Gerri's gone to school with many of these kids since the beginning grades but nobody's a little kid anymore. Some are uncharacteristically fun and charming. Others can't seem to get the hang of being cool and fall prey to the ultimate fear of every teenager, where self-esteem can be shredded and the pieces cast into the hallways' shadows of a private hell.

But this is exciting! This could mean that Betsy Alder, who just happens to be the most popular girl in the whole school, wants to be friends with Gerri. Gerri's never been in Betsy's clique of friends or any clique of friends for that matter but now maybe that's all about to change. Gerri tries to imagine who may be at Betsy's party and that throws her fantasy meter into overdrive. What may happen during the party? Dance? Make out? What if somebody really cool wants her to go out to one of the parked cars? Will someone want her to go all the way? What if she really likes a boy but he doesn't think she's cute? What if it's one of the basketball players? They'll probably all be ...

"Geraldine? Geraldine? What *are* you doing? Are you paying attention? Did you even hear my question?"

Wow. Moldy looks irritated and Gerri hopes she didn't see the card.

"Yes, Ma'am, Miss Morris. I'm paying attention. I just don't quite understand the question. Would you repeat it please?"

13

"Yes. Now *everybody.* Eyes up here. Now, please listen...what do you believe was the reason..."

Gerri can barely concentrate. She's still reeling from the surprise of the party invitation and how much fun this party will be. Gerri is trying to picture what can happen after a few Cokes, everybody's dancing and then who might pair with her for the rest of the evening. Gerri's never been in Betsy's house but she's sure lights get less and less until there are discreet corners and places for some serious smooching. Gerri likes the kissing and for sure some guys are better than others. There are still some minor inefficiencies that hopefully will work out with more practice. The awkward moments when approaching the kiss and both tilt the same way a couple of times or clunking of front teeth or a pair of glasses knocked sideways or all of those in one futile attempt to be cool and romantic. But the actual kissing gets better as techniques are discussed and giggled about in the hallway, making terms like French-kissing, deep, open-lips, trading gum and swapping spit the language du jour. And though Gerri has heard warnings in health classes about petting, she can't imagine based on her experience how it can be anything but exciting fun. Girls now talk about "going all the way" and "doing it" or "coming close" more openly and they speculate constantly about what boys talk about after parties.

At lunch Gerri spots a table with at least a couple of familiar faces.

"Over here, Gerri. Got a spot for you."

"Thanks, Barb. Whew. What a day. Sooo boring. Last hour I made a list of all the guys in school...well all of them are juniors and seniors, who might have a chance at being cool in this lifetime. Small list."

Everybody laughs. "So what qualifies somebody to be on the list? Looks, being smart?"

14

"Let's face it. Good looking has to be the top of the list. I mean can you imagine making out with some guy and you open your eyes and see somebody who looks like Frankenstein?"

"Yeah or like Frankenstein with zits. Like Paul Hopper? Don told me the other day Paul looks like his face caught on fire and somebody put it out with an icepick."

"Oh God. Cruel! But I heard somebody the other day refer to him as crater face. Ughh."

Gerri looks up from her lunch, "Yeah, cruel but true. Can you imagine? Oooo-ie!"

"So who's on your list Gerri?"

"Right. Like I'm gonna tell you so you can try to take them all away before I even have a chance."

"I'll bet Ronny is at the top, Eric Stanton, Mike Decker…"

"I'm not sayin."

"Sandy Sadler leans in to the table group, "But it's all guys you'd do it with if you had the chance. Right?"

Gerri brings a small explosion of laughter, "Absolutely. But not all of them at the same time. I'm not even sure that's possible. Well, let me think about that…maybe anything's possible."

"God. Gerri that's hilarious. Just imagine."

"No thanks. Best just leave it right there."

Gerri loves being center stage even though it's often such different groups of acquaintances. . "Well, I'm only half-kidding. I know next year is Senior year and then out of school. High school is the best chance any of us will ever have to find the guy who may be Prince Charming. Don't have to get

15

married right away but if you don't go to college where are you gonna meet guys after high school? So, boring days at school give time to make the shopping list for the future."

Janet Baker, usually very quiet and absorbent offers her opinion, "Ya know what, Gerri. That makes more sense than you can imagine. I'm not planning to go to college and that's exactly the way I look at my future. It's like it's in high gear right now to do something or suffer the consequences . If I can find someone this year or next that will be good. And if not, well I'm just not going to let that happen because I will find somebody. I'm not gonna be an old maid like the "Old Hen"."

Their attention shifts toward a disturbance in the lunchroom. A couple of boys surrounded by a growing crowd around them signal a likely fight. There's as much pushing and shoving in the crowd of spectators competing for a good spot to watch the action as there is by the participants.

With enough crowd goading, "Fight! Fight! C'mon!" the fists fly and the crowd oohs and ahhs it's gladiatorial approval particularly when a table gets knocked askew with trays and plates flying.

"Let's go see who it is!" Gerri jumps up from the table followed by the others. It's a mob scene as students are straining to see the action while others in the crowd are turned in the opposite direction, laughing and talking loudly about anything and everything. Fights are a fairly common occurrence as the teen aged bandy roosters test their metal over trivial matters of pride, offhand remarks and of course puppy love. A small brigade of teachers quickly arrive and break it up and the centers of attention are taken away in less gladiatorial pomp, heads bowed, little more physical damage than hair messed up and crestfallen pride. Disproportionate justice will surely follow. But they go along peacefully and without further incident.

"Who was it anyhow?"

Gerri shrugs, "Have no idea." She returns to her table and the others follow.

"I'm pretty tall and all I could see was the crowd until Mr Betts got in there. It looked like Sonny O'Day and I couldn't see who else."

16

"Oh, too bad, Gerri. Sonny may be out of school for a few days and surely Sonny O'Day is high on your list of eligibles?"

"Gad no! I'm sure you're kidding. He's not real bright or good looking so there's my gift to you all for today. Go after that Sonny. On second thought here's a second gift from Gerri… strike him off everybody's list."

And so the days go on and on as social skills are caught between fantasies of self-centered primping and others who struggle just to function from day to day. The teens are rough years and not very compassionate around the periphery.

CHAPTER 2

SOCIAL GRACES

After lunch as Gerri settles in for her fourth hour World Geography class, awaiting the bell, one of her classmates, Mike Decker, locks his gaze on Gerri, makes a deliberate turn and walks directly toward her. Mike walks in awkward, jerky movements, weaving in and out as he picks his way toward her through students talking before class begins. Gerri looks up into Mike's smiling, pimply face and at first she looks surprised and then gives him her big, delayed smile and obviously immobilizes him. Why has he planted himself right in front of her almost like he's standing at military attention with his mouth agape as if he's forgotten what he wanted to say? He looks nervous and his lip is quivering. He bends slightly down and forward toward Gerri and in a hushed voice, "Gerri, I was hoping to see you earlier today but haven't had a chance."

"Yeah, I've just been hurrying from class to class. You okay, Mike?" Gerri giggles at his paralytic shyness but is puzzled by why he's presented himself in such a fashion.

"Yeah. I'm doing okay…well, Gerri…I've got to hurry before the bell but I was wondering…if you don't …haven't had anyone…well, I was wondering if you'd go to the sock hop with me next week."

Gerri is stunned. She certainly wasn't expecting this.   She's gone to school with Mike since first grade but he's no longer the little boy he used to be. Just within the last year he's gotten tall, now probably six - two or three and he's one of the star players on the varsity basketball team.   Everybody likes Mike but he remains shy and nondescript except for his pimples and playing basketball. She knows she has to say something, "Uh, well, Mike, I'm just surprised. I wasn't expecting you to ask. I'll see if I can go. Okay? I'll have to tell you later. Okay?"

"Sure. That's fine, Gerri. I just thought…well, ya know…it should be fun. I was hoping no one had asked you yet and all. But let me know. Okay?"

More potential awkwardness is saved by the bell and Gerri blurts out, "Oops. The bell, Mike. Talk to ya later."

Gerri has no idea what she should have or could have said next. She watches Mike with his back toward her as he goes to his desk across the room. His clothes are not attractive, plaid shirt that looks a little small for him, shirt tail out on one side, blue jeans with the cuffs rolled up and black tennis shoes. Mike has a regular haircut that he parts and combs over and his hair shines like its carrying a fair share of hair cream. Gerri can't help herself to think of Mike any other way except the way he's always been to her. He's a friend. He's just a bashful friend. Now he's a tall, bashful friend. Mike is very plain.

Gerri feels a conflicted excitement. On one hand she's excited that she's invited to something, anything, by a boy. She's been invited to parties but always by the person having the party and all the parties she's attended have been given by girls. She's never been specifically

19

asked to any high school dance or event by a boy. This would be like a real date. But on the other hand it's not exciting that her very first real date would be with Mike Decker? That seems less and less appealing with every second that ticks past and though Gerri has no brother, if she did he'd likely be a Mike. Gerri tries to recall what she told Mike. She didn't really say yes or no...did she? Gerri can't recall her exact words and she's already looking for an escape hatch.

Then she recalls her words," I'll see if I can go."

Gerri quietly groans. " Please, God, help me get outta this. Please."

She'd love to go to the sock hop but not with Mike. Not that he isn't a boy and he's even popular at school because he plays basketball but the more she stares at Mike's hunched over posture in his desk the more Gerri is sure she doesn't want to go anywhere with Mike Decker. He'd probably wear what he's wearing today. He's a really nice guy, always has been, but since he grew up so tall, so quickly, his clothes always look too small for him and he's awkward. Mike's okay as a friend, even a brother but she is not attracted to him at all. Mike's definitely not a Prince Charming candidate.

Gerri takes a deep breath and seizes on her plan for Mike. She'll wait until tomorrow and then simply tell him she can't go to the sock hop. That way there won't be any misunderstanding and he can ask somebody else if he wants. Gerri shakes her head in disbelief. She can't imagine Mike dancing with anyone.

Gerri feels confident in her strategy to stop Mike's invitation but as she thinks through the consequences she has an "oops that won't work" moment. What if she says she can't go and then someone really cool asks her at Betsy's party? Or worse, what if Mike tells some of the other guys that he'd asked Gerri and she can't go. Then she'll get no other invitations. First they would all assume she can't go, so why ask? Second, and worse, the other guys may assume Gerri would have gone with Mike if she could so now she's sort of Mike's girl.

Gerri knows this won't be as simple as she originally thought. She's got to think of a better plan. Gerri settles into her seat as if she's listening to Mr. Betts about geography but she's actually engrossed in figuring out a plan to get out of Mike's invitation.

As Gerri gets to the last class of the day, Mr. Penn's language Arts Class, she is reeling from the day's excitement and now she'll be able to finish the day with the gorgeous Mr. Penn. When the bell rings for class to be over, Mr. Penn walks toward the door and happens to precede Gerri as she approaches, "Gerri, I wonder if I could have a word with you. Won't take but a minute or two. Can you?"

"Sure, Mr. Penn." Gerri walks to the front of the room and puts her books on one of the front desks, waiting impatiently near the front of Mr. Penn's desk. She straightens her skirt and checks that her blouse is tucked in properly. She glances at her blurry image in an outside window reflection and that's about the best she can do in the few seconds before he finally bids goodbye to the students and returns to his desk.

"Well, Gerri. You're looking happy today."

"Yeah. I'm doing okay."

"Listen Gerri, I know you don't have much time and you've just been in my class for the last hour but I'd like to have a quick word and ask a favor. It's no problem. So don't be alarmed or worried. Just a favor I'm hoping you can do. Okay?"

"Sure. If I can."

What could he want? Why his sudden friendliness? She wonders if it has anything to do with her dad also being a teacher. Maybe her dad asked Mr. Penn to be nice and keep an eye on her. That could be it. Maybe her dad isn't sure if he can trust Gerri any longer and he won't take the time to find out for himself so he asks others, like Mr. Penn, to occupy her time.

Mr. Penn smiles and silently motions for her to sit at one of the desks up front. As he takes a seat in a desk across from her she can't help but think how different this is than sitting across from any of the other teachers. Mr. Penn is totally different. This is deliciously enjoyable…dreamy! As Gerri looks at him she thinks with a little imagination he really doesn't seem that much older than any of her classmates, but yet he's a grown man. Is he ever! She loves his sheepish, innocent grin, almost like a little boy who's done something naughty. He looks directly at her when he talks and she can see his big blue eyes make contact with hers even at a distance. That impish grin is so handsome when it breaks into a big toothy smile. And he has the most beautiful sandy, brown hair combed back on the sides a little like some of the really popular movie stars. He's a little taller than her dad and a lot thinner. He's just plain handsome. He dresses different than the school principal, Mr. Landers, or the rest of the men teachers. He wears a tie every day but it's never knotted tight on his neck and never a perfect knot. Gerri ought to know about the details of how he dresses. She's studied every inch of him, head to toe. She's never noticed much about his shoes but she can't recall him ever wearing any shoes except penny loafers. He can dress a little casual or even wrinkled and it looks really, really cool. He's dreamy and just talking to him puts her on cloud nine.

"Gerri, first I want to be sure you are perfectly at ease with this conversation. I hope I didn't frighten you or lead you to think there is anything wrong. I simply need a favor. Also, let me compliment you on being a fine student and a mature, attractive young lady. I often

22

think I know students a little better by just casually observing their friends. But I must confess you have me stumped in that area. Of course I don't wish to imply that I spy on students. That's not it at all. I simply see lots of students on a daily basis and my mental picture of them as individuals usually includes images of their best and closest friends, usually groups of friends. Again, you've got me stumped."

"Oh, I know lots of kids in fact I probably know most everybody. I've gone to school with lots of these kids ever since first grade but I wouldn't say I'm close friends with many of them, like a group or anything. Ya know…not really what you'd call close."

"N- no, let me finish. I didn't mean to even suggest it's any sort of problem. It's just that at this stage of your life you want to choose your friends carefully and of course everyone, kids, teens, twenties, thirties and even old folks all need good solid friends. When I mentioned you to a couple of other teachers also didn't seem to know any group of schoolmates with whom you consistently hang around…not that you don't have friends …it's just that the teachers to whom I spoke aren't sure all those friends are the very best influence. I'm concerned that as a bright, smart young lady in this stage of your life, growing up into the attractive young woman you're becoming…well I must correct myself. I need to say the attractive young woman you are, I imagine at times it may be difficult to know all the right choices to make. And in many cases, right or wrong it's our friends where we get advice and ideas. Make sense?"

"Well, I guess so. There are always choices and decisions. Choices and decisions at home. Choices and decisions at school."

"That's very, very true. And some of the friends we pick today and some of the choices we make today can stay with us for a long time to come. Sometimes that's for the good and sometimes not so good. Choices equal results and consequences."

Mr. Penn looks piercingly into Gerri's eyes, "And I just want to talk with you today to let you know that I have taken notice of you and a professional interest in you and without being too nosy I've reviewed your school records and sort of observed from afar. Now here's my offer. If you want, and only if you want, I'd like to apply for the job to be… to be a very good friend to you, call it a coach…or mentor. That's a little unusual for me to be saying this. I mean me, a male-teacher and you, a female-student but I just know you have such great potential as a student, unusual maturity as a young woman and I want to make myself available for you to call upon for any advice, friendship or in fact, anything at all. I just wonder if you'd like that."

Finally! Gerri's hearing the first words of support for **Gerri**. She can't believe Mr. Penn is saying this. She barely knows him and that's only as a teacher at her school. She knows her face must be red as a beet from blushing. Her heart is pounding and her breathing is shallow and quick. She stutters her response, "We -w -w -well, Mr. Penn, I have you for sixth hour but I can't imagine that you know me very well…but you're right about my friends. I know a lot of kids and I suppose some aren't the best for really caring for important stuff. And some people I know aren't considered good kids all the time."

"Well, it doesn't require much to begin a friendship. Mostly just get to know one another a bit better. That's why I was wondering if you'd do me a favor. Now before I tell you, this is strictly a favor so if you don't have the time or if you simply don't want to do it just say so and no harm done. Okay?"

"Sure. What is it?"

"I am stuck here sometimes later than I want to be, mostly grading papers and I was wondering if you'd help me wrap things up each day. If you want, after sixth hour you could take a little break and then just come back in my room to help me for maybe thirty minutes or so. Maybe grade a few papers and that sort of thing. What do you think?"

"Gee whiz! Of course. I can do that? I mean help you?"

"Yes ma'am, It would be a big help and at the same time we can get to know each other better. So is that a yes?"

"Oh yes, Mr. Penn. Thank you so much. It will be a pleasure."

"I'm not sure it's possible to know what another person is always going through. And I'm just saying I will try very, very hard to be a good friend to you and anytime you ever feel like talking you can come in here and we can talk. That a deal?"

Gerri is nodding her head vigorously, "Oh yes. Thank you."

"Okay, I'll let Mr. Landers know and then I'll let you know if it's all set by tomorrow. I'll have a note brought to you or I'll let you know one way or the other tomorrow."

Gerri suddenly feels like a weight is lifted from her and she's about to levitate above the desk where she's sitting.

"Okay, then maybe we'll get together again as early as tomorrow…well you know, I'll see you in the sixth hour but I won't ask you to do anything to help until after school until it's all okayed on the up-and-up. "

"Mr. Penn laughs and is obviously delighted that Gerri wants to do this and that she is even a little bashful around him. They both get up and Mr. Penn walks ahead of Gerri and opens the door for her.

"Good night."

"Yes. Goodnight, Mr. Penn."

CHAPTER 3

HOME AGAIN, HOME AGAIN

After leaving Mr. Penn's room Gerri takes a long deep breath. School is really over for the day and it's been a good day for Gerri. A boring day in class but a good day to socialize, daydream and fantasize. Gerri's walking home as usual and she's thinking that with every day that passes going to school may be boring but it's a lot more fun than spending time at home. It hasn't always been that way but since being in high school her mother and father hardly notice her.

She laughs a little as she thinks her parents will never ask but at the moment Gerri would be hard pressed to tell them, or anyone, anything about any part of today's studies. Her mind is a jumble of faces, profiles, lips, hips in Levis, tee shirts with rolled up sleeves and hair slicked back on the sides in ducktails. Occasionally there are guys who wear slacks, white buck shoes and pastel-colored button down shirts. Everything's changing so fast and it's cool just being at school. She laughs again, "But nobody cares."

Gerri's not breaking any speed records but the time and distance pass quickly. She crosses to the other side of Van Ness Street, rounds the corner onto Vassar Avenue and slowly walks the last block toward home. There's little reason to overthink the view of her street and her house because to Gerri her home simply looks like everybody else's. In 1955, Fresno, California. Most kids' parents would describe these as good times. The Second World War, the Korean War and the Russian cold war threats are occasionally mentioned by adults but seldom is there remote interest in world events by kids in high school because frankly the kids have more important things about which to worry. The houses in this neighborhood are almost all single story with plaster exteriors, driveways consisting of two cement strips on the side of houses and in the front a couple of steps that lead to concrete porches and front doors. Most are light brown or a beige color and they were post-war homes so the trees and shrubs are beginning to fill in to make the neighborhood look a bit more established.

Gerri's street, Vassar, is a little unusual because there are houses built only on one side of the street and the other side is yet to be developed. So it makes a nice view out the front to see a wooded area instead of just more cookie-cutter houses. The woods has been a place where neighborhood kids have played hide-and-seek but as most of the neighborhood kids grow older the woods sits idle except for amorous adventurers after the sun goes down.

The DeMore family car, a black Chevrolet four-door sedan, is in the driveway and that means her dad is home. This is becoming more and more unusual because her dad, Stephen, finds reason after reason to come home later each day. When her dad comes home late it rankles Gerri's mom, Susie, more than Gerri. Her dad is a math teacher at Calway High School while Gerri attends Fresno Central High School. Gerri's mom is very, very pregnant and her dad says he'd prefer to come home earlier but feels it more important to get papers graded and next day preparations complete before coming home.

Gerri goes up the three concrete steps to the small front porch and she notices nothing unusual that the screen door is closed but it is a little strange that the front door is wide open. As she reaches for the screen door she hears voices so she pauses, leans with her ear near the door and listens.

"Stephen, on top of never being home you've become secretive and downright sneaky and I don't like it. Even when you are home you act like you really would rather be anyplace other than here with Gerri and me. I'm sure you find me unattractive in my current state and you would not have been home today until hours from now if I hadn't called and pleaded for you to come help me."

"Look Susie, I've told you a hundred times, I'll come home anytime you need me. No need to worry. Just don't cry wolf too often. Lucky I was able to get here as quickly as I did. Bill Ellington was on break so he took my class. That should at least make you feel better that I can react when necessary."

"You'll come home when I need you? You think I was crying wolf? I had unusual and very severe pains. I'm so relieved they stopped and

28

I'm sorry you think I did this just to see if you'd come home. You so much as admit you really don't feel any desire to be here, just show up if needed. And I suppose now that you've dutifully come home when beckoned and found I'm not dying, you'll hurry back to your wonderful school as quickly as you can?"

"Yep. Sure. You bet. Whatever you say. I'm not going to stand here and argue with you, Susie. You called before classes were even over and I dropped everything and came home. I guess I passed that part of your test. Now, class is over but I left everything in a jumble so I've got to take care of some things before tomorrow. Sooo, yes. I'm going back to school now and I'll see you later. Trying to do my job and being grilled by you is not the prescription for putting me in a great mood."

"See ya later. See ya later. I'm not amused by your attitude. What's the use? You don't care about anything except getting back to your precious school and whatever or *whoever* is more important than your family. But nothing too different about that drama is there? Nothing too different at all. Starts with a lack of interest at home, then the sneaking about, all make up a familiar result- cheating."

Gerri's mom uses a tone of voice that doesn't conceal her anger. There have been lots of little arguments over the past few months but they seem angrier on the part of her mom and sarcastically condescending on the part of her dad. With every successive argument Gerri solidifies in her mind that her future is tied less and less to her disintegrating family. It depresses her to think that probably every other kid she knows doesn't go through anything like this and that makes her even more resentful. Oh sure, kids talk about their problems at school but Gerri's sure she's the only one feeling like she's invisible in her own family.

Gone are the days when all three of them would spend the evenings and weekends enjoying the time together. Gerri wonders how much her mom's pregnancy causes her to be more edgy than usual or perhaps her dad's worry makes him edgy on the rare occasions when he's home. But in the general scheme of things Gerri sides more with her mom on most issues. So the result of overhearing her mom and dad argue causes her to bristle. The atmosphere is certainly not civil so she's feeling downright rebellious and she'd like to take a verbal shot at her dad as well.

She can hear her dad coming toward the door so she makes a little extra noise as she pulls open the screen door and enters the house. Her dad is near the door as she enters.

Stephen DeMore is a thirty-eight year old, very distinguished looking high school mathematics teacher. His dark, wavy hair is always combed straight back with seldom a hair out of place. It compliments his pleasant, handsome face and sort of big nose that her mom jokingly refers to as a royal, aquiline nose. He's an inch or so taller than her mother and the results of good food and comfort are beginning to show in his mid-section. Her dad's one of those dedicated individuals, born to be a teacher. He has the patience of a saint with his students and no matter what problems come his way, he ignores them and laughs them away. He looks a little bit straight-laced in his usual Stephen-uniform of a starched, white shirt and solid-colored tie every day. As far back as Gerri can remember her dad seemed so comfortable in his clothes that often at home he remained dressed in his white shirt and tie until bedtime.. His clothes, at school and at home, never look even slightly wrinkled and that has historically been thanks to her mom but that's all changed recently. Pregnancy and bed rest prevent her mom from doing all the usual chores around the house like cooking, cleaning, laundry and ironing. Lately by the time Stephen comes home he looks like his shirts have passed their useful wear-life by a couple of days. His usually never-out-of-place hair looks like it's tousled. Gerri knows her mom's condition is adding a stressful toll on all of them.

Even though Gerri's dad teaches at a high school different than she attends she's heard that at his high school, students want into her dad's classes because of his reputation as the easiest math teacher and he's always so happy-go-lucky with the students. Gerri thinks she wouldn't describe him as happy-go-lucky at home but then she doesn't spend that much time with him and usually he barely has more than a couple words to say and it's as if he feels obligated and strained to even say that much.

Her dad's reputation also extends to parents of Calway High students. They love Stephen as a math teacher because he would have them believe that their son or daughter is a gifted math student and he never says anything negative about any of their children. It's as if all his students do well all the time. Gerri believes that's an academic impossibility and she's not run across other teachers that likely accept Stephen's conclusions particularly at her high school.

"Good day at school, Gerri?"

"Good day at school? Well, hello and good to see you too, Dad. School, school, school. There's more to life than school…for me anyhow. There. I guess that will be the extent of our father-daughter conversation for the day so I should feel lucky. And even more lucky because you tried to ask me two questions. Question one, a good day? Yeah, it was alright. Second question, good day at school? Yeah, it was enjoyable because of my friends and talking to them and stuff like that. No other reason. I suppose after my hard day at school I should enjoy being at home with my family but there's not much going on in our home except for Mom and me. You're not really here even when you're here…but even that's seldom. So, home for a bit today and then whoosh, off again, huh? Let's see. Where are ya going, Dad? Let me guess. Back to *school*? Wow. Lucky guess on my part? Oh well, you better hurry so ya don't miss something much more exciting than here. "

Stephen shows his displeasure with a lingering frown, "Geez! You must have been waiting to offload all that for a while. And thank you for being a loving daughter. Hmmm. You're turning into quite the smarty-pants, huh? Why is it so difficult to get a civil response from you? Your demeanor and respect are in a nose-dive and that's not good. You'd best get control of that attitude of yours."

Gerri smirks and shrugs her shoulders to show she is not concerned with his assessment.

Stephen continues, "Well, I *am* on my way out so pay attention to your mom until I get home. I thought she was bound for the hospital this afternoon- lots of pain. She thought it was labor pains but whatever caused her scare seems to have passed. Anyhow, just keep an eye on her and help her any way you can. And if she has more of the severe pains you can call me on the number of the school hallway payphone. I left the number by our phone and if you have to call just let it ring. It takes me time to hear it, get out in the hall and answer it. Okay?"

"Sure, Dad. You totter off to school now and don't you worry about a thing which I'm sure you won't. You work real hard during your evening at school and Mom and I will be here doing whatever it is we're supposed to be doing."

Gerri rolls her eyes up in boring disgust but her dad doesn't seem to pay much attention other than to sarcastically toss it back to Gerri.

"Oh thanks again. Now I have two of you razzin me when all I'm trying to do is my job. Your mom's condition is worry enough so I can do without your sassy attitude. "

With that Stephen shakes his head in disgust and skips down the front steps where he climbs into the car. A couple of labored growls, a couple of mechanical grunts, a belch of black smoke and soon the big black Chevy is lumbering its way into the street, the exhaust black smoke cloud slowly dissipating to once again expose the driveway.

Gerri returns inside and after settling into her after-school routine she fixes her mom a toasted cheese sandwich and glass of milk. Gerri joins her mom in the bedroom for the same bill of fare and some promised time together but Gerri's mom is very tired and she dozes in and out of sleep. Gerri can't help but stare at her mom as she sleeps and think how different and helpless she looks lying there. That's not the mom, Susie DeMore that Gerri used to know.

Growing up in the very rural Ozarks of Missouri, Susie DeMore's acclaim as a striking beauty was never confined by rural boundaries. During her teen years she was consistently proclaimed queen of virtually every school event, county fair, regional celebration or holiday parade far and wide. Susie is five-eight flat-footed with long flowing strawberry blond hair, big brown eyes, beautiful facial features and a natural skin tint that appears to be a perpetual, exotic suntan. Susie could always be expected in short shorts or pedal pusher pants that accentuate her long shapely legs and phenomenal curves of femininity. She's always turned heads whether at the market, at a school function or working in the yard.

In the early stages of her pregnancy she still looked terrific but the last several weeks brought some unspecified but physically stressful challenges and as a result she's on bed rest. She looks gaunt and tired, face drawn and wrinkles from the corners of her mouth. Gerri imagines she'll bounce back to her old self after the baby is born. But for now she looks at her mom and misses that old look and fun personality of a few very short years ago.

Gerri picks up the bed tray with the plates and glasses and starts out of the bedroom to return the tray to the kitchen. She expects to go to her room and at least look through her assigned homework but Susie opens her eyes, "Sorry, Gerri. I must have fallen asleep. I keep falling asleep and for the life of me I can't tell if I've been asleep for ten seconds , ten minutes or an hour. Very strange. Your father isn't home yet is he?"

"Nope. You sort of lost a couple minutes but that's all. But no, he's not home yet and probably won't be for a while. Getting to be a habit with him. He's the only teacher I know who stays at school until eight or nine o'clock at night. Maybe he's not as smart as I always thought and that's why it takes him longer than other teachers. Maybe he's a math teacher who forgot how to do math. What else could take so much time to grade high school papers? He spends more time grading stuff than the kids spend taking his tests. And, I guarantee the kids in his math classes don't care whether their papers are graded or not. They know he's going to give them all good grades anyhow. What a pushover!"

"Now Gerri, that's not nice to say and it shouldn't be your concern how much time your dad is at home. That's my department and I actually tried to talk to him today before you got home and surprise, surprise, that got me nowhere. I still have a few words left for him, so promise me that if I happen to be asleep when he comes home tonight you'll wake me. I want to finish our little talk. Or at least try."

"Sure, Mom. Gonna give him the old business, huh?" Gerri laughs and thinks it is sort of funny that she and her mom seem to be on the same side- at least for this evening. Get Dad- Stephen.

"Never you mind, Gerri. Just wake me please."

"Sure." Gerri takes the trays with the dishes back into the kitchen, runs some warm water in the sink and washes the plates and glasses she and her mom used. Gerri smiles a devilish smile when she thinks of her dad coming home later. He'll expect something to eat all ready and waiting for him. Well, tonight Gerri is not going to fix anything for him. That can be surprise number two. Surprise number one is waiting in his bedroom to finish her mom's little talk. Gerri turns out the kitchen lights so it feels even less hospitable for her dad's late arrival.

Gerri avoids homework as long as possible but eventually she begins to thumb through some of the assignments. She's keeping an ear tuned for their car. Eventually she hears the creak of worn out shock absorbers as the car lumbers over the curb and into the driveway. The engine falls silent. She dashes to the light switch in her room, switches off the light and returns to her bedroom window that overlooks the driveway. She watches her dad exit the car and she's sure he can't see her looking directly down on him from the darkened window.

Spying can be boring but tonight it has its rewards as her dad does something odd. He gets out of the car, goes around to the passenger side, looks all around as if someone might be watching from the bushes, opens the passenger door and then bends down searching inside the car as if he's lost something on or under the passenger seat. He searches and searches around the front seat until he seems to have located the object of his search and whatever it happens to be is shoved into his suit, coat pocket. Stephen looks around some more, closes the passenger door and makes his way up the steps to the front door.

When Gerri hears the front door opening she goes back across the room, switches on her bedroom light and goes out her door toward the front of the house.

When Stephen enters through the front door she's startles him by suddenly appearing in front of him.

"Did you lose something in the car, Dad? "

35

"What?"

"I just asked if you lost something in the front seat of our car?"

"Oh , no, uh, ah I thought I dropped a pen and it may have rolled onto the floor that's all. Why?"

"Well, you were standing on your head looking for something in the car and I wondered why. That's all. Just sort of weird."

"Nope. Just a pen or something."

Stephen stops and looks directly at Gerri with a serious look. "Wait a second. Were you watching me? Spying from your room? What's gotten into you lately? I get smart alec questions from you and sassy answers from you if I ask something. I'd imagine you have more important things to do than spy on me. Have you been taking care of your mom? "

Gerri knows her dad well enough that he'll seldom answer anything directly. He's good at answering a question with a question or switch to another subject. Turning the tables on Gerri with the subject of taking care of her mother is supposed to be the stone wall. But for once Gerri feels like she's helping defend her mother and she doesn't intend to let it drop.

 "Sooo. Did you find your pen, Dad? Is that what you shoved into that coat pocket?" Gerri points at the pocket of Stephen's suit jacket.

"Hey. That's the end of it, Young Lady. Forget my pen and answer my question. Have you been taking care of your mother?"

"Yeah, Dad. She's been fine. I sat with her almost the whole time you were gone and we've eaten…seems like hours ago. But I'd still like to know, why do you always come home so late? Other teachers don't stay at school so late? I don't know why you don't want to be at home."

"Look. I just do what I think's best rather than drag a lot of schoolwork home. Now, I'm hungry and tired after today and I'm going to bed in a few minutes after I grab a bite to eat... say, I'll tell you what. Let's make peace...okay? How about if tomorrow I pick you up after school and we ride home together? Maybe we'll pick up something special, maybe some ice cream, to bring home to your mom. How's that?"

Gerri is certain her dad thinks he's successfully bamboozled her by diverting her questions. Her mistrust shows by her monotone response, "Yeah, that's fine. How long should I wait if you don't show?"

"You're impossible. But I'll plan on being there after you get out. So, then it's a date for tomorrow." Stephen breathes a sigh of relief as if he's brought this conversation to a successful close. But Gerri doesn't retreat from the kitchen and looks him directly in the eyes to re-open the inquisition.

"By the way, Mom ask me to be sure she's awake when you get home because she needs to talk to you... well what she said is , she *really*... needs to talk to you." Gerri raises her eyebrows a couple of times and gives her dad a sinister, smirky smile like she's gloating over an errant little brother being sent to the proverbial woodshed.

Stephen, obviously caught off guard, "Why? What's the problem?"

"Problem? I couldn't say. Anyhow, not my problem, Dad. Maybe your problem. Dunno. Mom just made me promise to be sure she's awake when you come home. For some reason she didn't seem all that happy and she's got to talk to you."

Stephen doesn't respond verbally to Gerri. He looks a little stunned, probably at her aggressive insubordination, shakes his head and gives her a disgusted look. He takes off his jacket, throws it over a chair, loosens his tie, pauses and takes a long deep breath and proceeds toward the bedroom.

Gerri knows her mom is awake when she hears her voice as he enters the bedroom and Gerri also knows her mom is angry because her voice doesn't sound the slightest bit weak.

"Stephen, please close the door. You left earlier before *we* finished. You avoid talking to me when I have concerns. That's not right and I don't like it one bit!"

"Oh, geez this sounds serious. Can I get something to eat or is this one of those things that just can't wait."

"Stephen, There you go again. Your reaction is always the same. Can't it wait? I'll just go get something to eat...I have to go back to school. Avoid talking. Avoid problems. You know because of my condition I'm not able to do much right now and I know that makes it tough on everybody. But I don't think it's too much to expect you to be here more. It's the same every night. I'm here waiting for you. Gerri is waiting for you. Gerri has homework but she takes care of me as well. And she never complains but I know it would be nice to have some help from you. She fixed a meal for us, came in here and talked with me and then I heard her clean it all up. You, on the other hand are not even on the premises. You do nothing to help out here at home. I just can't imagine what you need to do until nearly nine o'clock every night. Every night. I don't like being forced into being a suspicious wife. I try not to be suspicious but when I see trouble brewing I will not put my head in the sand like an ostrich. I want an answer and I deserve an answer. You're a high school math teacher for heaven's sake and you can surely add up two and two and arrive at the same conclusions I do.

So, I'm asking you for an explanation, a truthful explanation. Where are you every evening, why so late coming home and most important what are you doing? Or more to the point, *who* are you with?"

"Fine. I'm a bad father, a rotten husband and I work too much. Fine, Susie, guilty. But right now I'm also tired and hungry. I prefer to get schoolwork done at school and not drag it home. That's it. Not your two plus two equals trouble. But somehow that's not good enough. So okay, you add up your facts and I'll keep trying to do the best I can. I hope it's enough to make you happy. If not, I don't really know what else to do. Sorry for trying to do the best I can!"

"So, a quick sorry is supposed to be the band aid to fix this? Not quite! Let's be clear about the facts. Let's add some detail to the nightly absenteeism. When you get home, you smell like perfume. I know what I smell on you and I know the smell of perfume. And I also know it's not a perfume from this house. So don't try to tell me it's on the papers you're grading. God knows I've tried very hard to trust you. We've had this problem twice before and you begged me to forgive and forget. You promised you'd never do anything ever again to hurt me or our family. But the more I try to overlook little tidbits you just keep throwing them back in my face. You've made it impossible to overlook all the odds and ends, here, not here, acting guilty, unhappy…it's like a jigsaw puzzle but I don't think it will be a pretty picture when it all fits together. I know the telltale signs and I'm telling you right here and now, I will not pretend any longer that everything is okay. Particularly right now. We are about to bring another child into this world and honestly, I do not trust you.

"Hmm. Well, sorry to disappoint you but I don't know about any of what you're talking about. You're riddles. Bits and pieces? Jigsaw puzzles? Guess it's over my head." Stephen shrugs his shoulders and tries to sound puzzled as if Susie's talking in a mysterious dialect.

"You do not treat me like your wife and I'm sure for you that creates a direct path to another woman. Me being pregnant has given you ample opportunity to go shopping again. You're a weak man, Stephen DeMore and I don't know what the future holds for us as a family."

"I think it's strange that you can even think any of this is true. Maybe it's all your hormones scattering about, but okay, I listened to you. None of it's true. None of it. Now, I'm hungry and tired. I hope you'll think about all the really terrible things you just said. Really not fair, Susie. Not fair at all."

"So I guess that's it. No discussion. Just deny it and clam up because of course you just want to avoid talking about it. Avoid it, deny it, ignore it like you do every other problem that comes up. I'm clearly at a disadvantage in my condition but that's you. Just stonewall it."

Without a response Gerri's dad pauses for a second and knits his brow to give his wife a puzzled look. He holds his arms stretched out to the sides in disbelief, shakes his head , opens the bedroom door and walks out leaving the door standing wide open with Susie obviously very upset.

Gerri's listening to it all but she jumps back in her room as she sees her father's leg exiting the bedroom. He passes her room and silently walks to the kitchen. She hears the refrigerator door opening and some dishes rattling.

Gerri can't believe what she just heard. Her mom suspects him of something with another woman? Perfume? Done this twice before? Gerri is shocked.

Gerri's seen her dad's reaction to problems before and though she's never ever heard anything like what she just witnessed, she's certain nothing more will be argued, discussed or likely ever mentioned again. Tonight two very different silences will surely finish the evening- her

40

mom's sadness in silence now that she's spilled it all out and her dad's pouting in silence. Tomorrow they're very likely to both play the DeMore family game, acting like nothing ever happened. This is the way her parents deal with issues. Uncomfortable issues are never resolved or discussed. Pout or bottle up hurt feelings in silence, the next day avoid the subject and sure enough it all goes away. Everyone is to put on a happy face and show the world and each other that everything is just fine. Tamp the explosive powder of denial deeper and deeper into the bombshell.

CHAPTER 4

REALITY CHECK

Gerri's surprised to hear her dad coming back down the hall toward the bedroom. He goes into the bedroom with her mom. Just as Gerri imagined. Not a word is spoken.

Suddenly Gerri hears her mom's voice in alarm, "Stephen. Ohh. Oh my gosh! The pain again! I'm having the terrible pains again. They're like contractions. Ohhh! This can't happen yet. Ohhh! Owww!"

"I'll try to get hold of Doctor Heinzen. Just try to relax. Gerri! Gerri! Come here quick!"

Gerri runs to her parents' bedroom. Her dad is coming out the door and Gerri sees her mom sitting up in bed with a pained, horrified expression.

"Oh, Mom! What can I do?"

Her mom's face is contorted with pain and she cries out again., "Ohhh I don't know. Stephen, I think I better just go. God, this is not good!"

Gerri's dad looks panicked and confused and now he reverses and rushes back to the bedside, "Right. No time to call. Let's just get going. We've got to get this checked out. It's way too early for the baby."

"You're telling me! It's almost two months too early. That's what scares me. Ohhh. It hurts so bad...ohhh! It comes in waves. It's like contractions but I hope it's not. This can't happen yet."

"Mom, tell me what I can do."

Gerri's dad is looking panicky, "Can you stand, Susie? Let's get something on you and get going for the hospital. Gerri, give me a hand to help your mom up."

"Gerri, just grab my housecoat. That'll have to do for now."

As Stephen steadies the unstable Susie, Gerri makes a quick move for the closet and gets her mom's housecoat. As they get Susie's arms into the housecoat, "Oh, Mom, this is so scary. Are you gonna be okay?"

"I hope so. I'm sure I will be. Probably a false alarm and at the moment the pain is getting worse. Horrible pains and I better go in and get some help to be sure everything's okay with the baby."

Gerri looks at her mother and suddenly worry comes crashing down on her. Pre-pregnancy Susie looked like a model on a magazine cover. Today the unmistakable beauty of her face is gone. Her mom's face is puffy and chalky-looking. Susie's left hand is on her hip and she's walking slowly toward the hall with her legs apart and crying out in pain with each step. It's almost like Susie can't possibly be her mom. The loose fitting housecoat is so different from the way Gerri always thinks of her mom -capri pants, blouse with the bottom front ends tied in a knot. Gerri's dad used to say Susie looked just like the model for Prell Shampoo. But not today.

Stephen nervously jingles the car keys in his left hand as he supports Susie with his right, "Okay. Let's get going. Gerri, please just stay home and... and stay off the phone. I'll call if it looks like we're going to be more than an hour or so. Just do your homework. Okay?"

"Sure, Dad. But do you want me to come along to help?"

"No, you better stay here for now."

"Okay, but I'd sure feel better if I could help."

"Nope. Better you stay here. But please make yourself useful and grab that little overnight case in the bathroom. Your mom's had it packed for just such events…so, just grab it and bring it to the car."

"Well, why do you need a suitcase if you're just going to get checked out?"

Stephen wheels around his eyes flashing with hysteria, an unfamiliar expression. He's obviously upset and afraid but there's hostility and a void of patience mixed into his look. Drops of spittle pop off his lips as he snarls at Gerri, "Look, Little-Miss Smart-Ass, you just do as I tell you. Don't stand here and question me. I ask you to do something."

How quickly resentment can come flooding back, "Yes-siree. Your Honor, sir." Gerri gets her mom's overnight case and looks at her mom and shrugs as she opens the door for her mom and dad to come outside.

Stephen has Susie by the arm helping her down the steps but he looks directly at Gerri showing his irritation. "Susie, just take it easy. That's it. Let's get you going before any more pains start. And as far as Little-Miss-Attitude…"

"Oh, Stephen, c'mon. Not now. Don't be cross with Gerri. We're all feeling stress at the moment." Susie turns toward Gerri and through the obvious pain tries to give her a smile but it melts into a pained grimace before it can form..

Gerri is scared to death. She'd like to remain angry and bristling with sarcasm but down deep inside Gerri's so frightened about her mom she can hardly contain herself. But one glance at her dad and the fear is joined by anger.

Whatever happened to the days when Gerri's dad was her hero? She dreamt of someday marrying a man as handsome and loving as her father. But now it seems she does nothing right in her dad's eyes and

44

in Gerri's mind that's cruel. It's his tone that ramps up her irritation quicker than anything else-condescending, superior, sarcastic, always ready to scold and belittle her. His tone of voice and choice of words addressing Gerri are embarrassing to Gerri and she's found she responds in kind automatically.

Gerri feels more bold each time there's an exchange of words. In Gerri's book, she's won confrontations where she stumps her dad into a loss of words and all he can do is give her that loser-look and walk away in silence. For now, Gerri stands on the sidewalk leading to the steps, waving to her mom who stares without expression at Gerri.

The car growls a couple of times and starts with the black cloud behind it. Her dad backs it out of the driveway and when Gerri makes eye contact with her mother she freezes. Her mom's face shows no expression and her eyes are fixed on Gerri's. Gerri feels an unusual sense of fear as she silently looks at her mother's mask-like appearance. She feels sad, frightened and very alone. Intuition is so new to Gerri she doesn't know when to trust it. So, with a false sense of denial she passes directly over her strong foreboding intuition. She tells herself there's no reason to believe anything too bad will happen. It never does. Even counting her mom's and dad's earlier argument and Gerri's irritating her dad, their life at home is shallow and irritating but sedate. Nothing ever turns completely topsy turvy.

A couple hours later, Gerri falls asleep on the sofa waiting for her mom and dad to return. She sits up startled as the key unlocks the front door. It's her dad and her mom isn't with him.

"What happened? Is Mom okay?"

"Yeah. Okay is the best we can do for now. Doctor Heinzen came in from home and said she seems okay but he thought it best if the hospital keeps an eye on her tonight. Then if all goes well tomorrow she can probably come home tomorrow afternoon. He's worried right now the baby was about to come early and that would be dangerous for the baby."

"Oh, I hate Mom being there all alone tonight. Can I stay home from school tomorrow and go see her?"

"No. Absolutely not. You're making too much out of this and we really don't have any reason to be overly concerned at this point. Doctor Heinzen is being cautious and as I said she'll likely be home tomorrow afternoon after I get home."

"How can that work? You never get home 'til eight or nine and…"

"Just stop! I try to treat you as an adult and tell you what's going on and you have to be a smart alec. You want to be treated like a child? I'm sure I can arrange it. Now, get ready for bed and up for school tomorrow and I'll let you know what's going on as *I* see fit from now on. Got that?"

"Sure. How could I not get it. You're very clear about where I stand even though I'm worried about my mother and think I have a right to know what's going on. But you do whatever you want to do. That's the way it is. "

"Believe me, I try to understand you but you sure make it tough. That's all I'm saying for now, I'm going to bed and I strongly suggest you do the same."

CHAPTER 5

SURPRISE!

The next morning, Gerri and her dad are out of the house as usual and headed for their respective schools. Gerri is thinking a lot about her mom and she sits passively in her first class.

On the way to her second class Gerri sees Mike Decker and when Mike knows he's caught her eye, he's all smiles. Gerri needs to give him a response today. Avoiding the problem doesn't seem to be working and yet she still hasn't figured out how to tell Mike she can't go and still protect herself in case a better offer comes along.

Mike comes straight up to her in the hall, walking with an air of confidence. He must be pretty sure of himself after the awkward way he handled himself yesterday. He quickly reaches toward her and gives her nose a gentle squeeze. When Gerri's hand instinctively goes up in defense Mike playfully pokes her in the ribs. He's lost any shyness since yesterday. Maybe he thinks Gerri's "his girl" now but he'll have to get past that real quick.

"Hi Gerri. How ya doin today?"

"Oh I'm fine Mike. But I have to get to class right now. Talk to you later. Okay?"

Before Gerri even waits for an answer she sees Mr. Penn about twenty feet away and he makes eye contact with her. Gerri freezes for a second and melts into a smile for Mr. Penn. Mike looks at Gerri and then follows where she's looking and realizes she's looking and smiling at the handsome teacher. Mike turns back to Gerri.

"Geez, Louise, Gerri! What's that? You flirtin with the Penn-man? I mean, c'mon, Gerri. He's a teacher. He's a geezer. He's old enough to be your grand dad."

Gerri is embarrassed by Mike's comment but seizes her red-face moment to ingeniously turn it into trumped-up, dramatic anger toward Mike.

"How dare you say something like that, Mike Decker. That's the way nasty rumors start and I don't like it one bit. Besides, you're acting jealous when you have absolutely no right or reason to act jealous. You don't own me. I'm not your girl. In fact I'm going on to my class now and that will give you some extra time. Why don't you take that extra time to find yourself a date for the sock hop…cause it's not going to be me. And close your mouth or you'll catch flies."

A few students passing in the hall catch the tail end of her tirade and laugh at Mike as he stands like a whipped puppy.

Mike has the open-mouth, gawky look he had the other morning. She's caught him with his proverbial pants around his ankles and he does not have any idea how to respond. So he silently stands, Gerri's sharp words pouring over him and dripping into his own pool of embarrassment.

Gerri wheels around, swings her hair and dramatically walks toward her class leaving Mike frozen in the hall. Gerri doesn't look back at him but pictures him standing, mouth open watching her sachet away as other students walk around him as if he's a permanently attached pole in the hallway. Her deliberate march down the hall takes her to the safety of her next class, heart pounding as she enters the room.

48

She's done it! It couldn't have worked out better. Besides she even got a smile and look from Mr. Penn in the process. Gerri is relieved and now she can spend this class thinking about Mr. Penn and studying the boys to see who might step up to be a possible date for the sock hop and Betsy's party.

Gerri thinks it's best if she avoids Mike and his close friends for a while and even though she'll likely see some of them at lunch, she must keep her distance. Maybe Mike's friends and the school gossip mill will be best to speculate and prosecute Mike for his assuming, forward actions. In Gerri's mind that would certainly be proper high school justice.

Maybe there's the possibility of a much happier life if she could go to more parties and spend less time stuck at home. In fact, a minimum amount of home life would be tolerable if she could be doing things constantly with friends because then it would be fine if her parents leave her alone. Maybe she's had this lack of attention by her parents all wrong. Maybe a lack of attention may not be so bad. She just has to increase her away-from-home social life so home life is basically sleeping, eating and a place to hang her clothes. Besides she needs to forget all the mess with her dad and get her mind off feeling sorry about her mom. Maybe the answer is to begin a truce with her dad and apply her energy to get out of the house more often. As she indulges in these feelings Gerri thinks she should begin her truce by taking an olive branch to her dad. She knows he's made lots of mistakes and is in the dog house with her mom but maybe he could do with a little kindness, phony or not.

After her third hour class Gerri detours to the principal's office and asks for a pass to go home for lunch. The attendance secretary knows Gerri because of Stephen teaching in the district. Besides if she goes home at lunch it removes the chance of seeing Mike and his friends in the cafeteria.

Miss Grace Stinson is a perfect image for a principal's office. She is a very nice looking, thirtyish, very trim young lady. She dresses impeccably in skirt and jacket business suit combinations and her auburn hair is likely very long but no one can tell because it's always tightly wound to the back in a French Roll. She wears cat-eye black glasses and is the consummate smiling and busy-looking professional.

Miss Stinson toys with Gerri, "So you think I can trust you to go home and get back after lunch before class time?"

"Yes Ma'am. It's because my mother had to go to the hospital yesterday and they kept her. So it's just my dad and me and I thought I'd get something to eat and sort of pick up the house a little. I hope my mom gets home today and if she does she sure won't be happy with my dad if she sees how the house looks after she's only been away one night. But if I go home, I can pick things up and still get back to school in time, Miss Stinson."

"Well, bless your heart, Gerri. You must be the perfect daughter. I hope your Susie gets to feeling better real soon. Here's your pass, Sweetie. Be careful walking. Bye, now."

"Thanks. I'm always careful and my house is pretty close. Bye, Miss Stinson." Gerri smiles to think how Miss Stinson still clings onto her as the perfect daughter and stellar student in spite of what seems like a determined effort on Gerri's part to erode those images.

Gerri walks quickly to save as much time as she can and soon she's turning the corner onto Vassar Avenue. She looks up toward her house and is surprised to see her dad's car in the driveway. Gerri can't imagine why he'd be home at this point during the day. Maybe he had the same idea to clean up the house, or maybe he knows Gerri's mom will be home this afternoon or maybe she's home now. He's probably worn out by the stress and Gerri always giving him a difficult time lately. He deserves every bit of it but this is time for the pretend-truce.   Gerri has a picture in her mind of opening the door find he's napping on the sofa. If that's the case maybe she can pick up the house a bit and fix the two of them some lunch just to show him the olive branch.

Gerri finds the front door unlocked and she opens it avoiding any noise. Her dad is not on the sofa so he's probably lying down on his bed because the house is dark and quiet.

She tiptoes quietly down the dark hallway past her room and as she reaches her parents' bedroom   door there's a sound she is not expecting. It certainly isn't snoring. It's quiet talk and a little laughing. At first Gerri feels a sudden surge of happiness because this must mean her mom's back home again.   She runs the last couple steps toward the master bedroom so she can see her mom but suddenly pulls her hand away from the door knob like pulling back from a hot stove.

It's not her mom's voice or laugh on the other side of that bedroom door. Her heart races and her stomach suddenly feels sick.   She freezes. Whoever's in the bedroom heard her last few thunderous steps and so the talking on the other side of the door stops.   Complete silence.   Gerri isn't sure how to react but she spins around and runs stumbling over a small stack of magazines and scattering them all over the hallway. She gets to her room as if it's a bastion of safety, slams the door, turns the key in the lock and puts her head to the door listening.

Gerri listens and hears the master bedroom door quickly open and quietly shut again. She hears light footsteps quickly going through the hall, into the bathroom and the bathroom door shuts. Gerri is shocked beyond belief and walks backward and clumsily sits on the edge of her bed, not breathing, not making a sound, her mind swirling in confusion

51

and shock. The only thing she knows for sure is that this is very, very wrong.

A white-hot rage overtakes her shock and sick feeling. Her mind is racing trying to figure out who could be in that room with her dad. Gerri says in a soft whisper, " It's not horrible enough that my dad's dragged some woman home. It's my mom's room. My mom's bed. Mom is right!"

Tears well up in her eyes as she pictures her mom innocently in the hospital. Her mom suspected something but she'd have no idea Stephen would be so callous as to bring someone into their home the very next day after she's entered the hospital. Gerri can't imagine what kind of woman comes to another woman's home or what kind of husband would bring another woman to her mother's bed...when her poor mother is due to have or maybe at this moment is having a baby? Their baby. The DeMores' family baby. What kind of family can be happy after that?

Shocking, unanswerable questions flood Gerri's mind and make it impossible to think clearly. She wonders how her mom will react when she finds this out. What if they get divorced? Will her mother still live in this house? Or will her mom move? Will Gerri go with her? She knows for sure she wouldn't stay with just her dad, the scoundrel. The cheater.

Knock, knock, knock. A light tapping on her door.

"Gerri? Gerri? Honey, is that you? "

"Who else would it be? And who's here in the house with you? *Who's here with you?*" Gerri sits on her bed screaming at him through the locked door.

Her dad jiggles the door knob and finds it locked. "Just calm down, Gerri. I'll explain it to you if you'll just open the door. Everything's fine. But what are you doing home from school? Are you okay? Gerri, can I come in?"

"No! I'm not fine. I'm not fine at school and I'm not fine at home. Who is that in my mom's bedroom? Just get away from my door and leave me alone! Get away!"

"Gerri, calm down and open your door. It's not what you think and I can explain. But you've got to open the door. I simply have a teacher-friend helping me get some clothes together for your mom. That's all. Nothing more. So, please open the door."

Gerri is close to hysteria, "Get away! I don't want to talk to you! I don't even want to look at you! Get away from my door and then I'll leave so you and whoever is there can do what you want. How could you do this to my mom? To us? The hallway stinks! Cheap perfume! Looking for your pen every night in the car, huh? Or maybe cleaning up to be sure no lipstick or earrings or anything else is left behind? I really don't want to see you or talk to you ever again. So get away from my door."

Her dad says nothing and soon she hears him return to his bedroom and the door closes gently. All without another word.

The woman, whoever it is, remains in the bathroom but Gerri's suddenly feeling a sense of urgency after all the shock and drama. She listens at her door again and she'll just have to stay in her room until the bathroom is clear. Some whore invader using her own bathroom! Gerri fumes in yet another level of outrage caused by her dad and the interloper.

The bathroom door quietly opens and a few seconds later she hears her mom's bedroom door open and shut as if trying to do it secretly. Gerri

53

quietly turns the key in her locked door and silently opens the door looking into the empty hall. She jerks open her door and flies across the hall into the bathroom, carefully locking the bathroom door, and suddenly confronted by the smell of strange perfume filling the air, repulsive smelling. Maybe that's the perfume her mom smelled before. No wonder she'd know it was not anything from their house.

Gerri finishes in the bathroom and again quietly unlocks the door, peeks out into the hallway to be sure her dad's not waiting there. When she sees the coast is clear she flings the bathroom door open. The door careens off the wall protector and rebounds shut with a shudder and a slam. She marches with the voracity of a stormtrooper out the front door stressing the hinges as she flings the door open and bursts onto the porch. She leaves the front door standing wide-open as she goes down the steps and onto the sidewalk.

*****

Gerri's head is spinning as she walks back to school. With her mom gone their home didn't seem all that happy last night and this morning. With the shock of her dad's infidelity right under her mom's nose and Gerri's nose, suddenly the feeling of being abandoned and all alone is reinforced. Today her entire world is upside down and her thoughts are scattered to every corner of ridiculous possibilities and "what-ifs". As she nears the school she hears the bell for the next hour and though she's late, she really does not care. Gerri has much bigger concerns than school.

Gerri's mind is still completely rattled even after the fourth hour class is over. She heads to fifth hour. What a day!

"Hey, Gerri! Gerri! Wait up for a second."

54

Gerri looks back over her shoulder and sees Betsy Alder rushing to catch up.. Gerri doesn't want to talk and she isn't feeling like a party mood at the moment but Betsy obviously has something to say. Yesterday this would have been so cool and exciting. Gerri's known Betsy since second grade and they've always been on friendly terms but Betsy hangs out with a clique of friends and Gerri up to this point has been on the outside. But now it looks as if Betsy really wants to talk.

"Oh, hi, Betsy. You looking for me?"

"Yeah, Gerri. I want to talk to you about the party.

Gerri's heart is pounding. After all she is very, very excited about the invitation and now she's standing here talking to Betsy like they're best friends. Popularity at school gets momentum from other kids seeing who's talking with whom and talking with Betsy is a noticeable event in this high school's social circles. This is the very thing Mr. Penn meant about having the right group of friends. Somehow in a twisted sort of way just standing here in front of everyone talking with Betsy puts Gerri's noontime shock on a back burner. Gerri loosens up a bit, " So, Betsy, I think you told me it's a guys and gals party and your mom and dad are okay with that?"

"Yeah, Gerri. My dad's total lack of interest guarantees parties at my house are fun. He doesn't care at all about anything just so nobody gets in a fight or causes a neighbor to complain. And my mom's fine with it. My mom's a teacher with your dad and she usually doesn't come home until late so it means I'm the chaperone. Cool, huh? She says as long as the lights stay on its okay…and well…she won't even be around until late and I don't think she cares anyhow so yeah, parties at my house are cool."

"How cool! That sounds great. Who all is coming?"

"Well, I shouldn't be going on and on about the party and all.   I'm having a little problem with something at the moment and that's why I needed to talk to you. There will be lots of other parties...I mean if you can't come to this one and I mean, I invited you to come, I guess... but if you can't, it's okay?

Gerri isn't sure what Betsy's trying to say but she's nervously talking fast and it doesn't seem to be heading in a favorable direction.

"Huh? C'mon, Betsy. You're talking so fast I'm not sure I understand. If you don't want me to come, just say it. I'm sure there will be others. Sounded like lots of fun and I'm...er was looking forward to it with all the guys and lots of girls but just tell me in plain English. Okay?"

"Well, it started off to be the same couples who are going to the sock hop but then you threw a bag over Mike's head on that issue today so at lunch I was going to look for another boy to come for you... an even number of guys and gals. That's probably not going to be possible since you told Mike to get lost. Oh, it's sort of silly but it's the thing how you dropped Mike and won't go to the sock hop with him. Well, Mike told all his jockstrap buddies and you know how they are. They sort of stick together and so then at lunch most of the other guys said they won't come if you're there with somebody else. And I'm guessing you're not going to change your mind just so you can go to my party with Mike who you don't want to be with. You know what I mean?"

Gerri was afraid there might be some backlash from turning down Mike but she never dreamed so much would blow up over the one little thing. Betsy wants to take back Gerri's invitation and is just trying to find the right words to do it.

As Betsy and Gerri are talking a small group of girls are standing close by, close enough that their voices distract Betsy and her rambling explanation to Gerri. Betsy turns her head toward them and realizes it's some of her friends so she smiles at them but looks annoyed.

"Well, actually Gerri, I guess that's all. I just wanted you to know about the party and I am sorry and all. It just doesn't look like it's possible. I just don't see how at least at this point."

"Geez. I'm sorry, too Betsy. I'll talk to ya later." Gerri is so disappointed she feels sick.

"Okay, Gerri, see ya."

As Gerri walks toward her room she's feels like she just got kicked in the stomach and yet she's still puzzled by the conversation. It seems like at the end Betsy said she didn't think so at this point and that sounds like maybe Betsy is still working on it or wanted to say something more. Maybe she isn't withdrawing the invitation a hundred percent just yet. There's a couple of minutes before the bell rings so Gerri thinks party or not she's now likely included in Betsy's world so she'll just hang out with this little group of Betsy's friends until class and maybe get a little better impression of what's happening.

The group of girls is still talking but Betsy heads for the restroom so Gerri is standing close to the group but physically a couple of feet from the little circle. Gerri leans in toward the group and clearly overhears Anne Tolbert who is oblivious that Gerri's standing close behind her, " I know it's got Betsy in a tailspin and it's really not something she should have had to worry about. Who of our friends even hangs around with Gerri DeMore or probably even likes her if they did hang around together. Really. She looks like a scarecrow with big knockers and she acts stuck up and never says two nice words to anybody. But Betsy's mom said she *had* to invite her because of Gerri's mom being sick and all that stuff. But it's really Gerri's dad... Betsy's mom teaches with him and they're like really close. Ya know, ooo laa laa kind of close. I think Gerri's dad probably leaned on Betsy's mom to invite her. Besides Mike told Eric that Gerri's been flirting with Mr. Penn. Can you believe that? Huh? And you know the sympathy thing for her mom and all that..."

Suddenly one of the others glances over at Gerri standing right there listening to them, "Shhh. Anne. Annie, shush."

Another leans to the girl talking ," Anne…stop…right behind you," and she tosses her head to indicate Gerri's right there as people say sometimes do when it's too late.

The group all turns toward Gerri and then turns back to their little circle. There's a soft dramatic squeal, "Oh, God!" Then more giggling and the three girls huddle together laughing and they move as a group quickly away, with their backs to Gerri.

Gerri's left standing there with insulting goop like Mike Decker got from her earlier today and it's as if it's just been poured over her head this time. No doubt at all they were talking about her. So Betsy was forced to invite her. Gerri feels like she's going to be sick. Her face feels like it's on fire and tears fill her eyes. As if it can't get any worse, Betsy comes hurrying by on the side unaware of what's just happened.

Through the blur of big tears Gerri looks directly at Betsy and no matter how she tries, she can't smile. The pain of rejection and the white-hot rage of embarrassment are about to boil over as lips twist and quiver, "You won't have to worry anymore, I won't be at your party… I'm not some charity case and...I'm sure you can fix Mike Decker up with one of your slutty friends. You probably have a bunch of em. Maybe they'll catch his zits. Who cares anyhow?"

Tears are about to explode and Gerri knows she can hardly hold it in any longer. Instead of turning toward the class Gerri goes quickly to the bathroom. As she nears the bathroom door, the bell rings but Gerri

58

shoves open the door and goes into the bathroom anyhow. Everyone already in the bathroom is hurrying to exit since hearing the bell so no one seems to notice her. She enters the end stall, locks the door and sits heavily on the seat with her head in her hands. How can this be happening? Gerri feels like she can't trust anyone anymore. The tears flow down her cheeks as she sits quietly in the locked stall. It seems to her that a bathroom stall can be almost like a private office...anyhow at school. Throughout her school years Gerri's found if she needed to be by herself during a school day, a locked stall is the only place to physically escape. Particularly a stall next to the wall. That's where she always heads if need be. It seems safe and secure.

Gerri's aware of the tardy bell ringing but she's ignoring it and taking a couple more minutes. She's thinking about how her world has been betrayed and become fearful just in one day. Today! No matter how strong or rebellious she feels or acts it doesn't ever cover the internal pain of feeling like she's abandoned by everyone.

Her fifth hour teacher, Mrs. Dugger always seems nice enough and she knows Gerri's dad is a teacher so Gerri's not worried about an excuse for Mrs. Dugger. Eventually she feels okay to go to class so she puts a little water on her hands and rubs it on her face. It feels good to her tearful eyes. Slowly she makes her way down the hall toward Mrs. Dugger's room and figures maybe if she turns the knob slowly and opens the door quietly she can just slip into her seat.

Unfortunately it's one of those moments that she envisions will happen isn't even close to what really happens. The door opens quietly. Though there isn't a sound, every head turns toward Gerri, including Mrs. Dugger, who stops in mid-sentence , removes her glasses and lets them hang on the chain around her neck.

"Well, Miss DeMore? You decided to join us?"

59

Gerri realizes she needs to get this over quickly. She starts for her desk, head bowed and walking quickly.

"Sorry. Didn't mean to interrupt."

"Young lady, wait just a second, please. May I have your attention right here, please?"

Gerri looks at Mrs. Dugger and her heart falls in fright. Mrs. Dugger is glaring at her with a very irritated look and pointing to her own chest demanding Gerri's undivided attention.

"Didn't mean to interrupt? You already have. You know, Miss DeMore, I try to be accommodating if someone needs a little time here or there but you just sachet' in here as if you don't care. Do you think you're privileged and don't have to follow the rules? You interrupt my class without so much as a how-do-ya-do. Lately you've been acting like the class clown whenever you can and I think it's high time you know these people around you aren't laughing with you. They're laughing at you. That's sad. So I think it's time you and I come to an understanding about your attitude and conduct but we've wasted enough of everyone else's time for now. As soon as classes are over today I expect you to come and have a visit with me. We'll see if maybe I can help you understand rules and a little respect. Got that?"

The entire class is staring at Gerri and a couple of soft giggles and "oooh"'s are heard. She tries to keep her gaze focused on Mrs. Dugger, realizing she's again the star of today's student entertainment and this time it's not fun at all. The tears roll down her cheeks and she can't control the loud sobs that follow. Mrs. Dugger's silhouette is all that's visible through her tears.

"I don't feel well at all. I need to be excused. "

Out the door and down the hall goes Gerri, half-walking, half-running. She reaches the bathroom and goes to the end stall, sitting down, leaning her head back against the hard wall and stretching her long legs out in front. So other girls think she looks like a scarecrow? How can Mrs. Dugger embarrass her in front of the entire class? She could have said something after class or anything other than just make her stand there like a dunce. How can anybody be so cruel? No one can possibly know the fear, guilt, anger that pervades Gerri's life because if they did realize it maybe there would be some sympathy. Oh, how Gerri hates Mrs.Dugger.

It seems today's the day everybody is just waiting for a chance to chop her legs from under her and embarrass her. Events are even more embarrassing when they're such a surprise that she can't even think what to say or how to defend herself. Like the hateful comments of Anne Tolbert and the other girls in the hall, Betsy's invitation and how Betsy was really just doing what her mother made her do, but she never really wanted Gerri to come to her party. Or, like Mike Decker whining to his buddies and of course they all take his side because he's a basketball player. Gerri hates his pimples and gangly physique more than ever. They're all horrible and two-faced. So now she's not tall and attractive, she's a scarecrow that nobody likes. Gerri pledges to never speak to any of them, ever again. She may have to be civil to Mrs. Dugger but only to get through her class. No smiles and just hate for what all of them have done.

Gerri's so filled with rage she can hardly breathe. The longer she sits in the stall the more she feels very close to being out of control. She wishes she could turn back the clock a couple of years, escape to home and be held in her mom's arms right at this minute. But old memories of love and security can never catch up to today's reality

The outer door to the bathroom opens and one of Gerri's classmates quietly calls out, "Gerri? You in here?"

Gerri recognizes Jill's voice. "Yeah."

"Mrs. Dugger told me if you need help I can get the nurse or if you need to you can stay here until the bell rings and she said you can just go on to your next class. She said you don't have to see her after school today, either. So do you need me to get the nurse?"

"No. I'm okay. I just need a little time. I'll be fine in a minute. "

"Okay. I'm gonna stay here for a couple more minutes and then I'll go back to class. God. She's so boring I was about to go to sleep anyhow. I hate Grave-Dugger's class. Maybe I'll stay here until the bell rings."

Gerri doesn't answer. She really doesn't care if Jill misses class or not, but in a few minutes Jill leaves without another comment. When the bell sounds for the end of the period, Gerri walks back to the room to get her books. She knows Mrs. Dugger sees her but acts like she doesn't and she doesn't say anything, and Gerri's not going to say anything either.

But as Gerri heads for the door Mrs. Dugger speaks in a voice that's obviously meant to sound kind and caring, "Geraldine, are you alright?"

"Yes ma'am."

"Okay. See you tomorrow."

Gerri's face feels hot as anger builds once again. Mrs. Dugger can take the time to verbally beat her up in class in front of everyone but then wants to sound all friendly and caring when there's nobody around. All Gerri can think is that the damage was done in class. All the kids in class will remember every embarrassing second. Mrs. Dugger will never get a smile from this day forward.

As Gerri enters the hallway and hears the door latch behind her she emphatically whispers, "Witch!"

In sixth hour Mr. Penn mentions to Gerri that he's still waiting for Mr. Lander's approval so they'll postpone the after-school assistance for another day.

Finally, the end of this day! Gerri pushes open the big double-doors and stands outside in the fresh air. She takes a deep breath. Her dad is nowhere in sight and she never really expected him to be waiting or to even remember. He probably wouldn't show his face this soon anyhow. Not after his noon-time performance. She figures there's no reason to wait so she's all set to walk home.

CHAPTER 6

A WALK ON THE WILD SIDE

Gerri turns toward a voice on the other side of the steps, "Hey. Hey, Gerri. You waitin around? Need a ride home?"

Gerri knows Connie Waltrip by sight and by name but little else. Connie moved into the school district during their freshman year and Connie has a couple of older brothers but Gerri knows nothing else about Connie or her family. She doesn't have any classes with Connie but she dresses a lot different and it stands out from other girls.

As Gerri walks toward Connie she can tell that Connie has a cigarette cupped secretly in her hand. Gerri looks around and at the school door, "Not afraid of getting caught with that?"

"Nah. You can stand under somebody's nose if you look like you're not nervous about something. No big deal."

Connie is leaning with one hip against and an elbow resting on the big cement banister of the steps and Gerri's first impression is that she's posed like a streetwalker. But Connie doesn't seem like she actually tries to be provocative or sexy. She dresses a little different, and acts older than her age. She's very good looking. She wears her coal black hair in a pixie cut so it looks like a bowl cut around the sides over her ears and bangs in the front. She has big brown eyes and overdoes the eyebrows too dark. She has a wonderful smile but most of the time the smile is not available for public viewing and never a laugh. Connie wears bright red lipstick and it's accentuated today with her white blouse. The collar of the blouse is turned up and the upper button is undone. Connie is one of the few others in high school that share Gerri's infamy of having abundant bosoms and Connie's narrow waist always cinched with a wide belt makes certain no one can possibly miss her natural endowment. Today as usual she wears a tight mid-calf length dark skirt and black plain shoes with nylons. No saddle-oxfords and bobbi socks for Connie.

On a mild day like today Connie simply looks mature. When it's chilly out she dresses the same but wears a waist-length, black leather motorcycle jacket all day in school and that's why most students would say Connie's a "hood", short for hoodlum or toughie. She has a sort of tough look and while friendly, Connie stays to herself fueling a bit of mystery and gossip about her. Current gossip about Connie is that she dates older guys and her current boyfriend is a gang member. Most students think Connie's rebellious appearance is very cool.

"So, how ya doin, Connie? I was just taking a little breather before heading home. Heck of a day, Connie. Heck of a day. I'm just glad it's done and now I'm collecting my I-don't-give-a-crap attitude for another exciting night of home life."

"No problem-o, Kiddo. I can dig that. Many of my days are like that and I feel the same way. Out of here at the end of the day and try to do something cool until I have to come back. My brother Jake is just driving up and I'm sure we can drop you home. Jake's cool. He'll give you some laughs and then your day will be better. How's that sound?"

"Well, I don't live that far. Just up on Vassar Avenue and I can just walk. It's okay. But thanks. Cool of you to ask."

"C'mon, Gerri. Don't be a drag. No problem and I have a feelin you'll like Jake and his car. He's cool. It's cool. Don't be scared and besides…who's gonna tell? You'll get home before anybody's even looking for ya. And I guarantee it'll be more fun than walkin home with the creeps and peeps on your parade route."

Gerri doesn't respond for a second. She takes a deep breath and feels a bit of exhilaration. Right there on the street in front of Fresno Central High School a transformation is taking place in Gerri DeMore. It's a liberating, exciting, cleansing. She's always the good girl until recently and even now she's just play-acting being somewhat of a rebel more so than truly being a rebel. The fact of the matter is she's never done anything too exciting. Never anything too far out of the ordinary. But right here, right now she's about to break a whole lot of rules all at once. Impulsive excitement and devil-may-care confidence trump all the cautious thoughts of life up to this moment.

"Sure. Why not? Who'll know? Who'll care anyhow? Sooo, sounds good, Connie. I'm cool with it and thanks for coming to my rescue. I could make the walk home but I'm dying of boredom."

The spotless, black 1950 Ford slows and pulls toward the curb where the two girls stand. There isn't a speck of dirt anywhere to be seen as the black and chrome of the car glistens in the afternoon sun.

Gerri notices the group of boys and girls standing nearby move slowly away from the car's curbside location. But Gerri's seen this many times after school. Whenever one of the local toughs arrives to chauffeur a girl, students standing near the curb nonchalantly move away from the general location to avoid any remote possibility of contact. Today Gerri's at the curb with Connie looking at people move

66

the other way and it's an exciting perspective. Gerri's never done anything like this.

Connie reaches in front of Gerri and opens the passenger door. She leans down, looks into the car at the driver and speaks excitedly, "Hey, Jakie. This is Gerri DeMore one of the coolest girls from my class. I told her she could come with us and then we can drop her at home. Okay?"

The driver leans to a nearly prone position from the steering wheel over toward the passenger window. He lifts his sunglasses to see the prospective passenger on the sidewalk. Now that he sees her up close he is obviously pleased. A smile breaks his expression. "Sure. You bet. On one condition."

"What condition, funny-man?"

"Well, you are my sister so Gerri will have to ride in the center, nice and close to me and you gotta ride shotgun."

Connie shakes her head feigning disgust and doesn't even respond to Jake. She takes Gerri by the arm and pushes her gently toward the open door.

Jake is sitting in the driver's seat with his left hand on the steering wheel and his right arm across the middle of the seat back. He looks over the top of his sunglasses and smiles a perfect teeth smile as Gerri enters the car. Gerri has recently seen the movies Rebel Without A Cause and Blackboard Jungle and she does a double-take at Jake. He looks like the twin of James Dean. Hair combed back on the sides and a huge curl slightly over his forehead, snow-white tee shirt and blue jeans. He's wearing black leather boots that hold his jeans just above the ankle. His nose fits his thin face perfectly and his lips have a bit of a puff to them. The one physical feature she can clearly see are his muscles that show from the outstretched forearm up to the biceps. If

67

Gerri were forced into a one word description it would be the word gorgeous.

"Well, hello, Miss Gerri. What's shakin, Kiddo? I'm Jake Waltrip… of Jake-the-Snake fame. Wowsie, little girl! You razzle my berries. Welcome to Jake's chariot. Where've you been hiding?"

Trying to act cool and even flirt a bit Gerri smiles at Jake, "Hiding? I haven't been hiding anywhere. Why would I hide? "

"C'mon, Gerri. I'm jokin ya. Ya know? Crackin wise, Junior. I'd have said I was pullin your leg but I only just met ya and touchin those legs would be a violation of the pure food and drug act and more excitement than I could handle as the driver. I'd have to ask for the **lay-away plan**. Oops. There I go again. You got me all flustered. Now, scoot over here. Up close. I promise not to bite."

"Don't pay any attention to him Gerri. Jake's a big flirt but not as bad as some of his friends. They're all a bunch of greasers and you get close to some of them and it's like being around an octopus with arms and hands grabbin' at you, touchin and stuff. I'll show you who to watch out for. Don't worry."

"C'mon, Connie. They're just guys. They're harmless and I'm sure Gerri-girl can take care of herself. Besides, nobody's gonna frost me so there ain't gonna be nobody mess with Jake's lady."

"I'm not worried." Gerri turns toward Connie and smiles. She's obviously excited about this ride and approving of the company.

"So where do you live, Miss Gerri?"

"Actually just a few blocks up Van Ness and then a right on Vassar…about half way up Vassar. Across from the woods."

"You live on the street with the woods? How bout that? I've been up there a couple of times and so you live over there? Heck, that's only a few minutes to get there and besides we haven't even had a chance to get acquainted. Tell ya what. I want to drop by Brentwood's at some point so let's do that before we take ya home. Cool with that?"

"Yeah, cool. I just have to watch the time a little bit. My mom may still be in the hospital unless my dad went to pick her up but even if he picked her up I'm pretty sure he isn't at home. I just can't be out for too long."

"Sure forty-five minutes, an hour tops and we can have ya at your door. Wow! Your mom in the hospital? Is she okay?"

"I think so. She's about to have a baby and she was having a little trouble last night so my dad took her in to Saint Joe's."

"Hope she's okay. I really hope everything comes out good for you and your family. Anyhow, I need to drop by and see my guys… a little meet-up with friends. But not a real social thing. We got some… uh, stuff shakin and I gotta keep these guys focused on what they need to be doin to keep the bread comin in.. Sometimes I gotta be the one to crack the whip and other times they need to be throttled back a little. Won't take long and besides I can introduce ya around. Connie says you're cool so I'm trustin her and after seeing you, I'd take you at your word anyhow. Ya can teach most people some stuff but ya can't teach 'em to be good lookin like you and cool at the same time. You got it made in the shade. Okay? So you cool with all this?"

"Sure, that's fine. It's cool. Just so I get home by five or five-thirty. I can walk from the corner and tell my parents I stayed after school to talk to a teacher."

Connie wiggles her eyebrows, looks at Gerri as if teasing and in a slow, raspy, dramatic voice, "Yeah, like stayin after school talkin to Mr.

69

Penn? Mr. Penn? Huh, Gerri? I'll bet you'd stay after school…anytime…just to be alone with him? Who knows…he may want you to help him after hours. Huh, Gerri? I'll bet he'd loosen his tie for you."

Jake leans toward the steering wheel and turns slightly to make eye contact with Connie. "Hey Connie. Careful. You know how jealous Roger gets about stuff you say so I wouldn't be makin comments about anybody.   Particularly that panty-waist, Penn- so if I were you I wouldn't say too much about him or anybody else around Rog. Rog is liable to catch him out somewhere and jump him for a little lesson of his own. Penn's a faggot, geezer, homo with a pocket full of Sunday school pins."

Gerri is a little surprised that Jake seems to know Mr. Penn by name but before she can dwell on it Connie comes to Mr. Penn's rescue, "He is not, Jake! And you don't need to warn me about Rog. You just be sure *you* don't say anything about Penn to set him off. And anyhow I was just thinking, Jake. When we get to Brentwood's, let Gerri wear your jacket so nobody will mess with her or say anything too… too… well, you know. Don't worry Gerri. It's just like I said. Some of these guys are a bit too forward around girls particularly when they've been drinking or smoking reefers and stuff. But being with Jakie means nobody will do nothin' at all. I should know. Being his sister has real advantages."

Jake reaches up to the side of his head and dramatically slicks his hair back on one side, "Yep. Connie's got it right. Somebody's gotta be big chief and that's me. Been me for the last couple of years and my plan is to keep it that way. So Gerri-girl, you just be cool and stay close, just be my lady for the day. Okay?"

"Sure. No problem, Jake."

As they drive into Fresno and away from the area familiar to Gerri, her heart is racing. This is certainly a lot more than just a ride home from school. It just keeps getting more exciting. She's never done anything like this. Now she needs to step up and play the role of an older girl hanging out with older guys. She can easily pass for eighteen and she can act like it as well. Time to try acting sexy and act like she's a girl who knows her way around.

By accepting Connie's invitation today, Gerri sees herself as part of an exciting, rebellious image. Jake's great looking, and exciting to be seen with today but Gerri's sure he's not ever going to make the grade as a Prince Charming. But she feels empowered to be hanging around with such a powerful group of people. All the guys at school will like her even more now when they find out she knows her way around one of the local gangs. Plus she'll get to wear Jake's jacket. She can hardly believe how this day turned out to have a bright spot after all.

Gerri has only heard the rumors about Connie's older brothers, Jake and Joey. The rumor is they are leaders of a local gang called the Fresno Kings. The gang logo on their jackets is a gold crown with scripted letters "F" and "K" The Kings are somehow supposed to be the enforcers for a local labor union and a private trucking company that hauls a lot of the field produce around Fresno and also into the San Francisco Bay area. The rumor is probably overrated to some extent by the high school age embellishment of anything exciting like a gang. The most immediate and factual notoriety of the gang is for burglary, fighting, drinking and even smoking reefers. High school boys make fun of the gang name but only in private. Instead of the Fresno Kings they substitute a famous four-letter word beginning with "f" in place of Fresno. But never is that mentioned except in the safety of the school halls. Outside the building, high school boys give gang members a wide, quiet berth and the girls walk past, giggling as they flirt a little.

The car slows as they get within sight of the neon "L" shaped sign similar to those seen on movie theaters. The vertical part of the sign says "Brentwood's" and the smaller horizontal bottom says "Pool & Billiards". In the front windows are small lit neon signs for Falstaff Beer and another for Carling Black Label but Gerri isn't familiar with the actual names or for that matter bars or drinking except a slight familiarity from advertising and movies.

The threesome exits the car after parking and Jake gets his jacket from the back seat and then gently drapes it over Gerri's shoulders. He quietly whispers as he straightens the jacket, "Nothing like wearing Superman's cape."

They make their way toward the entrance, a massive wooden door with a small shaded window in the top. Jake is obviously in the lead and as he reaches the door he pulls it open. Gerri tries not to gasp as she's confronted for the first time by totally foreign atmosphere in the form of a cloud of cigarette smoke, the stench of stale beer, the clunking of pool balls, the jagged noise of a blaring juke box and people shouting to be heard above all the other noise.

"Hey, Jakie!"

"Hey, Norvel." The huge man sitting part-way on a red vinyl stool near the front door is for sure the bouncer. Gerri's heard the term and although she's never actually seen a bouncer, there's no guessing- Norvel is a bouncer. He's so fat his eyes are like horizontal slits over his puffy, rosy cheeks. He's huge horizontally and even though he's sitting, vertically as well. His black tee-shirt has a pelt of chest hair hanging over the top edge and with its sleeves cut off it shows massive arms with lots of red and blue ink to fill up the surfaces of the arms. Norvel turns his head to one side to cough and exposes two large rolls of muscle or fat between the back of his huge head and his shoulders. Norvel looks at the two girls as Jake motions for them to come inside.

Norvel looks like it's an effort but he begins to slide off his stool onto his feet, arms still folded in front as if to take a closer look at the two young girls but Jake is quick to stifle the action.

"It's okay, Norv. I've got my sis, Connie and her friend Gerri. They're cool. You know my sis' friends are Jake's friends. Cool?"

"I dig ya Daddy-o. You say it's cool is good enough for me but the cops have been givin us shit. So, it's cool as long as I'm here by the door. If you get em something to drink it's cool, man but put it on a table. Don't let em carry it around drinkin. If one of the inspectors comes in, I flip on the bright lights over the bar. If that happens just keep the girls away from the table with the drinks. If anybody asks whose drinks are on the table, nobody knows nothing. Okay? And if those lights go on get rid of anything else that would get us popped…ya know reefers and shit.The pilgrims downtown are watching us pretty close these days. You know the drill, Jake."

"I know, but we ain't gonna make you break a sweat, man. We're just gonna be here a couple minutes. I gotta see a couple of my guys and I'm gonna get em back in that corner to talk for a sec so I'll keep an eye up here and over the bar. Okay? "

Jake slips Norvel some sort of money almost as if it's just a worthless little love note and Gerri can't make out what it is but she thinks it's maybe a ten dollar bill. She doesn't see those very often.

"Okay, okay. Let's go back over here. Let's see who's here. Connie, you and Gerri want a beer or a coke or something else?"

Connie looks and acts as if the surroundings are very familiar but Gerri's taking it in like watching an exciting movie. Except Gerri feels like this time she's actually in the movie.

"Coke is fine with me. How bout you, Gerri?"

73

"Yeah. Coke would be great."

"Okay, so Coke it is." Jake heads for the bar. He quickly returns with two cokes and a beer. Jake dramatically clinks his beer bottle on each of their glasses, pulls his pack of Camel cigarettes out of his rolled up tee-shirt sleeve, shakes out one cigarette and obsessively packs it on his lighter. For the first time Gerri hears an unmistakable clink of a Zippo lighter as Jake opens it and rakes the flint wheel across his jeans to light the lighter. Jake never unlocks his gaze into Gerri's eyes and she gives Jake a big smile of approval because he's absolutely cool and sexy cute.

After about twenty minutes Jake returns from his meeting in the back corner and soon after, Connie and Roger find their way to a booth, talking privately, and Jake turns his undivided attention to Gerri. Jake strikes his sexiest pose for Gerri by leaning with his back against the bar, elbows on it supporting his weight, one foot resting on the footrest.

"Hey Kiddo. I promised to get you home and it's getting dark. You cool to stay a little or need to get going? You just say the word. By the way, like that coke?"

"Yeah, it's fine. Tastes good. Why? You don't think I know you put something in it?"

Jake laughs, "Very light. Very light. Just a little nectar of the gods to take the chill outta the night air. I'm careful. Not much in it. A little sloe gin. Most girls like it. Want another one?"

"Sure, why not?"

Gerri is enjoying this more moment by moment. Jake is exciting and handsome, the special coke he got her tastes great, she's got his coat around her shoulders, he's acting like the perfect gentleman and they are in a forbidden place. And she is handling it just fine. Gerri can't even imagine what percent of girls in high school have ever been inside a place like Brentwood's or had a drink with alcohol. She likes the atmosphere and can't believe how strangely relaxed she is. Her head has a little floating sensation but it feels good and she feels perfectly and confidently in control. The smell seems to be gone or she's used to it and the smoke and noise don't seem so bad. The music is exciting. The banter among the guys is very, very exciting. These are older guys probably early to mid- twenties and they are all dressed like hoods. Gerri realizes they aren't just dressed like hoods. They are the real thing. A few guys in her school try to dress like this but they are pretending and could never measure up to this. These are real men.

After Gerri works her way through about half of another doctored Coke she smiles at Jake, "I can stay a little longer but I guess I should be getting home before too long. But are you finished with what you needed to do?"

"Yeah. It's cool. Everybody's got their instructions and Jake's got his money. That's the way the world of Jake-the-Snake works, Gerri-girl. So, okay, then. We don't need to hang around here. Let's split."

Gerri looks over at the booth where Rog and Connie are sitting, "Connie ready?"

"Oh she's gonna stick around with Rog for a bit." Jake puts his face close to Gerri's, firmly puts his arm around her waist and pulls her close. "It'll be okay with just you and me...okay? You're not scared are ya?" Jake looks directly into Gerri's eyes like he's going to kiss her.

Gerri's complete lack of experience with alcohol and inability to recognize that her inhibitions are gone glides effortlessly into a false sense of control as she stares into Jake's eyes and responds with confidence, compliments of her clouded senses. "Scared? Me? Scared of what?"

Gerri leans forward and gives Jake a quick kiss on the lips, then pulls away and giggles.

Jake looks pleased. "Oh, look at you. Playin around, huh? That's good. Real good."

As they walk out the door, "See ya Norv. Gotta get this one home. Can't have too much excitement in one day."

"Watch yourself, Brother. See ya later?"

"Maybe. I might be back after I drop her home."

Gerri has Jake's coat around her shoulders and as they walk out the door, Jake puts his arm around her, sliding his arm under the jacket and as he pulls her closer, Gerri can feel Jake's hand gently touching her breast. Gerri pulls closer to Jake, looks at him and laughs.

Gerri taunts Jake, "Hey. Not scared are ya, Jakie?"

Jake laughs so hard he has to remove his arm from around Gerri, "Wow! Lady, you are one cool lassie."

As they get to Jake's car, he walks around with her to the passenger side and opens the door for her. She turns toward him before getting in the car and they embrace and a long passionate kiss follows. Jake guides Gerri's shoulders toward the car and she gets in. Gerri is dismissing any effect the alcohol is having but she feels so relaxed, excited and any remaining inhibitions are out the window. She really doesn't care about anything except where she is right now at this moment. And where she is right now is the front seat of Jake's car and she quickly and willingly participates in passionate kissing and touching. They spend a few minutes in the parking lot making out and

76

Jake straightens up in the seat, puts his right hand behind Gerri's head, running his fingers through her long hair and gently caresses one of her ears. Gerri is on fire!

"We really should get out of this parking lot, Gerri. I don't want anyone coming by and seeing us too close. Okay? We'll go someplace else. Okay?"

"Yeah. That's fine, Jake. You're driving."

Gerri sits close as they slowly make their way back to Gerri's neighborhood.

Jake turns the corner and as they proceed up Gerri's street she remarks," Geez. Why should I be surprised? House is dark, so my mom's not home and no car, so my dad's still gone. Guess we didn't need to be in a hurry after all."

"Well then, Let's just pull over here across from your house into this little woods. It's private enough and I'll try to park where we can see your house in case somebody comes home."

"Yeah, I don't care. Sounds fine to me." Gerri is sitting with her hips touching Jake's.

As they come to a halt and Jake turns off the engine and the lights. They resume the heavy kissing and embraces.

They quickly go beyond the quasi-innocent touching Gerri's toyed with at some of the parties but Gerri is strangely and willingly powerless. She's anxiously compliant at Jake's tugging at her clothes and where he has his hands. Jake knows what he wants and is not shy about making bold moves. Gerri is not resisting any of the touching or caressing.

Jake draws back from a long kiss and stares into Gerri's eyes. He's unsnapped her bra in the back and Gerri's providing unrestricted access

77

for Jake. He has his hands on the upper part of Gerri's thighs and as she feels him tugging at the waist of her underpants she raises up to help with the removal process. With her panties around one ankle they begin the deep passionate kissing again and Gerri feels like being in a dream. She glances through the trees and across the field of weeds toward her house and it all looks a bit blurry but that is a passing interruption and soon she's back to the enjoyment. This is wonderful and Gerri 's somewhat diminished mental state seizes on, "what's the harm? And besides, who cares?"

Jake reaches across her with his left hand and arm, pulling her toward a position of being on his lap facing him. She helps lift her skirt so it's not in the way of her straddling his legs with hers. As they passionately kiss and embrace Jake takes hold of the top of Gerri's hips gently lifting and resettling her onto his lap and quite suddenly Gerri is shocked at what she feels. There is immediate physical discomfort as she is pulled down firmly onto Jake.

"Ow. Jake! Ow. That's hurting me. Don't!"

But Jake's not stopping, and he's not unsure of what he's doing. Jake is kissing her even more aggressively and along with the unceasing deep kisses there's suddenly no mystery to Gerri of what is happening.

This doesn't feel good at all. It hurts. Gerri pulls back a little but Jake's kissing continues, now it's less affectionate and more raw. Gerri can feel what's happening and she's moving around trying to get more at ease or at least make it less uncomfortable. She groans and tries to pull away but Jake has his hands firmly on her hips holding her close to him as he moves in thrusting movements up and down beneath her.

Gerri makes more noises of protest but they are smothered in the kissing and Jake's heavy breathing. As Gerri gathers strength to pull away Jake clutches her so tight she can hardly breathe and he lurches awkwardly, his eyes widen and he exhales in a couple of rapid gasps and then he stops moving.

It's too late to stop Jake, and Gerri knows very well what just happened. The pain from penetration stops but Gerri feels a burst of panic and worry from a lot more than physical discomfort.

"Oh God, Jake. Why'd you do that? I can't believe it. Am I gonna be okay? What if…"

"C'mon. You'll be fine, yeah, you're fine. Just…" Jake still breathing hard, gently pushes Gerri off his lap back over into the passenger seat and then he suddenly freezes looking out his side of the car.

"What the…" Jake's head still turned toward the driver's window as he's frantically and awkwardly zipping his pants and smoothing his hair back on the sides.

Gerri is in shock and confused by his scrambling to get his clothes back in order. She suddenly feels nauseated probably from the fear of repercussions and the ever present lingering effects of her drinks. This is not fun in any way shape or form. She grabs and pulls her skirt down covering her legs and she's still trying to come back to the reality of what just happened and trying to figure out how to reconstitute herself and clothes when she sees flashes of very bright light across the dashboard.

Whack- whack- whack! Sharp, loud noise. Something hitting the driver's window. Instantly a stark, bright light floods the entire front seat of the car. Gerri freezes. The car doors quickly open on both sides of the car.

Gerri squints at the blinding light in her eyes and as the light moves a bit she knows immediately it's uniformed policemen. Her heart is racing.

79

Gerri knows what just happened with Jake and a wave of nausea sweeps across her. Fear, shock, surprise. She's one big stomach knot. And her panties are still around the ankle of her right foot.

Gerri stares toward the light as it moves from her eyes down her body and stops briefly on the panties around her ankle.

"Please just stay seated, Ma'am and do me a favor…put your hands on the dashboard."

The light briefly shines from Gerri across to Jake who is being removed from the car.

"Well, well. We thought it looked like your jalopy parked back here, Jakey boy. Let's go back to the patrol car and have a chat. C'mon. Nice and easy. You just stay real friendly."

Neither Jake nor Gerri say a word as Jake is taken to the patrol car parked about a car length or so behind Jake's car. Jake and Gerri were totally unaware of the police car's approach while they were involved.

Gerri has her hands on the dash as instructed but she turns her head watching Jake being taken away and she sees a new set of headlights pull up behind the dark patrol car. She can tell by the profile of the car's top it has a raised light so she assumes it's another police car. Gerri turns her head back around facing front in the seat. Both police cars now have their red lights flashing and everything in Jake's car interior turns a dull, slow flickering red color, alternating with darkness as the lights blink away in the night. She is so frightened she can't breathe. She thinks she's probably being arrested and headed for jail while only a hundred yards or so from her own house.

The officer who was on her side of the car now returns and with the light again in her face, "Okay, now what's your name and where are you from?"

"My name's Gerri...Geraldine. Geraldine DeMore."

"Alrighty then, Miss Geraldine, I'm going to need to see a driver's' license if you please."

"I don't have one."

"You don't, huh? How old are you anyhow?"

"I'm sixteen."

The policeman is silent for a second and then, "Okay, Miss. Is there a reason you don't have a license to show me? By the way, confirm your age again for me."

"I'm sixteen and I've had my permit for a year but I just have never taken the test."

"Okay, then. You just stay right where you are for a minute. I'm going to walk back to the patrol car but you just sit still, okay?"

"Yes Sir."

A couple minutes later two policemen are standing by Gerri.

"Do you have any kind of identification on you...school ID card or anything like that?"

"Yeah, I probably have my school ID in my purse."

"Okay is that your purse on the floor? Go ahead pick it up and take out your ID for me."

As Gerri reaches for her purse she takes hold of her panties first and pulls them up as far as she can. Then with hands shaking so badly she can hardly hold the purse she lifts it into her lap. As she opens her purse and tries to take out the ID she drops everything from the purse scattering it all over the floorboard.

Like a lightning bolt the image goes through her mind of her dad looking for something on the floor of the family car. At this point this evening her dad's car searches seem inconsequential.

Sensing her nervousness, the policeman says, "Look Geraldine, I'm officer Ferguson. My intention is to get this all sorted out and you safely home as quickly as possible. I know you're feeling pretty scared right now but just bear with us and we'll get you home as quickly as we can. That right there looks like your ID so would you just hand it to me please."

Gerri picks up her ID and with her hands shaking, she holds it out to Officer Ferguson.

Officer Ferguson shines the flashlight on the card and looks back at Gerri, "And where do you live, Miss DeMore?"

Gerri points in the direction of her house. She can see the porch light of the house next door. "Right across the street. Right over there. See the light that's on. Over there."

"You want to tell us about what happened tonight?"

"What do you mean, what happened? Nothing happened." Though not convincing, Gerri is too frightened to even admit to herself what she knows all too well actually happened. She cannot imagine what sort of laws she's broken and what will happen to her. She will not even allow herself to think of the consequences of her time in the car with Jake. It makes her feel sick. Physically sick.

Officer Ferguson shines the light down to the edge of the seat where Gerri tries to conceal her panties but they obviously still show.

"Geraldine, I'm trying to be helpful here. If Jake forced himself on you I need to know. Even if he didn't force you to do something against your will and let's say things just got a little hot and heavy and something happened, he's still in big trouble. He's well over eighteen and you're well under. That makes it a crime for him to be physically involved with you to any extent or for him to even attempt to be physically involved with you. So once more I'd like for you to answer me. What happened here tonight with you and Jake?"

Gerri's reply is instantaneous and in true DeMore family tradition of denial, "Why do you ask me the same question again? I answered before. Nothing. Nothing happened."

"Well, let's see about getting you home and perhaps you and your parents can figure out the rest of it."

"I just live right over there. I can walk home."

Officer Ferguson laughs a bit, "Nah. That's not how this works, Miss DeMore. I'm going to **take** you home to your parents. You get straightened up and pick up your belongings from the car. I'll wait. Then you and I will take that long ride across the street and in my car this time. All safe and sound for your delivery home."

Gerri says nothing. She can't believe this nightmare is happening. She gathers her things and straightens her clothes as best she can. Now Gerri's focus is to get home before her dad happens to get there.

The patrol car with Jake in it is still sitting in the woods with the red light flashing but Officer Ferguson turns off the flashing light on his car as they start the short drive to Gerri's house.

The police car pulls across the street and parks in front of Gerri's home and there on Gerri's front steps sits the DeMore's next door neighbor, Paulette Guthrie. Paulette is unmistakable. At sixteen, Gerri's head and shoulders taller than Paulette's five feet one inch frame. But Paulette's characteristic   loud, raspy, smoker's voice makes her presence seem a lot larger. Paulette always wears either white short shorts with an over blouse or she wears a denim skirt and red checked blouse. But it's Paulette's accessories and style that make her really stand out. Even if she's mowing her lawn, she wears either bright gold or sequined slippers or sandals. Her latest glasses are red exaggerated cat-eye glasses. For Paulette, the more exotic, the better. Her bright red hair is pageboy style but she's never seen without a scarf that wraps from under her hair in the back and ties in a knot on the top front in sort of a "Rosie-The-Riveter look.

Paulette is nosy so she probably noticed the police activity across the street and since the DeMores weren't home she decided to use their steps to check out the excitement. She couldn't have known that Gerri was part of that excitement. But there she sits on the steps,. As the patrol car stops at the curb, Paulette stands. At first Gerri can't imagine what a complication this will be. Then it dawns on Gerri that Paulette knows her mom is in the hospital and promised to keep an eye on Gerri and the house during this time. She's probably just concerned because Gerri didn't get home from school before dark and hasn't heard from Stephen. Gerri is grateful that at least her dad isn't home yet.

As Officer Ferguson comes around the front of the patrol car to escort Gerri toward her house Gerri seizes a last ditch effort and in desperation walks quickly toward Paulette and blurts out, "Mom, I'm so sorry. I should have let you know I'd be late."

Gerri wonders if Paulette will look all around, dumbfounded and not catch on and ask what in the world she's talking about.

 But Paulette is up to the challenge. Without a second of hesitation, Paulette walks straight over to Gerri and Officer Ferguson and throws her arms around Gerri.

"Never you mind, Sweetie. I'm just glad you're here safe and sound." Paulette looks at the policeman, "Thank you for the escort. Was there a problem, Officer?" Paulette turns her attention to the policeman.

He stands before Gerri and Paulette nearly at attention, looking slightly unsure or ill at ease. That may be why he has his hat on with the visor low enough he can obviously see out from under but others can't really see his eyes. It's clear enough to see he's an all-American looking guy with hair buzzed on the sides, clean-shaven and his gray and blue uniform looks like it is all starch and not a wrinkle to be seen. He smiles with his lips drawn tight and his overall demeanor seems like he's the kind of young guy who's still trying to get comfortable being in a position of authority. As much of his face as is possible to see shows a handsomeness that than anything gives an immediate impression of sincerity and trust.

 "Well, Ma'am, Geraldine was across the street in a car with a man and although we didn't witness any actual physical contact, let's just say she, at sixteen years of age, was in a very compromised, vulnerable position with a man 22 years old. We're arresting him on suspicion of statutory rape but that will likely be determined by you and Geraldine. I'm going to give you the card of Detective Edward Schmidt and you need to call him within the next 24 hours and let him know if you wish to press charges or not. Even if you don't press charges Ed's…er Detective Schmidt's investigation and the prosecutor will determine if there's evidence enough that Mr. Waltrip can be charged. We'll either formally charge Jake Waltrip at that point or if you do not press charges and our investigation lacks evidence then we'll probably have to release him."

Paulette looks in shock at Gerri and then back at Officer Ferguson. Paulette stammers, "Compromised…a guy twenty-two years old? Well, uh, okay, then, uh… okay. Gerri and I have some talking to do. Is that it then for tonight?"

85

"Yes, Ma'am. Again, I'm Officer Ferguson and if you need to reach me just call the precinct. But most likely you'll want to talk to Detective Schmidt. But if I can help, I'll help any way I can. And I sincerely mean that. I'm on your side. But for now, I think I'd best leave it to you folks to work through the events and what you want to do . Ma'am, Geraldine, goodnight."

As Officer Ferguson courteously tips the bill of his uniform hat with his fingertips Paulette stands with her mouth open looking at Gerri. Gerri is sure Paulette would never have gotten involved if she'd known what was really in play.

Paulette breaks her hypnotic gaze at Gerri and replies to the policeman, "Yes, goodnight and thank you."

As Officer Ferguson walks toward his car, Paulette takes Gerri by the arm and guides her up the steps of Gerri's house. "Let's walk up here toward your front door, Gerri. Wouldn't want to break up this little act. Certainly no reason to do anything else stupid tonight is there?

They proceed up the steps and Gerri starts to reach for the house key under the doormat but Paulette quickly pulls up on her arm.

"Just hold on a second, Gerri. Let's just stand here and have a little animated discussion like I'm giving you a real blessing. Got it? Wait until he drives away to get the key. Remember? This is *our* house, remember? I wouldn't likely lock the door just to come out and sit on *our* steps."

"Oh yeah. Thanks."

Paulette pauses, touches Gerri's arm and stiffens a bit, "Hey, you're not getting off that easy, Young lady. Seems to me you owe me a little explanation. You're walking and acting slow. I can smell something other than Dentyne gum on your breath. Let me guess…a little alcohol? Seems obvious to me but at least the cop didn't mention that."

Gerri looks at Paulette but remains silent. Paulette shrugs and motions for Gerri to proceed with an explanation.

Gerri looks for some sympathy but begins, "You want me to tell you what happened? Right now?"

" Sure, speak right up. That would be a nice gesture on your part, particularly since I'm sure I could be put in the slammer for what I just did to get you out of a jam. So yeah, spill it."

" Look, Paulette. I'll tell you but I can't explain any of this to my dad or dad and mom if he brings her home. Okay? I'm sorry I had to get you in the middle of this but it's all I could think of at the moment. So, please, Paulette…please just between us?"

"Ya know you are really something! And you know that of course. I'll bet if a thousand teenagers had the same situation and saw a neighbor sittin on their steps they wouldn't have thought to do what you did. Actually I'm impressed. Kinda fun if I do say so myself. Ballsy, my dear, real ballsy. Hell, you don't even know what ballsy is do ya?"

"Of course I do. I'm not eight years old."

Paulette almost smiles, "Okay, I'll give you that. You're not eight years old."

The patrol car turns around in the DeMore driveway and then disappears down the street. Gerri glances across the street at the woods and there are no flashing lights. She unlocks the door , turns on the outside light and as she and Paulette go into the DeMore house she looks once again across the street to see the remaining police car turn from the woods road onto her street and then it too disappears down the street. Gerri figures Jake is in the car. She wonders what he'll tell the police. He might tell it all. But right now her troubles are still inside her sixteen year old body and her mind is in pure chaos. Where should she even begin to think through all that's happened? Why did she ever get in that car this afternoon? The shame and guilt of it!

"Tell you what, Gerri. You go ahead and turn on whatever house lights you want on and then come back over to my place. Who knows? They may release your mom this evening and even if they decide to keep her one more night, we can talk and you won't be alone. If it gets too late, you can go home and I can stay over with you until somebody gets home. Okay?"

"Sure, that sounds good.

CHAPTER 7

UH OH, TRUST?

Gerri turns on the outside lights of her house and returns to Paulette's. Paulette's house has a natural gravitational pull toward the kitchen table. The house is Paulette's personality. The kitchen has white cabinets and a bright red vinyl top table with chrome legs and vinyl chairs to match. Prominent on the table is an ashtray the size of a dinner plate, empty at the moment, but remnant ashes still in place. A carton of Lucky Strike cigarettes is on the countertop next to the sink and an open pack is on the table with a book of matches stuffed down the cellophane cover of the pack.

"Coffee or something else?"

"No, thanks, Paulette, I really don't feel very good at the moment so I'll pass for now."

Paulette shakes out a cigarette, packs it on her bright red polished thumbnail and with a small gesture lands it on the edge of her lips. She methodically lights a match, sucks on the cigarette so that there's not a wisp of smoke at first and then she exhales a cloud that's quite impressive for a little woman. Gerri fights the image of Jake lighting cigarettes by clinking open his Zippo and raking it across his jeans.

"Okay, so you're not eight years old. Want a cigarette?"

"No thanks. That I've not tried but I'm sure I will sooner or later. A lot of the boys smoke at school and actually quite a few girls smoke if their boyfriends smoke. But I guess right now I don't need anything else on my breath. Right?"

"Oh yeah, thanks for reminding me. Paulette goes to a kitchen cabinet and takes out a Hershey bar. She slides it across the table to Gerri.

"Eat a little of this if you can. It'll kill that alcohol smell as quick as anything. And by the way, you can begin talking any old time. You can eat while you're telling me what the heck happened tonight."

Gerri begins to tear at the Hershey bar, "Well, I got finished with school and my dad said yesterday he'd pick me up from school today as long as he didn't have to pick up my mom at the hospital or anything else that might conveniently come up. Naturally, he was nowhere in sight and I have no idea if he's at school, the hospital or where he might be. And I really don't care. Anyhow, after school when he wasn't there I figured I had to walk home to an empty house so I had some goof-off time."

"Gosh, Dear, I feel so bad about Susie…er your mom's not having an easy time of this. And I know you and your dad are feeling it as well."

"Paulette, you don't even know the half of it. You wanted to hear so I'm gonna tell. My dad is only at home long enough to change clothes, get some sleep, grab a sandwich and leave the dirty dishes and oh yeah, he does only what he absolutely has to for Mom. And then only if she asks him, otherwise nothing. He never spends any time talking to her, and he never, ever talks to me except to let me know I'm a brat and shouldn't question anything."

"Yeah, yeah, yeah, Gerri. I'm sure your mom gets bored being in bed all the time and I ought to make it a point to come over more often and sit with her. I'm sure a lot of the way you see all this right now is what you're going through during this stage of your innocent little life. Well, I'll hold off on the innocent until I get the rest of the story. So go ahead and give me your version of what happened this afternoon and tonight."

"Well, this afternoon after school when I came out the school doors there was this girl I know, Connie, and she said her big brother, Jake was coming by to pick her up and I could ride home. About that time he pulled up in this really cool car. I mean everybody who was around was eyeing that car."

"Okay. Then?"

"Well, Connie's brother agreed to take me home and when we got in the car he said he had to stop by and see some guys for a few minutes. So I said that was cool…fine. Well, we stopped by and I had a coke. Well, then we left and he was bringing me home. I told Jake our car

90

wasn't here and no lights, so no one was at home yet. So, we went just across the street to talk. Well, you know a little kissin and stuff but I swear, Paulette that's it. Then the cops came and here I am. I'm so sorry but please don't tell my dad or mom. I won't ever do that again."

Paulette is silent. She seems sympathetic. She smiles a forgiving smile. But Gerri can't read Paulette's feelings. Paulette knows she just got the quick sanitized version and there just has to be lots more to the story.

"Well, okay. If you say that's it and it was all perfectly innocent then I guess that's it. Right?" Paulette takes a long drag off her Lucky and turns her head to one side as she exhales a cloud. Then she turns toward Gerri and stares intently into Gerri's eyes.

Gerri wants out of this now. She doesn't like Paulette's look.

"Yep, that's it."

"Okay. You are certainly welcome to stay here with me for a while until your dad or parents come home or if you have things to do you can go on home if you want. I just want you to trust me when I tell you that I'd do anything for you, Kiddo. You can always talk to me about anything. And I do mean, anything. What we talk about stays between you and me unless you talk about it to someone else. Okay? I just want to say it so you know."

Gerri takes a deep breath. She wants so badly to talk more but she just cannot at this moment. She's so frightened about what might be the results of this night she can't bring herself to talk about it out loud. Best to act as if nothing else happened, get home and take a bath. Gerri wonders if a hot bath can prevent pregnancy. Maybe all this will seem better in the morning.

"I know, Paulette. And thanks for listening. I think I'll go on home, take a bath and go to bed. Another exciting school day tomorrow."

"Yeah, Kid. You had quite the day today. Brought home in a limo…so to speak. Maybe you can get a ride home with the mayor tomorrow." Paulette snuffs out her cigarette and walks with Gerri to the front door.

"You go on ahead and start running your bath. I'll be right over and I'll holler when I come in the front door. Just a couple of minutes. Least I can do is stay with you until they get home. If you go to sleep, that's fine. I'll just stick around. My pleasure." Paulette holds out her arms for a hug.

"Okay. Thanks for being here, Paulette." Gerri hugs Paulette so tight she can feel Paulette wince. Without another word Gerri leaves Paulette's house and walks across the yard to the DeMore house. As soon as Gerri is in her house she goes into the bathroom and looks in the mirror. Perhaps she doesn't look any different but she sees herself a totally different person. Gerri's major-life-events clock can never have the hands reversed from today. Time to brush her teeth and take a bath. Then she can have another look to see if it's truly a metamorphosis of her looks or if she's reading too much into the straggly hair and slightly smeared lipstick.

She begins to draw a bath and undress, dropping her clothes unceremoniously on the floor. She thinks it's a bit ironic how quickly she can drop her underpants to the floor. Somehow it always took a couple of downward tugs before. Now a tug on one side and a hip wiggle lands them right at her feet ready to step out. Gerri looks at her pile of clothes and she bends down, picking up her underpants and looking at them inside and out. A shock goes through her body. The reality of what happened with Jake is evident and very obvious by the looks of her pants. Gerri wads them into a little ball and runs naked into the kitchen and there's nothing romantic or sexy about holding her pants out from her and making a face as if they are disgusting or toxic. She has to hurry because this would be difficult to explain if the front door suddenly opens and Paulette or her parents saw her exhibition of streaking around the house carrying underwear. She grabs a piece of newspaper from the trashcan under the sink and wraps her panties in it. She stuffs the wadded up paper as deep into the trash as she can and makes a mental note to "help out" in the morning by dumping the kitchen trash before school.

Gerri hurries back to the bathroom, brushes her teeth and uses cold cream to take off lipstick and the small amount of makeup she uses. Paulette announces her arrival so Gerri feels relieved her timing was okay with the underwear. She steps into the tub and slowly slides down into the warm water. The effect is very, very comforting. She soaks for a long, soothing period trying to disengage her mind from anything unpleasant. No thoughts about her dad. No worry for the moment about her mother. No thoughts of Jake. No thoughts of Connie. Gerri sits up in the tub and her body tingles. Thinking about Mr. Penn is different. Gerri wonders how he might treat her if he knew she was now an experienced woman.

Her fantasy is shattered like a bolt of lightning when she whispers to herself, "What if I'm pregnant?"

This is exactly how it happens. Maybe there's some way to know. She slides back down into the water, muttering quietly to herself, "Just stop! You've got to put all this out of your mind. Act like nothing happened. You know exactly how Mom and Dad treat stuff like this. Deny it, ignore it and act as if nothing is wrong. Nine times out of ten it will just blow over. Nothing."

The bath makes Gerri feel back to normal, at least visibly normal. She's preoccupied to the point of becoming obsessive about repercussions of her sexual fiasco. Every time she tries to think about something else her heart begins to pound and her thoughts regress to worry. Gerri wonders if this is how every waking minute is going to be until she knows for sure. Pregnancy. It has such frightening connotations to it and particularly since she's witnessed her mother's round of weakness and struggles. At sixteen years old she simply can't imagine how any of it could work. It would be a disaster. Total disaster.

Gerri finally emerges from her room in pajamas. She and Paulette sit on the sofa together and Paulette obviously is still interested in what is happening with Gerri.

"Okay, Princess, aside from what I know of tonight how's the rest of your life going? I hope it's phenomenal."

"Well, that's certainly not the way I'd describe this week…or last…or the ones before that. Wait until you hear the rest."

"Good Lord! There's more? Well, give it to me straight up on the rocks."

"Huh?" Gerri smiles at Paulette, settles against her shoulder and begins, "First off, at school, a girl in my class, Betsy Alder, the most popular girl in school, invited me to a party at her house. That was so cool! But then later in the day she basically withdrew the invitation because I turned down some guy who asked me to a dance. But I couldn't believe it. One minute here's a written invitation and the next minute oops, so sorry."

Paulette listens intently and nods, "Pretty rude if you asked me."

" Anyhow between classes she was trying to figure out a nice way to dis-invite me and I was a little confused about what she was really trying to do. She went off to the bathroom or somewhere so I walked up to join three of her other friends who were standing close by in the

94

hallway. They didn't know I was so close but I could clearly hear they were talking about me and saying really horrible things. They said I look ugly. Like a scarecrow with boobs. They said I was only invited to the party because Betsy's mom made her invite me and nobody really likes me. I was so embarrassed I started to cry. Then I was late for class and when I walked in the teacher singled me out in front of everybody and I couldn't help it. I ran from the room back to the bathroom. I was just trying to get through the day so I could see my mom this afternoon but she's still in the hospital and now if mom has the baby tonight she'll be there for another week before I can see her. I feel so lost and alone!"

"My gosh, girl. You had a bad day! Sometimes things all seem to happen at once and I know you 'll find this hard to believe but sometimes girls can be just plain mean. I don't think a lot of them intend to be that way but they get picked on by somebody or they aren't feelin' good or something and then they just pounce on the first victim they run across. Now present company excepted, I've never been mean, catty or bitchy to anybody in my entire life...well maybe once, or twice, or a couple thousand times, but that's all. I'm sorry those things happened but sometimes you gotta let stuff just go in one ear and out the other as if they don't have any idea what they're even talkin' about. And that goes for the teacher as well. She might have been having a bad day of her own and you just happen to come in a little late. Just let it go, Gerri. There's a lot worse stuff in this world. I know it made you feel bad but just try to let it go for what it was. Probably their problem that caused it, not yours. Okay?"

"I know. Let it go. But I can only let so much go. Besides, there's more. Oh, there's more, much, much more. You sure you're ready for all this?"

"Go ahead and shoot. I'm all ears. And by the way. How long were you gonna store all this and just let it cause you grief? That really

95

makes me feel bad. I'll always be here for you, Gerri. I just always thought that you and Susie were so close that you didn't need me horning in with my two cents."

"Paulette, if you only knew. I love my mom more than anything in the whole world and I want to be just like her ...except she's got the same bad habit as my dad. Nobody in our house ever talks about anything that's real life. Just smile and act like nothing happened. I've learned the few things I know about my body and what to expect like periods, pregnancy and all that from overhearing jokes and stories at school. Mom always says there's plenty of time to talk about all that stuff and so I'm probably the stupidest girl around when it comes to the real truth about girl-stuff."

"I'm willin' to give you the doctor's degree in Paulette's course about sex, human body, at least the way I see it and anything else I can help with. Just between you and me that birds and bees stuff is a fairy tale. Who can learn about their body and babies and womanhood by hearing about little fuzzy critters with a stinger? But I will admit I've dated some guys in my early days that would fit that description. Well, anyhow we can talk about anything you want and I won't withhold anything. Language may be a little rougher than you're used to but I'll sure tell you as much as I know. I've got my own fair share of scrapes and bruises from learning some things the hard way so if any of my mistakes help you, kid you got it."

Gerri continues telling Paulette about her verbal jousting becoming more intense with her dad and what she overheard her mom say how he'd done some bad things before."

"Well, maybe that's none of my business and you'd rather not talk about those sorts of details."

Gerri continues, "No, Paulette. It feels good to say out loud what I've been hearing and seeing for quite a while now. It's all part of why I feel so miserable and alone. Anyhow, here's what you don't know. Earlier I didn't tell you everything that built up to tonight. This morning at school I suppose I was feeling a little guilty about the way I've treated my dad or at least I wanted to make a peace treaty if possible so I got permission to come home for lunch. I was going to pick up the house and even fix him some lunch if he happened to come home during the lunch hour. As I came around the corner, there was our car in the driveway.

I thought maybe my dad was tired, or sick or something so I came in the house trying not to make any noise. He wasn't on the sofa like I thought he'd be and he wasn't in the kitchen. So, I went down the hall, quietly so I wouldn't wake him if he was sleeping. Then I heard his voice and a woman's voice talking quietly in my mom and dad's bedroom. Paulette, I couldn't believe it. At first I thought maybe Mom was home from the hospital but real quick I could tell it wasn't her in that room. It was my dad with another woman and the door was closed and they were laughing real quietly and talking real low."

"Oh my God, honey. Mercy me. I am so sorry. What'd you do?"

"That was the last thing in the world I expected and I was just standing there with my mouth hanging open. Then I got mad, really, really mad. I went into my room and slammed the door so loud it must have echoed through the whole neighborhood. I made sure they heard me. I banged the doors and knocked stuff around. I heard the bathroom door shut and then my dad knocked on my door asking if I was alright. I screamed at him to get away and leave me alone. He never said another word and he went back in his bedroom and closed the door. That's my dad for you.

Later I heard whoever it was in the bathroom quietly open the door and sneak back to my mom and dad's room. I finally went out the front door and left it standing wide open. I was so mad at him and whoever that was with him. My poor mother is in the hospital and that's how he treats her? That's just not right and he knows it. It makes me feel sick at my stomach just to think of it. And that's another reason I had little expectation of him showing up to give me a ride home after school."

"Gerri, I had no idea. Your dad always seems so loving toward your mom. Do you think there's any way you may be misunderstanding what you think you saw?"

"Paulette. I know what I saw...well what I heard. They were in my mother's bedroom laughing and talking all quiet and low. When I made noise, there was a mad scramble and the woman went into the bathroom afraid to come out. So I couldn't see who it was. Dad was trying to be so gentle and nice knocking on my door. He knows for sure that I know. I don't know what my mom will do when she finds out. What do you think she will do?"

"Well, that's hard to say. And he never had anything else to say about it since it happened?"

"Oh, yes. When he was knocking on my door he told me I misunderstood. He said it was a teacher from his school helping him get some clothes for my mom, I suppose to wear home from the hospital. What a liar!"

"And you don't think that's a likely story?"

"Gosh no. Come on Paulette. Mom was so careful what she packed...two weeks ago at least. She wouldn't want anybody else picking out clothes for her to wear. And I guarantee you my dad would be the last person she'd ask if she needed more clothes or makeup. No. That was a very weak, stupid try for an alibi."

"Yeah, his story sounds pretty soft and that's a real shame, Hon. Surely he knows he's been caught red-handed and his story is weak sounding."

"Well, I don't know what Mom will do. Should I tell her what I heard and saw when she comes home?"

"Young lady, you're in dangerous territory with me on this. I suppose my advice may not be what you want to hear but my advice is to watch and wait patiently. I think it will be pretty clear if he does tell her and probably just as clear if he doesn't. I'd give it a week or two, just to see. Your mama doesn't need to have you unload that on her as she walks in the door with a new baby. I expect since he knows that you know and how angry you are, he'll want to be the one to tell his side of it before she finds out from you. So, just be patient. It's for them to work out and I'm sure you and your mom will eventually get the chance to set all the facts straight. Just don't rush it. Okay?"

"Yeah, fine. Anyhow, I told you earlier about the ride home after school. Actually, there's a little more to it. I told you that before heading home I paused on the school steps outside and that's when this girl I know, Connie Waltrip, said her older brother was coming by to pick her up and I could get a ride home with them. It sounded harmless enough and besides I felt like doing something a little bit over the top just to get even with what my dad's done. And, as I told you her brother, Jake, arrived in this really, really cool black car and we left school and went to some pool hall, Brentwood's or something."

"Good God Almighty. You went to Brentwood's? No, you sure left that out the first time. Gerri, what in the living hell would a girl like you be in such a place? That's a hangout for hoodlums of all sizes and shapes. Holy smokes! You have no business being anywhere around a place like that. Oh, sorry. Go ahead with your story."

99

"Well, you're right it is a hangout but kinda cool once you're inside. Connie's brother, Jake, is leader of a gang, the Fresno Kings and he had me wear his leather jacket in the bar so no one would mess with me or anything. And they didn't. In fact a couple of guys walked way around so they wouldn't even come near me. Anyhow, Jake asked if I wanted a Coke and I said sure. I had no idea what it was the guy at the bar put in it but I watched him pour it. It was some red sweet stuff in my Coke and it was actually really good. After a while I was laughing and talking. When I asked Jake he said it's called sloe gin. I really felt good."

"Of course you felt good at the moment. At least until it wears off. What a scum. He knows better than to give teenagers alcohol."

"I know what you think but Jake was actually very mannerly and nice. He also looks exactly like James Dean. How cool is that? So when Jake was going to bring me home, Connie decided to stay behind with her boyfriend and so it was just Jake and me. When we got on our street I could see our car wasn't home so Jake said we could go across the street into the woods and that's what we did."

Gerri is feeling like she's unburdening herself with details but a feeling of uncertainty sweeps over her as she's talking. Just how many more details should she'll divulge. Suddenly she draws her story to an end. Some things she just can't admit just yet.

"And it's like I told you we were kissing and stuff and then all of a sudden the police were right there. And they made such a big deal out of it, but nothing else happened, Paulette. I may not know much but I do know that much. All around bad day."

Paulette is staring into Gerri's eyes like she did earlier. It's seems to Gerri that Paulette can look into her and know she's not telling the entire story. But Gerri isn't ready to admit to anything else. The fear must continue and so must the lie at least for now.

"Anyhow, I'm so angry at him. Have you ever heard of somebody doing something this lousy?"

"Who are we talking about? Are you angry at your dad? Or this guy Jake? Who ?"

"My dad, Paulette. My dad who's a cheater and liar!"

"Gerri, Honey, there isn't anybody who can get in the middle of something like this with your mom and dad. It's up to them...particularly your momma to decide if they're having a little trouble that's fixable or a whole lot of trouble that can't be fixed. I'm just very, very sorry you had to stumble across it like this. I'm usually the one who wants to hit problems head-on but this is one of those cases where that's not the right thing to do."

"Oh, I know, Paulette. I'm really not expecting you to be able to solve my mom and dad's problems."

"You're correct there. Again, it's a problem for them to work through or handle however they can. How I'd handle something that has to do with your parents doesn't count. It's their lives and I need to keep my big nose out of it. And by the way Gerri, that's why I said it's probably better for you to let your dad have a chance to talk with your mom about this. He's probably scared out of his wits that somehow you'll tell her before he has a chance so I'd be pretty certain that she'll know pretty darn quick. From what you said your mama already has suspicions but who knows for sure? How you and your dad get along in the meantime is a rough situation for both of you. I'm not making excuses for him but you know he may be very, very sorry for what's happened and doesn't want it to affect you. That would be my guess."

"Affect me? What he did, *does* affect me! Of course it does. He hurt my mommy and sneaked around behind her back and hurt her. I hate him. That's how it affects me."

"Well, I know you're angry but don't let your anger make the entire house impossible to live in once your mama's home. Maybe take a lead from her about how to act. You know how sweet and wonderful Susie is, just seeing how she treats your dad. She may be mad at him or worse. She may play nice and let him earn his way back into her good graces. You'll just have to see."

"Well that'll be a change for me...for sure. Even if I get angry and say something to him he just gets sarcastic with me and then changes the subject. I just go to my room and slam the door. I don't feel bad for doing that but I think down deep he just gets scared whenever he has to face anything bad. But I think you're right and I'll see how Mom acts with him...the jerk."

Paulette laughs. She's impressed how this "little girl" is shouldering so much and yet able to express her anger and feelings. But Paulette believes there may be more she's not hearing. Maybe that will come in time.

Gerri and Paulette continue to talk and eventually as it gets much later they both fall asleep on the sofa.

CHAPTER 8

GERRI'S WORLD IMPLODES

At the sound of the car in the driveway, Gerri springs off the sofa and is out the door and down the steps. After all the waiting and blaming her father for so much suspicion what she wants now more than anything is the safety, the security of her mother's and father's love. Gerri runs straight to Stephen and throws her body into his arms. She looks up at him wanting so badly for her happy fantasy to rekindle but she's surprised because he's avoiding looking at her. Stephen DeMore stares straight ahead.

"Oh, Daddy, I was so scared. Why didn't you call? Paulette's here but you should have called. I was so worried about Mom."

Suddenly Gerri realizes her father's hug is weak and pulling away from her. She pulls back from the remnants of her father's seemingly unemotional embrace and she sees a startled, shocked look on his grimacing face. He has not spoken a single word.

"Daddy? What's happened? What's wrong?"

Stephen doesn't say anything. Then he clutches onto Gerri so tight she can scarcely breathe. Stephen quietly sobs.

Finally, Stephen takes a loud, long deep breath. He gently releases his bear hug on her and without a spoken word, puts his hands on her shoulders, turns her around facing the house and guides her toward the steps.

"Come on. We'd better go inside."

Paulette removes her glasses and rubs her eyes. She's senses something horrible has happened.

"Listen you two, I'm gonna leave you alone and go home. Stephen, I'm a hundred feet away and I'll do anything you need. Please let me know what's going on when you can and let me help if I can."

Stephen doesn't say anything but Gerri sees him give Paulette a nod and tearful half-smile.

Gerri's stomach feels sick. She can't imagine why all this drama and why her father hasn't mentioned her mother or the new baby.

"But Dad. What's happened? Is Mommy okay? You have to tell me. What's happening?"

"C'mon, let's just go inside. I need to sit down. Come on, now… just come on in with me."

Stephen has his arm around Gerri's shoulder and Gerri puts her arm around Stephen's waist, an embrace so important to Gerri but so awkward they have difficulty maneuvering up the steps. Stephen pulls away from Gerri to open the front door and motions for her to go inside.

Stephen slowly and quietly closes the front door and the latch makes what is usually a comforting, routine click but for some reason at this instant everything sounds sharp and raw to her. For an instant Stephen and Gerri stand silently just inside the door of the quiet house.

"Come over here and sit down with me, Gerri."

They move to the sofa, take a seat next to each other and Gerri looks into her father's face. Stephen's eyes are red from crying. But he isn't crying now and he doesn't seem as nervous or tense as when he first arrived. For a split-second Gerri thinks maybe she is misunderstanding and perhaps nothing too bad has happened particularly because her dad takes a deep breath and seems more calm. Gerri is so close to her dad's face she can see the stubble beard and smell medicine or rubbing alcohol or maybe that's just a hospital smell. His breath reeks of stale coffee and it's very unpleasant to her but at this moment Gerri just wants him to talk. Just talk!

"Geraldine, I've been at the hospital the whole time since early this afternoon and have been with your mother most of that time, at least when they'd leave me in the room and not push me out into the hall. It certainly wasn't what anyone wanted but the baby was coming early. Gerri, your mother had very, very low blood pressure and had some trouble in delivery. The baby was born but it was just too early for him and he didn't have enough strength to make it. It was a beautiful little boy. He never breathed on his own. He just wasn't strong enough. The doctors and nurses wouldn't let me see him but I know they were doing everything they could. But in the end it wasn't enough. There was nothing else they could do."

"Ahhh! Oh no! Oh, Daddy...No. It can't be true. Oh, Daddy! It can't be true! Mommy must be so sad." She grabs the long hair on each side of her head and pulls it straight out to the sides partly yelling from the pain and crying from the sadness. She can't imagine how to bear the thought of the loss of the baby.

"My poor Mommy! She must be so sad. Daddy, I've got to see her!"

Stephen chokes back a sob and wipes his eyes, "Gerri. Come here close to me and look at me. You've got to know about this. It's so bad I can hardly say it."

He breaks down and cries out loud. Gerri's terrified. She's never experienced anything like this in her family. Gerri squeezes her eyes shut and begins to cry along with her father.

Little could Gerri know that there can be no preparation when lightning strikes the same place twice.

"Gerri, when Dr. Heinzen was explaining about our little boy, his nurse came running out of the room where they had just moved Susie and the nurse was screaming for the doctor. Something else had happened...I had no idea what. They both ran back to Susie's room along with several other hospital staff and closed the door. They wouldn't let me in. Gerri, can you imagine? I'm just left standing in the hall and they wouldn't let me in. When the Doctor finally came out he... and told...he told me that Sus...your mother...well, her heart failed and they couldn't revive her...she passed away...and I didn't even get to talk to her after the baby was born. I never even got to see her alive again. I just can't believe it. They're both gone. Gerri...they're gone. Oh God, Gerri. What will we do? They're both gone."

Stephen is mopping at his tear-filled, swollen eyes and he pulls away from Gerri. He gets a serious look, almost a trance on his face. Gerri winces, startled as Stephen groans loudly as if he's straining to lift something. He raises his clenched fists in the air.

"*Awwww!* I can't talk about it anymore. I just can't. I can't explain any of it. It's a nightmare. It's not true! I just can't talk about it anymore."

Gerri stares straight at her dad, paralyzed in disbelief. Her breath is very quick and shallow. Shattered from the emotional bomb that just went off inside her head, Stephen suddenly looks unreal, like the negative of a black and white photograph. Gerri's breathing short little breaths and her stomach feels fluttery. Her father's words seem to get

106

farther and farther away until they sound like echoes in a hollow cave. Then everything gets quiet and black as Gerri faints from shock.

Everything is lost in time and space as Gerri slowly starts to regain consciousness. At first she can't unscramble what's happened or whose voice she faintly hears. It's a little like the confusion while waking from a dream. Then the pain floods over her entire body and mind again with more intensity than before. Gerri gasps for breath.

"Just stay where you are!. Don't try to get up just yet. I'll get you a glass of water. Stay here."

Death? Died? She's heard in the past of relatives who died but she's never been near when it happened. A kaleidoscope of terror, horror, ghoulish jigsaw pieces of memories swirl in Gerri's mind. She can't speak. She can't think.

Stephen brings a glass of water and sits down by her feet. His hand is shaking so badly a little of the water slops out. "Here ya go. Maybe this will help a little."

Gerri looks intently at her father. His hair is tousled. It looks so strange. It's greasy and straggly. His tie is off and his wrinkled white shirt has the top button undone. This is so unusual. But Stephen DeMore is not himself tonight. Somehow Gerri senses her world is not the same at this moment and it will never, ever be the same ever again.

"This is so hard to even understand. It just can't be any worse for us right now. I don't want to risk you fainting again or getting sick so maybe in a bit you should get ready for bed. You can stay up for a while if you like but eventually you'll have to try to get some sleep and we'll talk about all this tomorrow."

Later Gerri stands silently, almost trance-like at the side of her bed. She's had her pajamas on for hours so she really has no reason to do anything else before bed. But going to bed doesn't seem possible at the moment. She pauses, just staring at the wall. Gerri's head feels numb. How can this be happening? Is it a dream? She's certain the answer to that is, no! For sure it's no dream and now what's she supposed to do? What will happen to them without her mom? Even now, she can't picture her father picking up the shattered pieces and taking control in a positive , comforting way. As she squeezes her eyes shut, she whispers, "Please God, let Dad make this all stop. He's got to help me. I'm so afraid. Just make this go away and bring back my mommy. Pleeease! I can't take this."

Eventually she lies down on her bed for some comfort but it feels so hard and cold. She sits up and reaches for a book but just as quickly tosses it aside. Her mind jumps from one horrible thought to another. Again, her breathing becomes quick and shallow. She feels light headed and nauseated..

As if she can make it all go away by talking aloud, "Please, please dear God, I know I've been a terrible daughter but please forgive me and bring my mother back. It's my fault, not hers…and the baby. I'll never ask for anything again except my mother."

With that Gerri throws herself across the bed and buries her face in the pillow. At least it blocks the light. Light seems to make the horror and sadness even worse. Gerri lies on top of her bedcovers and slowly turns toward the bedside lamp, switching it off.

As Gerri lies in the dark silence she can't remember what her mother's face looks like. She vividly recalls her mother's beautiful hair, and she knows her mother's face is so beautiful but she can't see it in her mind.

" Oh God, why am I doing this? Am I going crazy? I never even saw my little brother and I don't even know how to imagine him. What was his face like? Did he look like me? Daddy? Mommy? This isn't fair and I know now I am going completely crazy."

The lights in the room make her feel horrible but when she turns out the lights, no matter how hard she tries, she can't remember her own mother's face. Gerri abruptly sits up and once again switches on the light. Feet on the floor, sliding her feet across the room, she picks up the picture of her mother and father and stares at it. Tears stream down her cheeks and her heart hurts from the searing pain of loss and tragedy. Gerri wonders if this is going to be her destiny of suffering for the rest of her life.

Gerri hears her dad stirring in the living room and with eyes swollen from tears and trying too hard to go to sleep, she goes to the living room to join her father.

"Oh, honey. I thought you went to bed. Can't sleep?"

"No, Dad. When I turn out the lights I can't." Gerri begins to cry, " I can't remember what Mommy looks like and I never knew what the baby looked like. It's just awful." She lunges toward her Dad and he holds her in his arms.

"I know. I know. But, Gerri, we've got to be strong. That's what your mother would have wanted. Things like falling asleep and dreaming will be difficult for a while but we'll get through it. Right?"

"I'm not so sure, Dad. What will happen to us?"

"Well, we aren't going anywhere and we just have to work our way through everything. I just can't think about all of it right at this moment. Would you mind if we talk in the morning...and for now maybe just try to go back and lie down and try to go to sleep?"

Gerri doesn't answer him. She turns and starts toward her room, thwarted again, no answers; always tomorrow, never just talk about problems. She gets to her room knowing this is her assigned spot for the night and it's not going to do any good at all to come out seeking comfort from her Dad. Gerri lies across her bed and cries. She feels so alone. It's like being dropped down a well and destined to live in her own solitary, horrible, dismal world.

CHAPTER 9

A BAD DREAM IS BORN

Gerri wakes with a start. It's her dad softly calling to her and knocking on her bedroom door. She yawns and stretches but it doesn't even feel like she's been to sleep. She feels dizzy and then it all comes rushing over her again as she recalls the panic last night of trying to remember her mom's face. Her head jerks around toward her mother and father's picture on the chest next to the bed. She stares at it in exhausted disbelief.

"Yes. I'm awake. You can come in."

Stephen opens the door slowly and comes over and sits on the edge of her bed. He puts his hand to her forehead and brushes her hair back, "Listen Gerri, dear, you rest as long as you need. When you get up you should try to eat something. It may make you feel a little better."

"No. I don't think I can eat anything. Oh Dad! This can't be happening. I can't believe it. I keep thinking I'm dreaming and I'll wake up. I feel so horrible. I feel sick and dizzy."

"Well, you just take your time. And Gerri even if you're not feeling hungry, at least try even if it's only a piece of toast. Believe me, it will

110

take away some of that sick feeling. And I suspect there may not be too much rest later today. We'll likely get over run here shortly."

"Over run? By what or who? What do you mean?"

"Well, as soon as word spreads about all of this, and it surely will spread like wildfire, people feel like they need to do something. They'll want to help if they possibly can.   It's customary that people call on the telephone and express sympathy and ask if there's anything they can do... and there will be some who will stop here at the house and visit for a second or two. Some will probably drop off food for us."

"They can bring my mommy back, Dad. That's what they can do." Sobbing, Gerri buries her face in the pillow.

"I know, honey. I'm trying to deal with the same shock you are. But I'm just telling you people will be calling and some will probably come by with cards or just to say something for a minute or two. So what I'm saying is when you do get up and get dressed, please dress sort of like you're going to church...you know, dressy.   I'm going to wear a suit today. It's just a nice thing to do out of respect for your mama and little brother."

"Oh, Dad, I don't know if I can do any of this. I don't want to face anybody and I don't want to talk to anybody about it. I just hurt so bad inside. My heart actually hurts and I just want to cry all the time. Dad, what will we do?"

"I know. I know. But up and at 'em...when you feel like it." And he turns and walks back to his bedroom.

Gerri finally drags out of bed and makes her way to the bathroom. She can see her father in her mother and dad's bedroom. He puts a tie around his neck and looks in the mirror. Gerri thinks it seems a little

111

strange. It's the exact way he looks in the mirror every single morning when he leaves for school. That's not the way he should act the day after her mother and little baby brother die. Not today!

She scoots her slippered feet toward the master bedroom doorway, "Dad? Did you and Mom have a name picked out for my little brother?" She got the question out but immediately her face twists into a tear-filled mess.

"Yes, Gerri. His name was to be Matthew Julian. We were going to give him Susie's father's name and my dad's name but that's not to be." Her dad lowers his head and she can see his head move up and down as he cries openly. Her heart is breaking and it hurts even worse when she sees her dad cry.

Gerri slowly returns to the bathroom to get cleaned up and dressed. She combs and brushes her hair and puts on her dark blue corduroy jumper and black patent leather shoes. She carefully pulls her hair back in a ponytail, and through tears she whispers to the mirror, "Ponytail, just like Mom likes."

It's as if people have a written agenda to follow because at almost exactly noon the phone begins ringing and no sooner is it hung up from one call it begins anew with an unbroken string of the DeMore ring on the eight-party phone line, one long ring followed by two short ones. *riiiiing-ring-ring, riiiiing-ring ring*.

Stephen answers every call and to Gerri it seems every conversation is identical. "Yes. I know. Well, thank you for your kind words. Yes. We appreciate it. No. I don't know of anything you can do but I do appreciate you asking. That's very kind. No. There haven't been any arrangements yet but we'll be taking care of that tomorrow and then we'll be sure you know. Okay. Thanks for calling. We appreciate your thoughts and prayers. Goodbye."

"Yes I know. Well, thank you for your kind words. Yes. We appreciate it. No. I don't know of anything you can do but I do appreciate you asking. That's very kind. No. There haven't been any arrangements yet but we'll be taking care of that today or tomorrow I'm sure and then we'll be sure to let you know. Okay. Thanks for calling. Goodbye."

With Stephen busy fielding all the phone calls Gerri slumps on the living room sofa so sad she can hardly stand it. The unbroken monotony of the phone calls is an endless reminder of the tragedy.

There's a knock at the door and Stephen is still on a phone call. Gerri wonders if maybe it's Paulette. She gets up from the sofa and opens the door to find two middle-aged ladies she's never seen before.

"Hello dear. You must be the daughter. We're so sorry for you but is your father able to come to the door and talk with us for a couple of seconds. We can't stay but we'd like to pay our respects."

As if on cue, Stephen appears right behind Gerri and gently scoots her out of the doorway.

"Hello, ladies. Millie, Joan."

The one my dad calls Millie begins, "Stephen, we are so sorry for you and your girl. We just brought a little food by to help get you through the next few days. I know just how you feel. When I lost my sister I just didn't think I could go on but of course here I stand today. Time surely heals all."

Well, thanks for your kind words and the food. Gerri, will you take these dishes to the kitchen? And would you ladies like to come in?"

Gerri is confused by how her father is so friendly and smiling...just slightly more subdued than if it had been a week ago before any of this tragedy. There is some little something that she doesn't trust or like about the two women. She simply can't articulate that what irritates her are jealousy and suspicion as if these visitors are raiding her mother's nest. Probably more than anything, Gerri doesn't like the condescending tone and "You must be the daughter" comment.

Gerri mutters as she dutifully takes the casserole dishes to the kitchen, " Don't they wonder if I have a name? Oh, no. I'm just the girl or the daughter. Looks to me like they wanted to flirt with my dad. Yuk. Old bags."

Gerri overhears a bit more of the small talk and mutters a whisper to herself in defiance, "So Clarabell-the-clown or whatever her name is thinks that because she lost a sister this is the same? Well, I've got news for her. It's not the same and she better not tell me it is. I really don't care about someone else's sister right now. I only care about my mommy."

As Gerri returns to the living room she surprises herself at the sudden anger about the women coming to the house. Her growing feeling of anger draws intensity from the overwhelming grief that's dominated her every waking minute of the day.

Then the phone rings again and as Gerri glances at her dad he motions for her to stay where she is and he'll answer the phone. That's fine with Gerri because she doesn't want to have to deal with Millie and Joan again so she looks at her dad and gives a little bow and sweeps her arm in the direction of the kitchen indicating her dad is most welcome to answer the phone.

The two women bid a quick farewell and as the door closes, Stephen rushes toward the ringing phone, Gerri shrugs her shoulders and lets her words follow him into the kitchen, "I have no idea what you want me to do. Get the door, get the phone, or just sit here. Whatever you want. I'm just the girl."

Stephen either doesn't hear Gerri or ignores her comments as he gets to the kitchen and is right on script for the phone call once again. Gerri thinks she'll not have the patience to listen to this all day.

"Okay. Goodbye." Stephen walks from the kitchen and cranes his posture toward the front window as if to see if anyone is coming up the front steps so he can get prepared for the next wave of dramatics. But before Gerri can say anything sarcastic her dad speaks up," See Gerri this is why I wanted us to be dressed and sitting out here. There's going to be plenty more people stopping by to pay their respects. It's sort of a tradition that people bring food. So we just need to be as pleasant as possible. You can sure help by taking any food and putting it away. That will give me a chance to talk with each of them a little bit and thank them."

" Sure, Dad. But I don't think it helps a whole lot to have strangers show up with food and act like they're doing us a favor, pretending to care...or at least care about you. I just feel constantly sick to my stomach. I don't want any of their stinky, icky old casseroles."

"Aw, c'mon, Gerrie. That's not my girly. Try to look and act a little more pleasant. I know this is very hard for you but it isn't easy for me either. So let's just get through it with a smile and then you and I can spend some time just sitting on the sofa together. Would you like that?"

"Oh yes, I would like that a lot. I just want to sit by you. I feel so sad I want to cry and my stomach is upset. But I can't cry and that makes me feel even worse. I feel dizzy all the time like I'm going to faint. I'm so scared and I don't know why I feel so strange. Am I sick? Am I gonna be okay, Daddy?"

115

Stephen's intended answer is interrupted by another knock on the door. "Oops. Well, here we go again, Gerri. We'll have plenty of time to talk tonight so for now let's just be pleasant and get through this afternoon."

Gerri doesn't know most of the people who come to the door and drop off food, flowers and cards. To her it seems people are there only to see Stephen but he insists that if he's on the phone Gerri should open the door and politely greet the people and offer to come and get him. A similar instruction applies if Stephen's at the door with someone and the phone rings. Gerri should answer the phone and then come and get Stephen. That gives him ample reason to end a call or visit. Those are his instructions but Gerri sees it as pre-planned, fake drama so he can make a breathless entrance to receive the hugs and handshakes or rush to the phone out of breath. Gerri thinks this charade is demeaning to her poor mother and little brother.

Stephen makes sure there's always something to check on so he never pauses long enough to answer the two main questions Gerri asks many times between visitors and phone calls, "What are we going to do without Mom? Are we gonna be okay?"

After observing the day's activities Gerri is certain there must be a secret instruction book people follow when there's a death. They memorize a few phrases to say on the phone or when they bring food to the door.

Over and over again the same phrases are repeated,

"I know just how you feel."

"When my mother died…"

"Well, when my husband passed away…"

"Time will heal all this."

116

"Next year this time you'll look back and…"

Periodically in one of his hurried trips from kitchen to door or vice versa, Stephen glances directly at Gerri, smiles an innocent little grin, rolls his eyes and shakes his head as if he's fatigued and can hardly keep up with the activity. Gerri feels a surge of rage every time he does it because he looks like he's enjoying the activity in a perverted sort of way. It happens again, "Whew! You okay. Kiddo?"

"Yes, Dad, I'm okay. No, Dad. I'm **not** okay." Then Gerri glares at him in mockery. She feels awkward and useless while Stephen is jumping from place to place piously accepting all the remarks of sympathy and relishing in the attention. As Gerri sits in a semi-pout on the sofa her thoughts drift to her own personal problem. Now without her mom what in the world will she do if she's pregnant? Gerri silently counts on her fingers the number of days when she should know one way or the other. Gerri walks to the front window and stands motionless peering out the window partly to look for anymore well-wishers but mostly to look at Paulette's house. Gerri would love to hug Paulette at this moment. She feels a strange closeness to Paulette that she hasn't even felt recently with her mom. And for certain Gerri has no real father-daughter bond.

By evening the refrigerator is full of baking dishes and platters of food. Around seven o'clock the phone calls slow and the visitors at the door are sparse. By eight it's quiet again except for phone calls that belong to someone else on their party line. Gerri figures it's the gossip news picking up after listening in on all the calls all day long.

Gerri throws her head back as if about to pass out, "Will this ever end? These people are so phony with their little comments."

During this long day, the only calls handled differently are those from relatives. Stephen assures relatives they don't need to try to come out to California because he wants to get this over and back to normal "for Geraldine's sake" as quickly as possible.

Gerri figures Stephen's talk of getting everything over and discouraging making a long trip are because her dad makes no pretense about his dislike of relatives. She knows there's some long standing friction on both sides of her family. Stephen never mentions his two brothers and sister or his nephews and nieces. It's as if they don't exist. Their calls today were probably forced to be polite but with little sincere sense of loss. Gerri's not even sure if her aunts and uncles on her dad's side knew her mom very well and Gerri's never met most of them and the ones she has met she can't remember.

There are also nasty feelings between her mother's relatives and her dad but Gerri's not sure of the reasons. At this time to have relatives surging into Fresno would be a mess because they'd likely stay at the DeMore's house for who knows how long until they finally return home. Gerri's heard her dad's discouragement of visitors around holidays and he once told her mom that on both sides of the family he was just as glad to be a few thousand miles away rather than have to be around that bunch of "backwoods hillbillies". Dad said that when Susie was a teenager, she was the prettiest girl in the county and had her heart set on becoming a movie star. Apparently it wasn't just a fantasy or dream. Susie was absolutely certain she'd get a break and become a big star. He joked she married him because he promised to get her to California. He delivered on his promise and they actually thought she'd be discovered for Hollywood but of course along came Gerri and that never happened. Gerri wonders now if maybe she had it all wrong. Maybe it's her dad who is ashamed to be around relatives because her mom never came close to being in the movies and just maybe what spoiled her chances was having Gerri. Maybe that's why her dad doesn't like to face the relatives and maybe just being around "his girl" is a constant reminder of what life could have been without her.

118

Stephen appears, suit coat removed, tie loosened, and looking very fatigued. Normally there's never a hair out of place but tonight it looks greasy, clumped and unkempt. His shirt looks like he slept in it, the starch long since softened by perspiration then later dried into creased wrinkles. But she's more concerned about not repeating this day again than how her father looks at the moment.

As the day comes to a close Gerri feels another wave of fright settling over her like a damp, cold, smothering blanket. It frightens her so badly to think of the unknown events to take place over the next few days, the continuing sadness of losing her mother and little Matthew Julian and a feeling of diminished worth as if she's perhaps a burden. But as the day closes Gerri believes there's about as much chance of affection from her dad as there is hope her sweet mother will come through the door holding her new brother.

Big teardrops suddenly form in her eyes and then race each other down her cheeks forming little sad icicles as they drip from her chin. She eventually drops off to sleep with her final thoughts of the day, so afraid and guilty for what she's done and so alone-so very alone in her own house.

CHAPTER 10

INTO THE UNKNOWN

Gerri slowly opens her eyes at the sound of soft knocking on her door. "Gerri? Gerri? Are you awake?" The knob turns and her door slowly opens.

"I'm awake now, Dad. What time is it?"

"It's a little after eight and we need to be ready to have more people calling and coming by today. So when you get up, might as well just go ahead and get that pretty dress on again today. Okay?"

"Oh, Dad, do we have to do this again? When will this stop?"

"Yes. It's important that we do this. It's as much for the people who make the effort as it is for us."

Gerri twists her face as if totally puzzled. She can't understand that statement but it's a little early to think too hard on any particular subject.

"Let's try to have you all dressed and ready by nine. Okay?"

"OOOkaaay."

After she gets dressed and has a glass of juice she wanders into the living room where Stephen is sitting on the sofa. Gerri thinks this might be a chance to talk and she sits down next to him, he looks at her with a little smile and he puts his arm around her shoulder. Oh, how wonderful this feels to be close to him. She leans her head over on his shoulder and gives a long deep sigh.

And then, before a word is spoken, he removes his arm from around her shoulder, Gerri sits up to see what's wrong but Stephen quickly stands and then nervously walks from the sofa to the front window. He pulls the curtain back and peers out.

"Oh, I heard a car but I guess it isn't stopping here. Just want to be ready. Right?"

"Oh, Dad. Why can't you just sit down for a minute or two."

"Well, I know how you feel and believe me I'm feeling horrible again today, too. I'm nervous and very anxious to get all this over with. I know it's going to be rough for a while but the sooner we can get ourselves back to normal, the better it will be for us. I'm sure of it."

"Back to normal? Dad, there won't ever be any normal for me again. Not without Mom. I will never get over this, no matter how long."

"Well, I think you will. But today..."

But this morning he changes the game plan a bit. "Today I'll need to go to the funeral home and make all the arrangements. I thought I'd have you stay here and..."

"Oh, Dad please don't make me stay home and have to face these awful people. Let me go with you. I want to help any way I can. But I don't

121

want to be left here alone. Dad, I feel so lonely and sad right now. I hurt inside and I don't think I'll ever, ever get over this."

"Aw right, then. We'll stay here together until noon, but then we'll lock it up, leave a note on the door and go to Wilson's Funeral Home over on North Teilman. I'll tell you before we go there, this will be really rough. I'm nervous about going. And by the way, you'll get past this. A little rain must fall into every life but there will be sunny days again."

Gerri snaps her head around toward Stephen in shock. Does he think some cute little cliché is going to make her feel better? That's like the clichés every well-wisher brought to the door yesterday. Meaningless words. Now her dad and his "a little rain must fall". This isn't a little rain. This is a hurricane, a tornado, an earthquake and a torrential downpour all at once. Life at home the last couple of years was slipping into disenchantment, but now the death of her mom makes certain every single thing Gerri counted on is devastated and blown out of her life. Gone. There is no hope for Gerri at the DeMore home. A little rain indeed!

After noon they lock the front door and drive to the funeral home. It's not too far away from their house but her dad drives slowly …and silently. Not a word is spoken between them. They pull into the Wilson Funeral Home parking lot and their car is the only one in the lot.

"Are you sure it's open today?"

"Yes, I talked to Mr. Wilson and he said to just come on in. He's here today all day and can take care of everything."

"Okay, if you say they're open, I guess they are."

122

As they walk toward the entrance the place at least from the outside doesn't look frightening. Gerri takes a little breath and sigh of relief, her fright defenses are totally disarmed by the innocent and professional look of the entrance.

As her dad opens the door and holds it for her to go in first, that innocence changes in a flash.   This is as shocking as going into Brentwood's Bar. It's a different environment, totally foreign and not a pleasant introduction as the smell and decor rush out the door, envelope her and grip her in it's claws. There's stone silence inside the entrance and everything looks one hundred percent perfect.   There's a sweet smell that's unlike any smell Gerri's ever encountered and it's very, very creepy. Her eyes scan the framed pictures. There's one of a green hillside with a flock of sheep and a huge picture of two little boys, backs turned walking on a tree lined path with a dog.   Too perfect. Her heart is pounding.

 From out of a lighted side office appears a heavy set, red-faced man in a spotless navy blue suit, "How do you do, I'm Herm Wilson and you must be the DeMores.   I'm here to help you any way I can?"

He's just slightly taller than Gerri but tens of pounds overweight. He has a big welcoming smile and it's difficult not to notice his face and bald head are red, very red but maybe his tie is just too tight. The top of his bald head glistens as if it's been waxed. His bushy gray eyebrows nearly bridge the gap across his nose and the two perfectly combed side tufts of gray hair over his ears give him a distinguished look. Though technically well-groomed, as he stands with light to his back it's hard to miss the small bushes of hair protruding from his ears. His clothes are without spot or wrinkle, almost too perfect.   Even his fat, wrinkly fingers and fingernails look like they've been scrubbed with bleach or maybe soaking in water a long time.

"Hello, Mr. Wilson. I'm Stephen DeMore and this is my daughter, Geraldine, uh Gerri."

"Nice to meet you, Stephen, and you, Gerri. I wish it was under other circumstances. Let me tell you how sorry I am for your loss. And I don't want you to have to be here with me any longer than is absolutely necessary so if it's okay with you and Gerri, Stephen, why don't we all go to my office. It's this way at the end of the hall. By the way, before we go any further, could I get either of you something to drink...coffee, soft drink, water, maybe a cookie to nibble on?"

"No, I'm fine, thanks. Gerri do you want anything?"

"No, thanks. I'm fine, too." But for once someone actually sees *her* and seems to care...at least a little bit.

The hallway carpets are so thick her feet feel wobbly and a little unsure of themselves. She's never walked on anything quite this luxurious. They enter Mr. Wilson's office and have a seat. Gerri and her dad sit across the desk from Herm Wilson and Gerri's beginning to think this may not be so creepy after all, except for that putrid smell. It's like a mix of fragrant flowers and squeaky clean but all overshadowed by a distinct scent of talcum powder. The smell is awful .

Mr. Wilson moves a few papers around on top of his desk and Gerri continues to carefully look him over. His appearance is striking. When he talks or smiles he looks directly at the eyes of the person with whom he's talking and he has a natural air of being in charge. It would be difficult to imagine him as anything other than a boss. Gerri wonders what he's like when he's out shopping or just at home but she can't imagine him in any setting other than this spook house. Gerri knows she'd be scared out of her wits if she ever had to be alone with Mr. Wilson.

He talks about the details to be decided for the funeral service. He covers the options for the date and time, viewing, music, chapel service, flowers, obituaries, and cemetery plot. He's very well-organized and as Mr. Wilson presents options for her dad, Gerri notices her dad nods or says yes in agreement to all Mr. Wilson's recommendations.

"Stephen, I'm sure you're very, very proud of your daughter. And Gerri, you're a beautiful young woman. I know this seems overwhelming at the moment but I hope you'll trust me when I say I want to take as much of the burden off the two of you as I can. Okay?"

Stephen nods his approval. Gerri simply looks without expression at Mr. Wilson but she's impressed. He's actually sincere. He cares! How nice of him. He's not so scary after all.

At last Mr. Wilson seems to be wrapping up the details for the funeral service. He double checks his desk full of forms and he leans forward," Shall we select the type of caskets you'd like?"

Gerri looks at her dad and he jumps like she caught him a million miles away, "Yes. I suppose we'd better do that whenever you say."

"Fine. We have quite a selection. I'll open this doorway, you'll be able to see the different models available and I'll explain everything about them in details so you'll feel confident you're selecting the ones you'll be proud of for your wife and infant and yet stay within a level of affordable comfort."

With that Mr. Wilson takes about three steps from his desk to a paneled wall that has a couple of pictures hanging on it. He apparently steps on a switch in the floor and the wall separates in the middle and begins to withdraw in two directions exposing a huge room stacked full of caskets. They are displayed in a soft light. Caskets are on the floor,

125

on pedestals and hanging on the walls at angles to show the insides, the outsides and cutaways to show how they are constructed.

The snow white carpet is so thick it continues to feel unnatural to walk on. There's soft music playing and the rush of air from the big showroom brings out a renewed blast of that unmistakable smell. Stephen and Gerri walk into this chamber of horrors and Mr. Wilson is determined to stand by each casket and explain the makeup of the coffin, the lining material, the beauty and of course the permanence for the "family's peace of mind."

Suddenly Gerri begins to breathe quickly and her heart is pounding. Her original thought was correct and this guy really is one-hundred percent creepy. He has such a gentle way and genuine smile but he really enjoys this stuff and this place. He has little terms he uses in explaining everything but it all comes back to one thing. Death is shocking and it's permanent. Gerri wonders if this day will ever end!

But it's way too soon for it to end. Life's worst cruelties seem to be just getting warmed up. Stephen selects copper colored, very plain coffins,one for her mom and one for Matthew. He turns to Gerri and mumbles something about whether she thinks his choices are correct. Gerri is in sensual shock and trying hard not to run out the door. She silently nods with closed eyes. That's the best she can do at the moment.

"Okay, I think that's all in here. Let's go back to my desk just for a couple of seconds. Gerri? Are you okay? I promise we'll be done in just a couple of minutes."

She nods at Mr. Wilson without saying a word.

They sit down once again, the doors slide shut as they return to the business office environment. Mr. Wilson goes over the contract and costs with Stephen, assuring him they'll work with whatever financial

126

arrangements that suit his comfort level. Gerri isn't paying a lot of attention but she hears a life insurance policy mentioned by Stephen. Mr. Wilson sits back for a second and looks a bit surprised about the fact there's a policy or perhaps it's the amount. Gerri isn't listening to the details. But Mr. Wilson asks Stephen again if he's sure he's satisfied with the caskets as if they should go choose something a little fancier. But Stephen says the selections are fine, he signs the papers without even reading them and then he leans back in the big leather chair while taking a deep breath.

"Now there's one last assignment I have for you and likely for the two of you. Perhaps you and Gerri can go have some lunch and discuss the attire you'd like to have for your wife. If you would be so kind as to make that a priority, it would be very helpful to us in meeting your expectations. Do you think you could decide on the clothes, collect them and bring them by later today for me?"

Stephen is clearly unprepared for this, chokes and hoarsely says, "Yes. I think we can do that. Gerri, we'll need to go home and look for special clothes in Mom's closet. Okay?"

The idea of gathering her mom's clothes shocks Gerri so badly she shivers shock and stares straight ahead. The caskets, collecting her mom's clothing. This is horrible. Her stomach hurts as if she's been punched. For a second Gerri thinks she's about to have a massive period and maybe leave a trail of blood on Mr. Wilson's perfect white carpet. But this isn't the same kind of cramps. She just wants out of this place. Now!

Tears stream down Gerri's face and she's in hysterics as they hurry from the building. Her dad dutifully puts his arm around her shoulder to walk to the car but she can tell by how stiff his arm feels he's more concerned with looking like he's comforting her than actually providing comfort. Not gentle, not helpful. Just one more first hand experience in her own private hell on earth.

Not a word is spoken as they drive home. After turning slowly into the driveway Stephen turns off the car engine and he and Gerri sit in the car as they both stare straight ahead, the sun coming through the windshield making it hot and uncomfortable.

"Well, Gerri. Let's get out of this hot car. Can you help me get some clothes together? Will you be up to it?"

Gerri nods, they enter their house without any conversation and both go down the hallway to the master bedroom. Stephen opens the blinds part way and rays of light blast through showing dust particles in the air. The room has a musty smell like a seldom used guest room that finally gets a chance to exhale its stored up, stagnate breath.

Stephen pulls hangars apart exposing her mom's clothes and Gerri touches and smells each dress, eyes squeezed tightly closed, imagining her mom in them . Stephen seems aloof or at best disinterested in putting much effort into the task but asks a couple of times, "what about this? Would this be appropriate?"

Gerri's responses are very weak, "I don't know. "I'm not sure."

Stephen lays four dresses out on the bed and Gerri pictures her mother in each of the dresses, lying back on the bed smiling at her. Gerri drifts into a sort of daze visualizing her mom's smiling face lying on the bed. Suddenly her daze is a shocking nightmare as her mom's image turns from a smile to a frightening, chalky-white, lifeless look with eyes wide open staring at Gerri. It brings a flashback of her mom's face from the other night when she and her dad drove to the hospital. Just blankly staring at Gerri out of the car window. Gerri gasps and takes a stumbling step to the side as if it's real. She turns and runs to the living room, falling face first onto the sofa, sobbing.

128

Eventually Stephen walks in, "Oh, there you are, Gerri. I know you're really having a tough time with all this and I understand. I feel the same but we just have to get through it. One step at a time. Can you help me decide on the clothes because Mr. Wilson is expecting us this afternoon."

"Dad, I don't care about Mr. Wilson or anybody else except my mom. I want to see her. I want to kiss her. I want her to smile and hug me. Oh, Dad, I miss her so much." She buries her face in her hands and openly weeps.

After a few moments crying Gerri lifts her face and realizes her dad already withdrew from the room and she can hear him rustling through the closet again. Why can't he just acknowledge her horrible pain, hug her, stroke her hair, kiss her forehead or even just allow her to sit touching him?

Stephen returns to the living room and lays one of Susie's dresses across the big chair. " I think this will do just fine. Don't you think so?"

Gerri lifts her swollen, tear-drenched face and stares at the dress and then turns toward her dad. "Where are her shoes, stockings, and underwear? And her jewelry? And her makeup? Dad, where's everything else?"

Stephen gives a dramatic sigh as if frustrated by the question and responds without thinking, "Oh, I don't think they need any of that stuff. It doesn't show and it's just going to be buried..." His voice trails off.

Those words were the trigger for Gerri coming apart at the emotional seams. She's crying hysterically but she sees her dad turn and leave the room once again.

Gerri is emotionally raw and blurts out, " Why would you leave me sitting here about to fall apart? Dad, do you know how alone I feel? Can't you just be my father? Ya know, Dad, be my father? Why won't you help me?"

There's no immediate reply to her outburst but in a matter of several seconds he emerges from the hallway with a small suitcase. "Look, sweetheart. I'm sorry. I just hadn't thought clearly about what all to take. I have everything now. "

Gerri doesn't doubt her dad has at least made an effort to put some of her mom's things together and she follows her dad out the front door to the car and without a word they return to the funeral home. Stephen realizes Gerri's close to the breaking point so he asks her to remain in the car. Gerri thinks that's wise and it will give her dad the chance to talk with Mr. Wilson without any embarrassing eruptions. Gerri's also grateful she can avoid smelling that awful horrible place and to avoid seeing the creepy Herm Wilson.

Finally her dad emerges from the funeral home, gets into the car, starts the engine, looks over at her and takes a long deep breath. "This is almost too much to handle isn't it, Gerri?"

She glances at her dad and then looks out the passenger window," Yeah. Except it's not *almost* too much. It *is* too much."

CHAPTER 11

FAMILY VISITORS

Though she's still in the fog of sleep, the next morning begins with her dad's soft knock on her bedroom door followed by his quiet voice about the agenda for the day.

"How about you get dressed and you don't have to be real fancy. We'll go over to the diner on Walsh and have a proper breakfast. Besides I'm

131

sort of keeping an eye open later today for your grandmother, Uncle Billy and Aunt June. They absolutely insisted on coming here and they said they'd get here in time for the funeral tomorrow. It's a long, long drive but knowing them they'll push it straight through. I was really hoping they wouldn't come because it can't be easy for them and driving like that can turn out disastrous. Besides, once they get here they are not easy people to be around, much less under the same roof. But we'll see. Usually it's a three day drive but we'll see how soon they make it. You probably don't remember too much about them ...you were so small. But they are odd to say the least. It's too bad they have to come visit under these conditions but mark my words you'll be ready for their visit to end by the time they leave to go home. Anyhow... you want to go get some breakfast with your dad?"

"Yeah. Sure. I'm not hungry but I'll go just to be with you and to get out of the house."

After breakfast with very few words spoken except for the bacon being good and the toast being burnt, Stephen and Gerri head home. Gerri's looking down when they turn the corner onto Vassar and she's somewhat startled by her dad, "Oh Dear God! Now it all begins. Hillbilly heaven!"

There's a car in the DeMore driveway, not just any car, a car with baggage tied to the top, a man with his hat tilted back on his head standing near the street with one foot resting on the back bumper. Another man leans the upper part of his body on the hood of the car like he's asleep standing up except for the toothpick and cigarette dangling from his lips and there are two very large women sitting on the porch steps. There's also an older woman in an ankle length dress walking from around the side of their house. As Stephen and Gerri come to a stop in front of their house Gerri recognizes the older woman walking beside the house. It's her grandmother. Two of the others must be Uncle Billy and Aunt June but that still leaves one extra

132

couple. Gerri shudders to think how all of them are going to squeeze into their house.

Stephen rolls his car window down and honks while waving out the window with his free arm. Gerri looks at him a little disgusted. He can be so phony. He has a big toothy smile from ear to ear as if he is extremely happy to see them but he mutters to Gerri through the smile, "Oh God, help us. The whole bunch came. The pestilence has descended."

With the relatives' car in the driveway, Stephen parks next to the curb.

"Hi, everybody," as her dad hops from the car and opens his arms wide as if to embrace them all at once.

Gerri's grandmother walks directly over toward Gerri and her dad but Gerri can't help but notice that Uncle Billy and Aunt June and the other two just remain sitting, leaning or standing and all absolutely expressionless.

Her grandmother isn't able to manage a smile with her greeting, "Hello Stephen. We are worn to a complete frazzle. Been driving non-stop except for toilet breaks and gasoline. I thought maybe you expected us but I guess not 'cause when we got here of course you and Geraldine were gone and the house was locked up tighter than a drum so we probably shocked some of your neighbors if they happened to be lookin out in your backyard. All of us had to go in the worst way so when one went we eventually all went but I'm not gonna say where out there. Sorry. But we couldn't hold it no longer."

"Well, of course. And I am sorry. I would have left the house open if I'd thought you'd get here this quick. I really didn't think you'd get here until tomorrow sometime. You drove straight through from Missouri?"

"Yep. As straight as the road would go."

133

Stephen steps forward and gives a brief polite hug to grandma. Gerri can't really hear what's said. It's sort of mumbling with "sorry" mixed in from each voice and a couple of pats on each other's backs. The greetings seem stiff, almost forced politeness.

"Billy? June? You look like you're worn out. Come on inside. Here, Gerri go open the door real quick. Ed, May don't fall asleep out here. Come on in."

Gerri bounds up the steps wondering why even her grandma never made any effort to say hello to her and for certain the rest don't appear to be very pleasant. Maybe they're just exhausted.

Gerri heard her dad use the names, Billy, June, May and Ed but she has no earthly idea which person belongs to which name. She knows that May is her mom's sister and Ed is May's husband. Billy is her mom's brother and June is Billy's wife but she can't recall seeing them before. They barely even look up as Gerri goes up the steps beside them. But soon the entire traveling party is inside the house. The weary travelers grab the closest chairs and sofas, flopping unceremoniously down with collective loud sighs of relief and groans.

"We'll get some food out for…just take a second. Friends brought lots of food and it will come in handy at this point. Come on. Loosen those shoes and get comfortable."

The very heavy woman Gerri realizes is May from the clue in her request, "It would be better if you'd show us where we'll be able to sleep and Ed can get our suitcases inside. I know I'd rather lie down and stretch out than eat anything at the moment. But maybe while Ed's bringin' in our stuff I will grab just a quick bite or two."

Gerri stares at May in disbelief that she can be her beautiful mother's younger sister. She is extremely overweight and her hair is sticking out in clumps so that it looks like it hasn't seen a comb or brush for some extended period of time. She hasn't smiled yet and looks like she's perpetually angry about something. Collectively the relatives and their clothes look like ragamuffins. The women's dresses look like they were homemade-and not by anyone with much sewing skill and Gerri figures they really don't care about personal appearance. Gerri is starting to understand her dad's comment about being glad by the time they leave. She has a feeling this is going to be a strained visit and as she glances once again at May she still can't believe this is her mother's sister. There is no resemblance at all.

May sees Gerri looking in her direction and without any pleasant tone or smile, "It's Geraldine, right? Look honey I'm your aunt May and I know you probably don't ever remember seeing me but you've been doing nothin' but gawk at me since we walked in here. You staring at me with that blank look makes me feel like you either don't approve of me or I'm scaring you or somethin. I don't scare you do I?"

"No. I just don't think I've actually seen you or Uncle Ed before." Gerri knows she shouldn't have been so obvious and she quickly looks away from May and heads for the kitchen.

Stephen begins the berthing process, "Okay, I figure Billy and June can go into my room, Mom Presley takes Gerri's room, Ed and May out on the sun porch on the daybed and a cot. Gerri and I will sleep on the living room sofas. So if you want to take a look at where you'll be and then start bringing suitcases in, by all means let's get it done."

Gerri never dreamed she was going to get tossed out of her own room. Just one of those little issues her dad forgot to tell her. He's figured this all out in advance and it's too bad he never bothered to mention it to Gerri. She could have at least gotten some of her things out before her grandma moves in. Her dad is really irritating her and she can't bear to look at him waving his arms with the directions and smiling as if this is some sort of pleasure vacation. Well it's not! Gerri feels very irritable and tired. What a houseful! And there is something about them that isn't friendly. Gerri thinks even some of the well-wisher strangers that came to the door over the last couple of days may have seemed phony but at least they were smiling and pleasant. These are relatives and they look like they're a bunch of grouches.

When the last suitcases, bags and boxes are in the house, it's a disaster area. Each begins sorting through the pile of baggage and traipsing off this way and that, taking suitcases to their nesting spots. Gerri stands idly in the kitchen, rinsing an occasional glass or plate and just watching. She's never, ever seen the house in this sort of disarray with everything so topsy-turvy. Remnants of food and garbage begin to appear from the travelers' car and it lands on the end of the sink as well as the dishes they are using and abandoning since their arrival. Gerri senses this mess is going to get a lot worse and she doesn't see any prospects of the house-guests helping. She considers the best she can do for the moment is try to beat a hasty retreat and...

A familiar voice quickly changes her escape plans," Gerri? Would you be a good girl and help clean up this mess in the kitchen. I'll get back and help you in a few minutes but let me get everybody settled, towels, sheets, all that. Okay?"

"Dad, " she whispers, "We can't do this every day. Look at this already. They haven't even been here an hour and look at the house. How long are they going to be here?"

"Shhh. We'll talk later but I'm sure they may want to stay a few days even after the funeral. I mean it's such a long way from Missouri to California and the road home will be just as long. We'll just do the best we can and try to stay ahead of the disorganization for a few days. "

" Disorganization? Is that what you call bringing half-eaten garbage out of a car and just leave it on the sink? Do they not even have trash cans in whatever woods they came out of?"

"Gerri! Don't talk like that. Let's just pull together and make the best of it. This is your mother's family and we have to remember that."

"I miss Mommy so much I can't stand it. And these people don't act anything like Mommy."

Stephen doesn't respond and he leaves the room to get away . Gerri's stuck with the mess so she sets about the cleanup chore and of course Stephen never makes it back to help. Gerri can hear him going from room to room and making small talk and more of the "sorry" words are exchanged.

Gerri wonders why her aunts or uncles can hardly even manage more than a semi-polite nod in her direction. None have used her name except May who didn't like Gerri staring at her. Then when Gerri is cleaning the kitchen mess her own grandmother really shows her lack of understanding of Gerri's grief with her attempt at comfort, " Honey, I'm real sorry and believe me I know the pain.   After all it is my daughter."

Gerri never even looks up from the dishwashing to acknowledge her comments but it sure makes her angry as she says silently to herself," Thanks a lot, Grandma. It just happens to be my mother **and** my little brother but I'm sure you don't really care how **I** feel and what it's doing to me inside."

Suddenly a chill comes over Gerri and drowns out every other thought. The reality of fear that she may have a baby of her own growing inside. Her mouth goes dry, she perspires, her heart races and her breath quickens. This fear is inescapable but she is unwilling to share her

137

problem and fear with anyone at this point. She must find a way to endure the fear without letting on something's wrong with her.

There are some occasional cameo-like appearances from assigned sleeping arrangements and passing through the kitchen and living room, but by and large the evening is about getting comfortable and pretty soon there is a mix of snoring and quiet conversations until finally her dad turns out the living room light. Gerri lies on one sofa and her eyes don't seem to be able to close. It's so frightening and sickening to think that her mom and little brother, at this very second, are somewhere across town in that funeral home. Are they lying on a bed or a table? What about the baby? She wonders if they have Matthew with her mom and not off by himself. It would be better if he were with their mom and not by himself, the tiny little guy. But at any rate they are there by themselves all alone in the dark. She feels so sad for her mom and Matthew. Gerri's mind races and she doubts if she'll ever go to sleep tonight but soon exhaustion trumps fear and sadness as she falls fast asleep.

✳✳✳✳✳

A loud noise startles Gerri awake as if from a nightmare. It's pots and skillets rattling and clanking in the kitchen. One little light over the stove is on and she sees her grandma in her housecoat doing something at the stove. She thinks if she lies very still she'll be left alone and won't have to get into any conversations or worse, get drawn into heavy kitchen labor.

"Ahhhh!" Gerri's hoarse, sleepy voice complains in protest and she squints her eyes as the bright overhead living room light snaps to life. No chance of playing possum now.

There stands her dad, stretching. " Almost six so I guess it's time we get up and at 'em, Gerri. Are you awake? Gerri? We'll need to pick up

138

our bedclothes and use the bathroom before everybody else gets up, so up and at 'em."

Gerri groans and raises up on one elbow. "I know. I know. Up and at 'em. It's not even daylight yet. That light's so bright. Hey, Dad? I'm not going back to school until all this is over, right? The days seem all mixed up but just so I know when I have to go back."

"Of course not, Gerri. I called Bill Landers at home and I told him not to expect you for a whole week. I think it's best if we just stay around here all this week with our visitors. Today's the funeral and wake but we'll need some time after that and nothing's planned as such but I expect your grandma, aunts and uncles will want to visit with us."

"I really doubt they want to visit, but fine, I'll stay home for the rest of the week. Besides, somebody has to be appointed slave to clean up after the hillbillies."

"Gerri! Shhh."

Gerri is still very, very tired. Not sleepy. Just plain tired. She yawns and sleepily rolls over on the sofa, nearly rolling off into the floor. She catches herself before rolling off the edge and sits up still squinting at the bright ceiling light.

Then the gruesome events of the day flood over her like a firehose bath of ice water. Today is the funeral. Just sitting here she feels faint from fright, the ever-present sense of loss and worst of all, the lingering fear of pregnancy. She doubts anybody even realizes or cares she hasn't seen her mother since the day she went to the hospital. This is so unbelievable but the reality of it is settling in like a dense fog over a humid marsh. What will it be like? What's she supposed to do? Does she have to say something in particular to people? What if she gets sick? Gerri figures this will be the absolute worst day of her life.

139

Gerri's grandma fixes breakfast for everyone and the eating lasts long enough until it's time to get ready for the funeral. The dishes and skillets are just left in the sink and on the table. At least today, her dad says some neighbors are going to come in during the funeral and clean up. That's so people can come over after the funeral, have more to eat and then they can leave a huge mess...so either way Gerri is certain to get stuck cleaning a mess either now or tomorrow.

While everyone takes turns in the bathroom and begins to dress, Stephen and Gerri are predictably and woefully silent. Stephen looks at his reflection in a mirror or window, straightens his tie, clears his throat, takes a few steps looking up at the ceiling and then repeats the process. Gerri senses her father is very, very upset and anxious. He probably has no idea what's supposed to happen today or how he'll be able to deal with it and that's certainly the way she feels.

Her dad is wearing his black suit and a dark blue tie. At least today his hair doesn't look greasy and tousled. Gerri wears her very best dress, a navy blue velveteen jumper with a white bib and patent leather shoes. As she brushes her hair and looks in the mirror she keeps asking herself the same questions over and over. What will she and her dad do in this quiet unhappy house without her mom and what will it be like if she turns out to be pregnant?

She wanders into the kitchen where Stephen seems to have stopped his nervous pacing and he's sitting at the table, head in hands.

"Dad, are you okay?"

"Yeah. Just thinking. This is the hardest part, Gerri and we just have to get through it today."

"I'm so scared about today but I'm also scared about tomorrow, the day after tomorrow and the day after that tomorrow. Will we be okay? What are we going to do without Mom?"

140

"Oh, we'll manage somehow. We just have to stick together. Like glue, Gerri."

She doesn't respond about his reference to sticking together but she's certain her perception of sticking together like glue is a lot different than her dad's. His idea is the glue is sticky or non-sticky at Stephen's convenience and most of the time, non-sticky. She feels a little bad for thinking in negative terms about her dad right now but it's hard for her to find forgiveness as she recalls how he tries to shovel problems off to some other time or place and all the while cheating with some floozie from school. Gerri's feeling very nervous and anxious stimulated by hurrying up to get dressed and then just waiting, waiting, waiting.

Stephen looks at his watch. "Okay, Gerri. It's time. We'd better go. We are supposed to meet with Mr. Wilson before people start arriving at the funeral home. So I guess we'd better get a move on."

CHAPTER 12

THE FUNERAL

Gerri and Stephen drive silently along Tielman Street and Gerri sees the Wilson Funeral Home sign in the distance. A knot starts in her stomach and she really doesn't want to go in the parking lot much less get out of the car. But she knows deep inside there are things she must do today that aren't options. The DeMore's car slows and turns into the parking lot. The Missouri car, packed with the Ozark hillbillies, still covered with mud and bugs, follows closely behind. A young man in a dark suit comes out of the funeral home and approaches. Gerri's heart is pounding, emotionally anxious and deeply fearful about the unknown events today. Stephen rolls down his window.

" Mr. DeMore?" Stephen nods. "Sir, I'm Jim, one of Mr. Wilson's Directors and I'd like to get you to line up in the parking lot so when we leave in the procession you'll be parked properly. If you would, please pull around and park next to the curb so you'll be the first car after the hearse. It's parked under the portico. See what I mean? By the way, is the car behind you immediate family as well?"

"Yes. It's my wife's mother, her brother and sister and their wife and husband and I think I see where you need us to park."

"That's fine I just wanted to be sure it's family and not just an early arrival. I'll meet you over by the hearse and show you all inside. Thank you, Mr. DeMore."

"You bet."

Stephen does as instructed and swings the car around edging it toward where the long black hearse is parked. Jim indicates when Stephen's close enough and Gerri is aware the engine is silent. She has a physical and emotional collapse at this moment and does not see how she can possibly do this. Jim quickly appears on the passenger side of the car, opens the door for Gerri, extends a warm smile and his hand and without thinking she feels her feet hit the ground and begin to walk. Except for the cold air she can't even feel her feet or legs but they must be working somehow because she's getting closer and closer to that horrible entry way.

Gerri takes her first step into the funeral home and gasps as if suffocating. There's Mr. Wilson right in front of her and several other
142

young people including Jim from the parking lot. They immediately stop talking, make eye contact and smile as Gerri enters. They all look pleasant and very businesslike. Their smiles are friendly but perhaps are more like polite requirements, as if Mr. Wilson gives the command to smile and they all do so. They're not big smiles, just the exactly perfect ones that Mr. Wilson demands. Mr. Wilson says the names of each of his staff members and exchanges introductions with Stephen, Gerri and all of Susie's family.

Mr. Wilson finishes the introductions and quickly gets down to business, "I wanted you to meet everyone here and be assured that if you need anything today just mention it to any of our staff members and we'll do our best to take care of it. Now there are a couple more things before we go in. First, there's a small lounge in the front of the chapel off to the side and that's reserved for the two of you, and your immediate family or special guests with whom you need to be alone. There are restrooms in the lobby hallway for visitors but you will find a private restroom in the lounge as well as a refrigerator stocked with plenty of cold water, soda and fruit juice. There's coffee on the counter and some cookies if you'd like a snack. That room is for you to simply step into when you feel the need for a little quiet or privacy. Okay?"

"Sure, thanks, Mister..."

"Please Stephen...Herm. Okay, then the main reason I wanted you to come early today is so you, as the immediate family, can go into the chapel together and privately be alone with your loved ones and see them, get a little more comfortable with the surroundings and that way it's not a surprise after the other guests begin to arrive. So..." He looks at each of them, " If you're ready you may follow me."

As Mr. Wilson slowly walks across the lobby, he opens the two double doors of the chapel. Gerri's knees suddenly feel like they can't

143

support her. First in view are the two coffins in the front and the flowers in the indirect light of four floor lamps. Gerri wouldn't normally even notice floor lamps but she's never seen lamps where the shades look like they're upside down. The soft gold light filtered through the bronze colored shades adds to the strange atmosphere. It's a sensory overload. It's a house of horrors.

Everywhere she looks it's shocking and startling and of course that shouldn't be unusual because she's never been to a funeral. It is truly a real live nightmare in Technicolor. In the front of the room is the center of attention, two shiny bronze-colored caskets. The lid is open on the large casket and she vaguely sees a silhouette of the person she's sure is her mother. To one side is a very small coffin with the lid closed and on top of it a vase with a single red rose bud.

Mr. Wilson indicates for everyone to follow him and he walks directly to the open lid of her mother's casket. He steps to one side, turns and Gerri's aware he's looking attentively at Stephen, Her dad quietly begins to weep, head bowed but Gerri just stands and stares-petrified. She feels like her head is going to explode and it makes her facial skin so tight she can't even blink or move her mouth.

"Arghhh! Oh God, Susan Jane! It can't be! Why you?"

Everyone jumps at the sound of the startling outburst. Gerri's body stiffens and she staggers back a step after the sudden piercing scream from her grandma. It's so loud even Mr. Wilson jumps and loses his little polite smile for an instant. Her grandma quickly turns away and Uncle Billy and Aunt June each put a hand under her arms and assist her toward a seat. Everyone standing next to the caskets take a deep breath.

"Stephen, Gerri, I hope you're pleased with what we've done to prepare Mrs. DeMore and your baby, Matthew for this day."

144

Neither Stephen nor Gerri give any sort of response to Mr. Wilson's request for affirmation that he and his staff have done a good job. Gerri can't do anything but stare at her mother's body and the tornado of emotions have her more in a state of catatonia than grief. The ultimate, horrific surprise is that her mother's body looks more like a plastic mannequin than her mom. The expression is like a tight-lipped smile that isn't any sort of expression Gerri ever saw on her beautiful mother. Her skin looks plastic and there are wrinkles on her neck and hands. Gerri can't recall wrinkles anywhere on her mother.

Stephen puts his arm around Gerri, "You okay?"

She shakes her head "no" because she's not at all "okay". But Gerri never says a word out loud.

Mr. Wilson intercedes so there's not much guesswork in what to do, "Now you two and your family just take your time in here and when you feel like it just take a little break over there in the lounge area. Then you'll be a little more ready to greet people as they begin to come in within the next little while."

He gestures toward the opposite end of the chapel from where they stand, " Guests should arrive from the back of the chapel and I'd expect some early ones at almost any time now. Ya know, there are some folks that if something starts at one they'll be here at twelve thirty and there are others that will be late for the whole service. Well, you just take your time."

With that, Mr. Wilson disappears off to the side through a door Gerri had not noticed was there. What a creepy place. Secret doors that lead to caskets, doors that let scary old Herm escape and reappear.

Stephen takes Gerri's arm and guides her toward the lounge and they barely start in that direction before there's talking at the entry to the chapel followed by people starting to drift inside. Gerri watches out of

145

curiosity as arriving guests look around, awkwardly figure out who will be first to sign the guest register and then hesitatingly walk toward the front of the chapel where the caskets are located. Judging from guests' jerky, awkward movements Gerri immediately suspects most people would just as soon avoid coming to Mr.Wilson's business place. Death, and the rituals around it, obviously scare people- and rightly so.

Women in hats with veils, dark dresses, dark suits and everybody wanting to hug and slap Stephen and Gerri on the back usually with a few unintelligible words probably meant to come out as, "Ohhh, Sweetie" or "Aww, there" or "I know, Hon, I know. It's hard".

During the obligatory hugs most don't make eye contact but look down especially if Gerri looks directly at them. There's a new smell that's really awful. There's the funeral home smell of talcum powder, squeaky clean and flowers mixed with perfume and now the new introduction to mix with all the rest, very strong soap. It must be Lifebuoy. So strong! It makes Gerri sneeze a couple of times.

After the hugs, people parade to the casket, stand there in silence for thirty seconds or so and then start drifting over looking at the flowers. After a few minutes of reading or pretending to read the cards on the flowers they meander toward a chapel seat.

Along with Stephen and the visiting relatives there is constant hub bub in the front by the caskets. Simple talking through endless introductions, saying names, repeating names and how someone knows the DeMores. A lot of the visitors are teachers from various schools.

Every chance Gerri edges her way to the lounge where she can shut the door, sit back in the big recliner and for a few fleeting seconds close her eyes and imagine she's somewhere else. Anywhere else. Sometimes there's a little knock on the door and it's someone sent by

Stephen to check to be sure Gerri's okay and that has to include the hug, the back slap and, "Aww" or "Ohh" or "I know".

Gerri's made four trips into the lounge in the first half hour or so but then her little sanctuary is discovered by someone else. The next time she slips into the lounge she finds the big leather chair occupied by her Aunt May. Though her Aunt May acts distraught and totally fatigued, she has enough strength and presence of mind to have a soft drink in one hand and a couple cookies in the other. Trying not to stare and be the repeat recipient of May's wrath Gerri doesn't say anything but peripherally watches her break one of the cookies into smaller pieces as if only to take a taste but one taste leads closely to another and another until cookie after cookie mysteriously disappears off the plate that she has relocated from the counter to the sofa next to her chair. Gerri's fascinated that May can devour an entire plate of cookies in short order, all in little innocent bites. May is in seventh heaven when one of the funeral home staff comes in to check on everything and quickly replenishes the plate with an even bigger mound of cookies. For a while Gerri thinks May could be at least an entertaining distraction from all the stuff in the chapel but Gerri knows she must do her duty and spend at least some time mingling with the visitors.

As Gerri returns to the chapel she's shocked at the number of people present. They are all hugging each other, shaking their heads as if in perpetual disbelief and when they see Gerri it looks to her like they stop talking and stare or stare a second and then whisper something to each other, probably about her. Maybe somehow someone knows about her being out with a gang member. Maybe there are rumors about the encounter with the police. Maybe there's a rumor about her being pregnant or worse, that some people can tell by looking at her. Maybe they think she's a rebellious tramp or even a hood. Probably something like, "well, the only reason she's here is because her dad's a teacher and she had to be invited." Just thinking that makes her so angry she could scream.

147

More of the obligatory hugs, and more parading up to the caskets by people she barely knows. Some are crying, sobbing and sniveling and Gerri's not sure what she's supposed to do with people like this. She stares at her mother's body and except for her eyes being closed Gerri thinks her expressionless face reminds her of how her mom looked when she stared at Gerri from the car window as they left for the hospital. The returning fright of that thought takes her breath and she gasps. What if somehow her mom mysteriously suspected she would never see Gerri, ever again. Suddenly Gerri feels very faint but she's not resisting the feeling. In fact, she doesn't mind the feeling of being a little woozie and floating all at once.

Gerri wishes all of this would stop. She's very sweaty and nauseated. Fainting would be okay but this sick feeling isn't good. Suddenly there's a firm, supporting hand under her arm and a comforting, raspy tobacco-smelling voice and warm breath on the side of her face. Oh God, how good that smells and feels. Trusty Paulette appears like a miracle when she sees Gerri at her emotional limit. She puts her arm around Gerri.

" C'mon Gerri. Let me help you find a place to sit down over here. We can go over to this little room to the side away from all the people."

Paulette walks her to the lounge and Gerri sits heavily into the big chair. "Okay, Gerri? Let me get you some water. Or I tell you what? Let me fix you a little coffee with some cream and sugar. That may help a little better than water."

"I don't even know what coffee tastes like. I don't think I'll like it cause it smells so bad. And if you want a cookie, Paulette you'd better grab one now because if piggy-May comes back in she'll likely clean that plate of em again."

" Oh Gerri. I didn't meet her I don't think. What's her name, Peggy May?"

Gerri giggles, "No, Paulette I said she's piggy May...ya know oink oink P-I-G-G-Y, not the name Peggy?"

" Oh my gosh, young lady! What if I'd have walked out of here and said you must be Peggy May? She'd have crowned both of us. Now would you like to try a little coffee? Just try a little and if you don't like it you can have water or some juice."

Paulette's right. Come to think of it, Paulette's always right. Gerri's lucky to have her and actually the coffee isn't bad. She sips the coffee and closes her eyes in instant relief. Eventually she looks at Paulette and smiles, "Okay, I guess we should go back in there and sit with everybody else. Do they have some church service or something next?"

"Yes, honey. There will be a little service in honor of your mother and little brother. Then we'll go in a procession of cars over to the cemetery. They do another little shorter service over there and then we'll go back to your house. I'll try to stay as close to you as I can today and if you need anything at all, sweetie, I'll try to take care of it for you. It's a long day for you, isn't it?"

"Yeah. Whew. A long day is right and with all these relatives at home there's hardly room to turn around. I'm glad they got to come but I'll sure be glad when they leave. Okay, I guess I'm ready to go back out there. Will this ever be over? "

Gerri gets up from the chair and follows Paulette into the chapel to a row of seats in the front.

As Gerri glances to the rear of the chapel her jaw drops and she gasps at the sight of Connie Waltrip. Gerri is suddenly fearful and panic

149

stricken. If Connie's here Jake might be here as well and she doesn't want to see him. Connie and Jake are really close as brother and sister and even though Gerri has a confused and surprised reaction at seeing Connie, Gerri does not want to lay eyes on Jake. Just seeing Connie sets off a physical panic attack. Connie makes eye contact with Gerri, gives a polite smile and begins to walk toward Gerri in the chapel front. Gerri's eyes are still searching for Jake but she doesn't see him. Connie is certainly attractive enough and today she's not wearing the tough-girl clothes she usually wears to school. She's got on a mid calf-length skirt, white blouse and the collar isn't even turned up. Her hair is nicely done and her bright red lipstick certainly don't present any image that might be in poor taste.

"God, Gerri. I'm so sorry. I had no idea until I heard at school. I mean. I knew your mom was in the hospital but I had no idea. I feel so bad for you." Connie begins to cry as she hugs Gerri.

"I know. I know. I don't know how I'll ever get past this, Connie. And my little baby brother, too."

Even though Gerri gently pushes away Connie holds onto Gerri's shoulders and continues the hug. Connie whispers, "I've got to talk to you somewhere we can be alone. Can you do it now? Just for a second?"

"Yeah. I guess so. What's the matter, Connie? You in trouble?"

"Just talk to me for a minute. Where can we go?"

Gerri motions toward the lounge area and as they enter the lounge, Connie looks nervously around, walks over and makes sure no ones in the restroom and then turns back to Gerri with a look of urgency.

"I'll be real quick about this. I don't know how much of this you know or not. That night the cops got you and Jake up the hill they took Jake in and beat him up really bad. He seems to be okay now but he's still bruised and stuff but the cops really did a dance on him."

"Oh my gosh!"

"Well, that isn't the worst of it. They were trying to get him to confess that he'd forced you, ya know, raped you and they were going to see he got thirty years or more in prison."

"Whaa?"

"Just listen. He wouldn't admit to anything but they told him your mom was taking you to the hospital to be examined and was going to press charges for rape or at the very least, statutory rape, because you aren't eighteen. His lawyer knows the judge or something so Jake's guys bonded him out awaiting trial and as soon as they did Jake went into hiding."

"Connie, my mom was in the hospital. I never told anybody anything and I never went to any hospital or doctor. But I haven't told a soul anything bad about Jake or what we did or didn't do. I told my next door neighbor, who the cops thought was my mom, I told her we were kissin and stuff but that's it and..."

"So you mean the cops were just trying to get Jake to admit to something that never happened?"

Gerri looks at Connie and Connie returns the look.

"Jesus, Gerri. You and Jake really... you really did it...but you never told anybody? Are you okay?"

"I'm scared out of my mind, Connie. I'll know by next week. But I'm not telling anybody anything."

151

Oh, Gerri. I feel so bad for you. And I can't believe how brave you are. Jake told me he figured you'd get pressured to make up a story to get him in trouble and yet all the time he really knew he did have something to worry about. And you haven't told anybody. You're amazing."

"Yeah. Well, for whatever that's worth."

"Wait til I tell Jake. I feel like beatin the shit outta him again. Ya know, it's you who ought to be leadin a gang. You're one tough, true-blue through-and-through cookie."

"Well, I'll tell you I'm not feelin very tough at the moment. I am scared outta my ever-lovin mind."

The lounge door opens and May begins her waddle to the big chair and likely a Coke and a bite or two of cookies.

"Hi Aunt May. This is one of my friends, Connie. This is my Aunt May."

"Hi ya Aunt May."

May raises one hand like a pathetic Queen-of-England wave as she lumbers past the two girls. There may have been a grunt but that would have been the most acknowledgement as May's focus is on sustenance.

Gerri and Connie return to the chapel and Connie leaves Gerri in the hugs of the endless supply of visitors. As Gerri watches Connie walking toward the back of the chapel she sees a young man sitting near the front looking directly at her. He's probably in his early twenties, crew cut, white shirt and tie and very handsome in a rugged sort of way. The five o'clock shadow is in contrast to the sharply pressed white shirt. But Gerri can't quite place him. Maybe he's another teacher but she can't recall. She keeps trying to place him and their eyes meet. He smiles and gestures with his head toward the end of his bench seat, then he looks back at Gerri and winks. She is baffled about who this is and why the strange actions.

While he still has her eyes engaged, he gets up from his seat and starts to walk forward toward Gerri. He gestures with his head again toward the end of the bench where Paulette is sitting and that's when it hits Gerri. It's the policeman who brought her home the other night and he recognizes Paulette. Not only does he recognize Paulette he's toying with Gerri to let her know he knows.

Gerri's look of shock must be obvious and he quickly walks forward, stretches open his arms and hugs Gerri very tight and close. Very tight. Very, very close.

"I'm so sorry about your mother, Geraldine. By the way, I'm Len Ferguson and I'm not here to do anything other than to tell you how sorry I am. That's it. So please don't worry. You made quite an impression on me and I have continued to think about you since the other night. You have plenty on your plate at the moment, so just know I'm here for you and I'm one-hundred percent in your corner."

As Len Ferguson continues to hug Gerri she doesn't even try to pull away. She openly sobs as he holds her. He puts his hand behind her head and comforts her, "Shhh. Shhhh. You just take your time. I can't possibly know what you're going through."

"Gerri draws back her head and then kisses him on the cheek in grateful appreciation. It feels so good just to be held by someone with her comfort in mind. She moves her head just slightly so she can see Paulette. Paulette suddenly makes the identity connection of the policeman and her reaction would be funny if it was anywhere or anytime other than the funeral. Paulette's eyes are as wide as physically possible, her mouth slightly open in what looks like she's been electrocuted. Gerri continues to enjoy the hug a few seconds longer and then both Gerri and Len pull their upper bodies back still holding around the shoulders and touching from the waist down.

"I'd better unhand you, you sweet girl. Liable to get carried away and cause you embarrassment and I wouldn't want…"

"Don't even think that. I am so surprised to see you and I couldn't place your face at first. Gotta be the uniform or I guess in this case not the uniform. Well, you know what I mean."

"I didn't want it to seem inappropriate for me to attend but when I heard your mom passed away I couldn't stay away. Look at my eyes so you know I'm pledging this…Okay… I will do anything…anything to help and support you during this very sad time. I don't wear a uniform twenty-four hours a day and I mean it…I will do anything you need or want whether I'm on duty or off-duty."

Gerri feels a warm glow over her body. How wonderful to have someone who really cares about her. "I can't tell you how much this means to me."

Len winks at Gerri and tosses his head in Paulette's direction, " And that goes for helping your entire family, even the red-head."

Gerri smiles. Len turns and moves toward the rear of the chapel. Gerri watches him and suddenly wonders if Len could be a possible competitor with Dan Penn. But these are strained circumstances and maybe she's just allowing the stress to cloud her emotions. It's true both men are handsome but confusing because here she stands, enduring the worst possible tragedy, sixteen years old, and at the same time worried about pregnancy by a hoodlum in his twenties and yet deeply, intoxicatingly, physically attracted to two older men, a cop and a teacher. Growing up is very strange and very, very confusing.

154

Gerri moves to join Paulette and whisper a few remarks about Len and she scans the room looking for her dad. She spots him talking with Dan Penn and her principal, Mister Landers. Gerri wonders if she'll get a big hug from Dan like she did from Len. Maybe Dan saw Len and knows Gerri is sophisticated enough to hold her own with a variety of men in her life. Gerri feels empowered by all this but that's superficial and the heartbreak of the event is still shackling her heart to pain and loneliness.

Stephen walks with the group of school colleagues toward the front and Dan veers off toward Gerri. He takes her hands in his, squeezes them and looks her in the eyes, "Gerri, Gerri. I am so sorry for you."

"Thanks, Mr. Penn. I appreciate seeing you today. You have no idea how I felt when I saw you back there talking to my dad."

Dan gives a quick glance around to know who may be within earshot and then quietly and tenderly, "I would give anything to hug you and hold you right at this moment but holding your hands will have to do for the time being. Just know how special you are to me and how I look forward to seeing you again very soon." One final hand-squeeze and Dan lets go, smiles and takes a couple of steps back from Gerri still with his eyes frozen on her. He turns toward Stephen, smiles and nods to him and then Dan makes his way to the rear and disappears either to the lobby or the parking lot.

The ever-present gloom of the funeral, the surprise appearances of Connie, Len and Dan leave Gerri's emotions stretched to the point of breaking. She joins Paulette and as she sits down Gerri gives a huge sigh. Her breath haltingly gasps aloud as she exhales. Paulette looks at her and puts her arm around Gerri's shoulders and bowed head.

People in the pews are waiting for the service to begin but a few remain milling about in the side aisles and up front by the caskets. Gerri

155

notices her dad walking alone on the other side of the room. He gives a couple of hugs to women Gerri doesn't know and the only thing for certain is they are not relatives or close friends she's ever met. Maybe those women are other teachers but Gerri gets a sudden and unsettling twinge of suspicion. Stephen never hugs Gerri like he's hugging the unknown women. She also knows from her prolonged hug by Len that there's some slightly erotic attachment to that sort of hugging. Gerri's sure her dad is playing all this to the hilt for his own perverted enjoyment. To Gerri his actions are inappropriate at her mother and brother's funeral.

Paulette is looking the other direction when Gerri slides across the seat to the aisle and strides directly across the front of the chapel and down the side aisle toward the back, making a beeline for her dad.

When she gets within a few feet of her dad and the small group of women, "Why are you doing this? Huh? Why would you do this?"

"Gerrie, sweetheart, why am I doing what?"

"Don't call me sweetheart. And you know very good and well what I mean. Her. Her. Her. You know, Dad, all the special, *hers*. Anybody besides me who has knockers and long hair. Hug. Kiss. Why are you doing this right in front of my mother? I think it's sick."

"Oh, God, Gerri, I know you're upset but don't do this. Let's go over and sit down. Let's just go over by Paulette."

"Sure. Sit down, Gerri. Don't embarrass me, Gerri. Well, you have it backwards. You're an embarrassment right here in the same room with my mother and brother."

Stephen painfully smiles and tries to reach for Gerri's arms to control her movements. He's so worried about what everybody else thinks he's probably going to try to wrap his arms around her as if he's

156

hugging her but Gerri isn't about to let that happen. She swats at his outstretched hands each time he reaches in her direction, pulling away every time he makes physical contact. Gerri can feel herself losing control and becoming emotionally unhinged. Her voice is progressively louder and it seems Stephen is making the situation worse by trying to physically touch her. He's keeps reaching for her, nervously smiling and looking all around at the crowd of people and shaking his head as if he can't understand why she's so upset.

Suddenly Paulette takes her hand and Gerri turns and looks at her. She surrenders to Paulette's tender touch but the floodgate of captured tears ruptures and she buries her head against Paulette's shoulder, sobbing. The crescendo of the devastating grief and raw emotions erupt.

Stephen makes a hasty retreat to the lounge, obviously shaken by the incident. Paulette and Gerri walk slowly to their seats and though Paulette is a tiny woman she's holding Gerri up from completely collapsing. Gerri sits quietly for a moment with her head bowed but then she turns her shoulders and looks around the chapel. As she looks her audience is looking at her. As she regains momentary control Gerri feels twinges of shame for the over-reaction but then she spots Stephen. He emerges from the lounge, walks down the side aisle and across the back of the chapel. He approaches a woman Gerri hasn't noticed before. The woman looks somewhat familiar but Gerri's certain she doesn't actually know her by name.

Stephen takes the woman by the arm and walks with her into the lobby of the funeral home. A few moments later he re-enters the chapel alone. Gerri struggles with an overwhelming instinct to repeat confrontation and outrage. She cannot fathom how a person can be so low she'll take up with a married man and show up at the funeral causing further disrespect to the wife and family.

Paulette senses the time bomb next to her is ticking and she grips Gerri's hand, shaking her head as if "don't" and gently restrains Gerri in her fully seated position. Gerri is overwhelmed by the awful pain in her heart and constant need to cry. She's emotionally shredded and exhausted. For now there's at least temporary comfort sitting quietly by Paulette. Stephen eventually slides in the other side of the seats next to Paulette and there the three of them sit in the front row of the chapel.

During most of the funeral service Gerri weeps, eyes closed and head nestled against Paulette's shoulder. Stephen stares straight ahead.

As the service concludes, Jim and another staff member of the funeral home enter from the back, march solemnly toward the front and as they reach the front of the chapel they stop at the row where Stephen, Paulette and Gerri sit. Jim bends down and says something to Stephen and he gets up and motions for Gerri to join him in the aisle.

Stephen bends over by Gerri and whispers, "They'll take us up front now."

Jim holds his arm out to escort Gerri and Stephen walks with the other staff member. No one else in the chapel is moving and it's so quiet the proverbial pin-drop could be heard.   Suddenly there they are, the four of them standing in front of the caskets, in a line as if to salute or bow or do something.   Jim steps in front to the side and faces Stephen and Gerri putting his face as close as he can to both.

"Stephen, Gerri. Ralph and I are going to step to the side for a moment and let the two of you say a final goodbye before we close the coffin. So take a moment with your loved ones and then we'll take you back to your seats." Jim and Ralph step to one side.

Being told "final goodbye" is like electrocuting Gerri. Her breath is suddenly in jerks and gasps. She wants to touch her mother but dare not. Her mouth is open like she's ready to scream. Gerri feels Jim's

158

arm underneath hers gently guiding her to turn back toward the seats. As she turns she's aware of everyone staring but it doesn't matter. She feels a light-headed, floating feeling and as they reach where Paulette is sitting Gerri jerks her head toward all the seated people in surprise because they all look very dark and getting darker. Oh, oh...their faces look like negatives of photographs. Gerri faints and drops to the floor.

CHAPTER 13

BURIAL

"Ahhhh! Ewwww!" Gerri hears her own voice cry out but can't connect to it or understand what's happening. She senses a very uncomfortable, sharp burning in her nose and she shakes her head from side to side.

She hears her dad's voice and sees him leaning over her, "That'll be better now. You'll be okay, Gerri. Those smelling salts are pretty tough."

She glances around the room and sees she's in the big leather chair in the lounge with her feet propped on an ottoman. She squirms and struggles to sit upright.

"Just stay there for a few seconds. We'll get everyone out of the chapel and on their way to line up for the procession. Then we can go out and get into your car, Stephen. If you'd like I'd suggest Ralph drive you and Gerri in your car to the cemetery? Then you can go on home from there and Ralph can ride back here with me."

"Sure, Jim. that'll be fine. You a little better now, Gerri?"

"Yeah. I'm okay." She pushes down on the chair arms and stands up. "What happened?"

"Well, you had a little fainting spell so take your time and don't rush it. If you need to sit for a couple more minutes it's fine. But at least you're getting some color back in your face now. As soon as you feel up to it, we'll go outside to the car. Fresh air will make you feel a bit better as well."

"No, I'm okay. I'm a little sweaty but otherwise I think I'm okay. We can go anytime."

They walk from the lounge and Gerri sees the chapel is completely empty of people, flowers and the coffins. Like nothing ever happened here. Even the lamps are turned out. The main source of light is the lobby and they gravitate toward it without being prompted. As they walk outside, the air feels cold against her perspiring skin. She realizes her clothes are damp and the cold air makes her shiver. Wow! What an ordeal. Ralph opens the back door of the car, Gerri slides in, and Ralph politely closes the door. Stephen scoots into the back seat from the other side and Ralph unceremoniously takes the wheel in the driver's seat.

The hearse begins to move and they follow, driving out of the parking lot ever so slow, the big black hearse in front and DeMore's car next. Gerri looks out the back window at all the cars following with their headlights glowing and little "FUNERAL" placards facing out through their windshields.

The procession snakes its way through town, not having to wait at intersections, stop signs or stop lights. All the usual traffic hindrances ignored by the slow, but apparently important, procession. There is a motorcycle policeman who dashes ahead of the procession, stopping traffic so the hearse and the cars following never have to stop. Gerri looks out the window, a tear runs down her cheek. How sad people have to wait until they die to be able to get respect and an escort like this.

"Do they do this for weddings, Dad?"

"What?"

"I just asked if you get the traffic to stop when you get married. Or when you have a baby or when you graduate? Or is it just done when somebody dies? "

"No, Gerri. I don't think so. I don't know. "

"You don't think so, what? Is it done other times or only when somebody dies?"

"Huh? Oh, Gerri, I don't know. What difference does it make? I just can't concentrate right now."

Well, that's clear enough Stephen is in his own world and won't talk. Gerri takes a deep breath, continues looking out the window and falls silent.

The hearse and procession turn through the big wrought iron arched gates of the cemetery, and Gerri's heart begins to pound in anticipation of the next events. She's sure this short ride of rest and isolation from grief is about over and there will be more horrible things in store. She wonders how much more of this she can take.

"Do I have to do anything here, Dad?"

"No, Gerri. I believe we just sit and the minister will say a few words and that's about it as far as I can remember how these things go. Then we'll go back to our house and many of these folks will stop by for a sandwich and a drink. Just for a little while."

Gerri stares at the reddish purple tent-looking structure among the tombstones and green grass, certain that's where they're heading but unsure of the formalities of getting to the tent. Another person she assumes is from the funeral home stands by the small line of folding chairs next to the tent across from where dirt is piled next to an elaborate hole in the ground. There's a big brass apparatus over the

162

hole and fake grass hanging over the edges so it looks less like actual dirt around the hole. All the flowers from the funeral home are piled high around the edges. A cadre of men from Stephen's school go to the rear of the hearse while everyone else stands in a group and watches. The men make two lines behind the hearse and her mother's coffin comes smoothly out into their waiting grips. They appear to struggle a little from the weight but carry her coffin toward the gravesite. Behind are two men carrying the tiny bronze coffin of her little brother. Stephen and Gerri, grandma, aunts and uncles and all the others in attendance walk behind the coffins toward the grave site.

Stephen, Gerri, Grandma, aunts and uncles sit in a row of folding chairs next to the grave. Paulette stands behind Gerri and Gerri puts her hand up on her shoulder so Paulette can hold it. Before the ceremony gets underway, Gerri is looking at the cars parked around the cemetery. Some as close as a few yards and others parked behind the hearse one behind the other snaking way off in the distance around the cemetery's big circular drive. There are still people arriving and hurrying for the ceremony. Paulette squeezes Gerri's hand a couple of times and when Gerri looks back Paulette is motioning with her head in the direction of some of the cars and Gerri spots Len Ferguson. Len has some sort of harness over his white shirt and as he walks toward the group he is slipping on a suit coat. From watching movies Gerri is sure Len is wearing a shoulder harness for a gun. She can't figure out why he'd do that. Then it hits her. Maybe Connie is right and Len is itching to spot Jake so he can arrest him or maybe even shoot him. She is filled with fear and anger that Jake would even think about showing up in the first place and also that Len thinks her mom's funeral is a place to do police business.

Gerri's overloaded and chaotic mind get her past the initial details of the ceremony and she begins to look around at the attendees. Just about the time Gerri's focus lands on Len and she notices he's looking in the opposite direction of the burial party, Paulette squeezes Gerri's

163

shoulders in an urgent manner. Paulette's moving her head and her eyes not in Len's direction but in front of the hearse where there are only three cars parked separated fifty yards or so from the rest.

Standing in a straight line by the three cars are eight guys as if standing at attention with one arm reaching across their chest, clenched fist over their heart. It's plain enough who they are because of the black leather jackets. Gerri recognizes Jake as the first in the line. She can't figure out why they would be here except as an attempted show of respect for her. At least Gerri sees it that way and can't help but feel a tenderness in her heart for the exhibition.

As Gerri glances back toward Len, he's no longer standing but walking in a quick pace away from the crowd around the grave and toward Jake's gang. Len has pulled back one flap of his suit jacket. Gerri isn't sure if she should do something or sit still. She feels a wave of fear and panic. Paulette's got both hands on Gerri's shoulders pushing firmly down so Gerri is sure Paulette's not about to let her get involved.

As soon as Len is away from the burial party headed for Jake, Jake and another guy get in the lead car and very quickly they are driving the short distance around the cemetery and obviously toward the front gate. The other gang members are no longer standing in a line but are milling around as if welcoming a confrontation with Len. But as soon as Len sees Jake getting away he reverses his course and runs for his own car. Unfortunately for Len, his car is nearly twice as far away as he's just walked. Len is jogging toward his car but Jake's long gone and now the other gang members get into the other two cars and slowly head around toward the entrance.

Len obviously thwarted in his display of heroism slows to a walk, kicks at the grass and continues slowly toward his car. Paulette lightly pats Gerri on the shoulders as if to say the danger has passed.

Gerri turns her attention back to the ceremony and realizes it's almost over and she doesn't even know what's happened. One-by-one people file past the coffin, some picking an occasional flower or petal off the baskets of flowers and placing it on the tops of the coffins, then making their way around past Stephen and Gerri. There are words muttered but it sounds like sad, sorry gibberish and only an occasional word is even recognizable. After all, what else can these same people say after already saying sorry at the house and again at the funeral home? More of the same. This is like a horror scene that never ends. What if these people just get back in line and keep coming through? It means none of this will ever end and Gerri will endure faceless people forever saying stuff in this foreign language of grief. Gerri is uncomfortable sitting trying to appear appreciative or happy that they make the effort to stop by and put their cold clammy hand in hers or worse against her face as if they care.

Soon it's just Stephen, Paulette, Gerri, a few stragglers, and Jim and Ralph. Jim and Ralph come up to Stephen and Gerri. They, smile politely and professionally, shake hands with their white gloves still on, and Jim bids them farewell from Wilson Funeral Home, "On behalf of Herman Wilson and the Wilson Funeral Home let me again express our deepest sympathy for your losses and sincerely thank you for allowing us to handle the details of this sad occasion for you."

Jim and Ralph walk back to the hearse as they strip off their gloves and talk quietly about something only audible to the two of them. It's over. Everybody turns, walks away and this is it.

Gerri notices two men standing some distance away by a tree smoking and watching. They're in work clothes and each has a shovel. They must be truly the final end to all this. How cold and crude to make all this big formal hoopla with everybody dressed up in their finest and then just walk away abandoning her mother and brother to two rough-looking laborers in overalls.

165

"Gerri, I guess we'd better get a move on. Some neighbors are already at our house by now greeting folks and I suppose we ought to get going as well." Stephen glances toward the burial area, takes a long, deep breath and when he lets it out, he's crying.

Gerri looks down at the ground and begins walking toward the car. She looks back and sees the two men putting out their cigarettes and starting toward the grave. She can't bear this and she gives in to hysteria. She points at the men and screams out loud like never before.

"Get away from them! You stay away from my mother and little brother! Don't you dare touch them! Get away!"

Her cries are so loud Stephen takes hold of her shoulder as if to console her but Gerri's letting it fly this time. She pulls violently away from her dad's grip and continues the hysterics all the while turned toward the two men and waving frantically at them to go away. They immediately stop, turn and walk briskly in retreat toward the safety of the tree. It's a small victory and she won't have to see whatever crass ceremony they hold to finally lower her mother and brother into the ground but far from any consolation, it just adds to the boiling over of grief.

CHAPTER 14

AFTERSHOCKS

Stephen, Gerri and Paulette return silently to the DeMore home. Cars are parked on both sides of the street but their driveway is left open for them to park so Stephen drives in and each get out heading toward the door. Suddenly Gerri feels absolutely exhausted as if she's trying to recover from a long illness. Just plain weak. The house is full of funeral and cemetery attendees still in their best clothes. Many people must have something in common with Aunt May namely that they can whip up a tornadic appetite over practically any excuse. People must be over their personal jitters of being in a funeral home because they've put the whispers and gaunt looks back into storage and are laughing and talking in regular voices. Gerri's having trouble reconciling the reasons for any of this. She asks herself why it's now time to have a party. Just act like nothing ever happened.

Gerri's feeling very edgy. She resolves to throw an absolute hissy-fit if she sees the mystery woman who her dad escorted to the funeral home lobby. She smirks a sinister grin thinking how she could disrupt things in a really proper explosion particularly if any of the kissy, huggy vultures show up and start their kissy huggy thing once again. Well, she'll just be on watch and if any of them step one foot into her mother's house and start pawing on her dad and him pawing back, she'll cause such a ruckus they won't know what to do. Gerri clenches her fists in defiance. They'll see a side of her they haven't seen before.

Gerri scans the growing throng of people and once again her take on this is it's hypocritical- from pious sadness to instant laughing and talking. Occasionally Gerri's pulled aside and reminded how she has to "be there " for her dad. She's told how well he's bearing up under the strain and how brave he is. Gerri restrains herself from making any seething responses. He's not brave. He's in full and complete denial and typically acting like it never happened. The real trouble is when he shuts out his personal pain he shuts Gerri out as well. She feels so very alone in their crowded, noisy house. Only once does anyone actually seek her out as an individual, calling her by name but then regressing to the cutting words, "You're going to have to help your dad a lot because he's gonna need it."

At first Gerri wonders why some people actually avoid being close to her but she suspects they're uncomfortable after her blow up at the funeral home and don't want to be the recipients of their own personal tirade. How unfair it is for people to assume it was her fault and Stephen is to be hugged and while out of her listening range he's probably given their sympathy for being saddled with a brat like Gerri. So apparently the future social pattern is to ostracize and isolate the brat even further. Today in Gerri's real-world the only people on whom she can count are as few as the fingers of one hand -Paulette, Connie, Jake, Len and Dan. What a strange group of misfits to call friends particularly since each is likely a destructive oil and water mix with most of the others.

Gerri goes to her room and closes the door for a minute trying to reset her emotions. Her jaw drops as she looks around. Her room is an absolute shambles where her grandmother's clothes and that smelly

168

perfume consume the entire space. It's like it's not even her room anymore but at least it's a quiet place in which to escape for a few minutes. She hears the muffled, but distinctive tone of women's voices in the hallway waiting to use the one bathroom. What a premium that bathroom is today! The sound of women's voices in the hall is comforting and she moves close to the door and presses her ear against it so she can soak up the comfort for a minute or two. This might be the best, most soothing thing she's experienced all day, or week for that matter.

"Well, Elizabeth told me he's been sneaking around seeing Beverly Alder for quite some time and I guess it's more than just seeing, ya know, a little oo-la-la ...know what I mean?" The women snicker at the remark.

From the other side of the door Gerri knits her brow in surprise.

Another voice, "Some people can't work together without getting involved and I suppose that's what happened. But who knows?"

"Well, I heard his daughter has been suspicious ever since Susie went into the hospital. And everybody saw her at Wilson's today. I'd say somebody better keep an eye on her. She seems a little bit over the top with the drama and hysterics. That's when some of today's teenagers get off with the wrong crowd. But she's just a kid and maybe she knows more than she should. I feel sorry for both of them. Susie would have been crushed. I hope she never knew."

"You've got to be joking. He's a two-timin' rat. He may be a teacher but he's a typical man. All phony family man but in the end he's like all the rest. Men only think with one thing and we all know what that is. And they don't care who gets hurt as long as they get you know what. And I'm guessing old Stephie-boy has been getting a-plenty."

169

"Well here's another thing I bet you didn't know. One evening my son, Mike, was waiting at Calway High for a ride after a basketball game. It was just after dark. He was sitting down on the curb by the faculty parking lot and he saw the two of them come out of the school together. He knows Stephen DeMore because Gerri and Mike have always been in school together and Mike recognized Beverly Alder because he's been to parties at the Alder home. Anyhow, he said they looked around very suspiciously and then walked across to a corner of the parking lot where one of them had obviously parked a car so it would be out of sight for their rendezvous. Anyhow, they got in the car and…well, my son was curious so he walked over close to the car and looked through the windows, but stayed out of sight. He said it was worse than a couple of teenagers in heat at the drive-in with lots of bare skin showing and all the accompanying moaning and groaning. Mike said he couldn't watch cause it was so dirty but knowing my Mike Decker, he's probably just not telling his mom everything. He probably watched as long as he could. But how disgusting is that? Right on the school grounds. They're gonna get caught and when they do I'll bet the school board will fire them. And you know it will happen. That's people out of control. Dogs in the street."

Gerri mouths the words, "Beverly Alder." Of course that's why she looked familiar at a distance earlier today. Betsy's mom and Gerri's dad! Now the party invitation makes more sense. Her own dad insisted Betsy invite Gerri probably to get her off his trail for a Friday night."

Just to shock the gossipers, Gerri opens the door and walks out, smiling.

"Excuse me, ladies."

There's a collective gasp of surprise by the three women in the hall. They look like they've seen a ghost. The hallway is absolutely silent

170

as Gerri walks back toward the kitchen. Now she knows the awful truth and she's seething with rage because now she knows other people know as well. Another mark of dishonor and disrespect toward her dear sweet mother.

She whispers and sighs in a clear voice," Will this ever end? "

Gerri returns to the group rummaging around the kitchen and pours a glass of Coke. As she turns Len is standing right behind her. He smiles and takes a step toward her, making him awkwardly too close for Gerri's comfort.

"Hey, little lady. You've been through the wringer haven't you? How ya holding up?"

Gerri tries to take a step back but bumps into the counter. "I'll be okay. I don't know when, but I'm sure I'll be okay."

Len is so close she can feel his breath and she feels trapped. "Well, maybe this isn't the time or place but I wanted to tell you again how you can call on me anytime. For anything. And I do mean **anything**. Sometimes you may just need a hug."

Gerri is uncomfortable having Len's face so close and is confused by his comment. She feels something is not so good in his mannerisms and tone. "Well, Mister…Offic…I'm really not sure what to call…"

"Call me Len. Don't get all tense and all. Okay? Okay?"

"Sure. Fine. Len."

"Look Gerri, I'm just trying to be your friend. That's all. Ya know it can't be all bad to have a cop for a friend. Right? Am I right?"

"Yeah, yeah…I guess so. I'm not really sure what you mean but listen, You're gonna have to excuse me. I 'm just tired and stressed

171

and I just need to go to my room for a while. It's not you. This day has just been too much for me to handle."

"Sure. Sure. Again. Sorry for your loss. And see you soon. Okay? Huh? Okay?"

Gerri looks at Len and there's something frightening about him. He's fidgety and his eyes are always looking around even when he's talking to her. Gerri quickly walks through a group in the kitchen and then hurries to her room, closes and locks the door. She listens to be certain Len doesn't follow her and there's no noise outside in the hallway except for the occasional person to use the bathroom. Gerri is panic stricken and she sits heavily on the edge of her bed.

✳✳✳✳✳✳

The day after the funeral and wake, the first vestiges of daylight rouse her from a nearly sleepless night on the living room sofa. She's turns her body from facing the back cushions. What a disaster! Dirty dishes, ash trays to their brims, half-eaten casseroles left out overnight, trash, suitcases sitting around open, clothes hung over chairs, and the house smells like old food, cigarettes, and enough cologne, perfume and soap smell to declare the area toxic. Gerri's mother would never leave an overnight mess to look like this.

Yesterday their small house was filled to the brim with sixty or so people all of whom ate, drank, spilled, and abandoned it all behind. After the last guest left, Stephen suggested they had all had a rough day and "we'll just clean it up in the morning". Gerri feels certain the result of his comment will not bring out a team effort to clean up but it will make a predictable, miserable morning for Gerri, the de facto house maid. After all, that's why her dad absolutely refused Paulette's offer to let Gerri stay with her while the visitors are in town. There wouldn't be anybody to clean up if Gerri wasn't available.

172

Grandma, aunts and uncles eventually prepare to leave the house after loud pot-clanging and adding more to the already horrendous mess. Now there's bacon sizzling grease-splatters all over the stove, sticky molasses puddles under a few abandoned spoons, and half-full coffee cups shoved in between remnants of last night's mess. Gerri is amazed when her grandmother and Aunt June roll out of bed, hair quadrupled in size with big curlers and they immediately prepare more food. Never a mention of cleaning up before preparing more, just pile it higher. Everything abandoned where last touched and never anything picked up. Gerri is under no illusions regarding who will clean the house and there's no relief in sight as long as the hillbillies occupy the DeMore house. She can almost hear the words, "Oh, the girl can do it. It'll be good for her."

What galls Gerri is that Stephen seems perfectly in agreement with it and never comes to her defense either to call her by name or to help with the work.

"Hey Steve. You and your daughter want to drive over by the cemetery for a bit? We thought it might be nice to go by…you know, the day after. Just to pay respects."

Stephen grimaces at being called Steve but remains ever the dutiful host, "No thanks, Bill. You all go right ahead. I think maybe it's best if Gerri and I stay here and clean up a little after the funeral and all the people being here yesterday. We can take care of the house but you guys please go right ahead."

Now it's Gerri's turn to grimace as she looks at all of them in disbelief. First, Gerri can't stand the thought that her mother and brother are in that place in the cold, damp ground. She also can't imagine why anyone would want to go back to that horrible cemetery today. Nope. She's not about to revisit yesterday's events this soon. The only thing appealing at all is to get out of this house even for an hour. Just to be

173

away from this mess would be wonderful, but certainly not worth it if getting away means to indulge this hopeless group. They are really strange.

Finally her relatives leave for their outing and there's more silence without even the mumbling from bedrooms- a totally quiet house. Friends and acquaintances are not expected to stop by the house today so it's just Stephen and Gerri. As angry and upset with her dad as she is, this feels better than preceding days. Maybe, just maybe, her dad will take a long deep breath and say, "Gerri, why don't we sit down together over here?"

Oh, if only they could just sit for a while and talk. Just the two of them. Gerri simply wants him to say he loves her.

"Gerri? Did I catch you daydreaming? Would you give a hand here to clean up from yesterday and breakfast? You know how to wash dishes so give me a little help here. Okay?"

Gerri is offended by his tone and what he says. She can't believe it. Now his way of talking to her is to imply she's lazy and daydreaming and then basically dump it on her to clean up the mess from this bunch of hillbilly slobs? Gerri's not a happy girl.

"Of course I'll clean it up. No one else is going to lift a finger to help. And by the way, I'm not daydreaming. Look at this sloppy mess! How can they just do all this and then walk out and go somewhere? How do they get along at home? Do they have someone who follows them around picking up after them. Or maybe they just don't care if it looks like a garbage dump and they just add to it until the house gets so full it just explodes."

"Oh, Gerri. They're your mother's folks and they are a little hicky but don't ever refer to them that way, or oh my God, they'd kill us both. No, just do your best like a little trooper, if you will."

174

"Okay I will... but Dad, since they're gone for a while and before I clean this up will you just sit on the sofa with me right now and talk to *me* for a while?"

"Actually, I told you earlier that I have work I need to do before school on Monday. I've missed this whole week and there's plenty of time for us to talk later after all this Missouri bunch leaves. It's a little difficult with everybody in and out right now but I'm sure we'll have lots of time together later this week. "

Gerri is physically and mentally depressed from the last several days but her face flushes red with renewal of hidden emotion-anger. But now it's back in full force. Why should she even try anymore?

Gerri tosses the dishrag on the sink, and leaves the dirty dishes and other mess, silently walking away from it all, escaping to her pigsty room. She closes the door and stands with clenched fists facing the window.

"Clean up the mess? Gerri can do it. Leave it for Gerri. Go back to work? Go back to school? Am I supposed to just "act" like nothing ever happened?"

Gerri lies on her bed and breathes deeply. Quickly she sits up, dramatically coughs and gags, shaking her head in disgust.

"Even my pillow stinks like Grandma's perfume and soap. Now even my own room isn't a place to get away for a couple of minutes."

There's a light knocking on Gerri's door.

"Gerri, c'mon, please. I asked if you'd help out and clean up the dishes? I wanted you to do it before Grandma and the rest get back. Okay? And if you see anything we need for groceries just jot it down. Okay? "

"Yeah. Yeah. Sure. Okay. I don't really care. I mean why should I care? I can clean up dishes. I can look at all the half-eaten stuff in and out of the refrigerator just waiting for someone to get poisoned. I can make the grocery list. I can do it all, Dad. Do I need to clean the bathroom, wash Aunt May's dirty underwear, dust the shelves and wash the windows, too?"

"Oh, Gerri. Don't get so down about everything. I'm trying to get past all this. You'll see. You'll get back in school next week and see all your friends, I'll get back to work and everything will get back to normal pretty soon. "

Gerri has her mouth open to counter what her dad said but she abruptly turns toward a noise at the front door.

"Oh my God. I can't believe it! I hear them. They can't possibly be back already. Oh God."

"Shhh. Gerri. Not so loud."

After being away from the DeMore house for an hour the Missouri travelers approach the front door .

"Hey. We're back from the cemetery. "

The front door swings open and an exhausted looking group of relatives giving painful sighs of relief begin plopping down on the sofas and chairs.

"I can't believe somebody already took all them tags off the flowers so who's to know who sent what? But who am I to say anything? Guess that's the way they do it here in Cal I-forn-i -aaa!"

"Billy, pipe down. You know how Stephen thinks we're all a bunch of hoosiers anyhow. I swan, ya don't need to give 'em more reason."

176

Stephen retains his role as host, " I hope you didn't have any trouble finding it and everything was okay?"

"Oh yeah, Steve. We found it. That's some cemetery. People pickin' blades of grass. Nothing out of place. Must cost a fortune to keep it up like that. We have plain ordinary people who volunteer to do that back home. But I guess that's just fancy California for ya. "

"I wasn't paying attention to how fancy the cemetery was for the last couple of days. I was busy burying a wife and son."

'Aw, c'mon Steve, I didn't intend nothin mean or nothin."

" Oh no. Of course not. And I never took it that way. I suppose it may be a little different for you."

Gerri listens and watches in some amazement. She notices an unusual emotion on her dad's face-he's angry. It may be because they are always complaining or making fun of California but more likely it's just the fact he really hates to be called Steve. These people seem to be oblivious to the rest of the world and have no cares about anyone except themselves. Gerri wonders why they drove all that way to come out here.

Most of what surprises Gerri is her grandma. Except for the initial view of her mom's body and the frightening outburst she just acts like it's any ordinary day and she's cruising along without any noticeable grief or cares. Other than that it seems her most stimulating topic of conversation is about how her butt got tired during the long trip to California and Gerri thinks there's been sufficient butt-recovery time and now they should leave.

Soon another lunch blossoms into full bloom with every conceivable dish dragged out of the refrigerator along with plates and silverware

177

and an added spectacular mess is born. They actually scoot dirty dishes and stack them higher to make room for a new mess.

Grandma lifts her face from her food with a cheery tone, "Why don't you all leave those dishes and I'll get 'em in just a bit?"

Gerri can't believe her ears. It must be a miracle because Grandma might actually do some dishes. But before she can give a sigh of relief, Grandma directs her conversation to Stephen and the result is predictable.

"So Stephen, Why don't you just sit down and visit. Gerri and I can knock these dishes out. Can't we, Gerri?"

Gerri can't even force a smile. She knows she's expected to say that's fine and then Grandma will find some excuse to disappear. She knows this is going to be another clever way to dump it all on her. As she seethes in irritation Gerri wonders if maybe she should watch and learn. This is probably the perfect lesson on how to succeed at being a fat, lazy hillbilly. Grandma or not, relatives or not, Gerri simply doesn't like any of these visitors.

Grandma suddenly has a better idea, "Ya know...I swan, but I admit that bein in this different time zone and all that drivin just to get here for a couple of days has me plum tuckered out. What if we all go and sit a spell on the back porch and then we can get them dishes and stuff when we come back inside. Just leave it for now."

Gerri boils over in sarcasm, "Naw that's perfectly okay. You all just go sit out on that there back porch and take a load off your mind and I'll just do what I enjoy by washin these dishes. Heck. My pleasure, Grandma. I love doing housework. It'll be good career experience, don't you think? Just like the Ozarks, huh?"

178

Gerri's grandmother doesn't miss the sarcasm in Gerri's tone and words. She pauses for an instant and then turns toward Stephen." Tell ya what I think. I think your girl is getting a right smart mouth on her. That's what I think. And you don't seem to be all that interested in correctin her. Old enough to show a little respect but then she's under your roof. Wouldn't happen but once under my roof. "

Then turning back to Gerri her grandma continues, "And I have no problem with answering your smart mouth by allowin you to go right on ahead and do the dishes. That's great. It'll be good for us to get a little fresh air and good for you to be where we don't have to listen to you run that mouth for a while."

There's silence. Stephen looks uncomfortable as he wears a little half-grin of embarrassment. Gerri realizes he'll not defend her and his look of embarrassment is for himself, not Gerri.

Billy breaks the silence looking toward Stephen, " And we'll probably be turnin' in early tonight so we can get an early start. We're gonna be headin' back tomorrow. Who knows if that car will get over the mountains again. But we got our desert water bag and I ain't sure how it works but I swear that water hangs in that canvas bag up in front of the car and it's as cold as ice when you want to drink some. I don't get it."

Stephen appears engaged with Billy's comment, "Oh Billy, it's just evaporation and it only works where the humidity is very low. It wouldn't work in Missouri. Too humid. Just basic science."

"Science my ass, Steve. I know you're a teacher and all but I just did what some folks back home told me to do. Fill the bag with water, hang it on the front of the car and as ya get close to Californ-I-A it gets cold. I did it, it works. Plain and simple. You can tell me all you want that it's science this or science that, and try to tell me all the scientific details but I don't care. All I care is that it works. So, I don't need any of your schooling on basic science, Steve."

Stephen's face turns crimson as if he'll blow up. At least that would be a sight to see. But then he takes a deep breath, smiles, silently turns and without a word walks toward the front door and stands looking out the window.

CHAPTER 15

OUT WITH THE TRASH

Half-whispering voices in the night. It's still dark. Gerri begins to wake. No mystery in her recognition of the voices. It's her grandma, aunts and uncles and they are bringing suitcases into the living room. Gerri listens and peeks with squinted eyes into the movement of people coming and going through the living room, just a few feet from her temporary bed on the sofa. If they're trying to be quiet, they're not succeeding, nor do they care. Gerri can see the mantle clock in the dim light and it's three-forty-five in the morning. She listens and tries to act as if she's still trying to sleep.

"Look Steve..."

Stephen wheels toward Gerri's grandma and glares at her, "Stephen... my name's *Stephen*. Okay?"

"Look we don't want to make this any worse than it is. We're just simple folks. You may not think we're real smart but I think you'll find...we're pretty dog gone smart when it comes to takin' care of family. Susie wrote to me that she was going to leave you and come home with your girl and the new one. There was a problem, Stephen, and it must have been a serious problem when a mother has to come home to be with her own ma and leave her husband behind. So look here. I'd never turn my back on my own daughter, granddaughter and at the time we didn't know, but a grandson. And just so you understand real good, Stephen, family is Susie and Geraldine and that baby. What *you* do is up to you but the others are *my* family. Susie's gone, baby's gone but Geraldine's still here. All I know is that Susie was havin' a problem with you and I don't need all the details why. Now, you're standing there shaking your head like it's not true. Well, it is true. It's a problem cause she said it's a problem. That's good 'nuff. Now the reason we're talkin' here is about Geraldine and her future. Whether she stays here or if it would be better for her to be with me back home."

Gerri is shocked! What are they talking about? Why are they talking about her? What does her grandma mean here or with Grandma?

Then Billy picks up the chorus, "Ya know Stephen, Susie wrote to Ma several times thinkin there would be a point... now...now don't hold up your hand to stop me from tellin you what you need to hear teacher or not, for once you just listen. Geraldine is family, and like Ma says, we are more than willin' to take good care of her and this part I want to be sure you understand."

Stephen looks angrier than Gerri's ever seen him, "Are you people nuts? You are not even making sense. You have no idea about anything. There was no letter about Susie leaving me."

"Well, there was. Most certainly was. In fact Susie was going to change the beneficiary on her big Hollywood star life insurance policy …change it to Ma. In fact there's a good possibility she already did make the changes."

"Aha! Ahhh Haaa! So, that's what this is all about. The life insurance. This is about money. Well, I have to hand it to you. You're right when you say you're good at taking care of family…like makin up some half-baked story about Susie leaving me and giving you the insurance money. Yep that money would go a long way in the Ozarks I guess… Well, listen to this you bunch of hillbillies…The life insurance policy says Stephen DeMore on it and not anything else. How 'dya like that?"

There's total silence in the room. Now Stephen is feeling like the winner, "So, Gerri's not going anywhere and neither is our money. We have a good life and this is a very tough time. But she's my daughter and you can't walk into my house…did you hear that? *My* house. You can't walk in here and act like you can take life insurance money and decide what's best for *my* daughter."

"Now, Stephen let me finish. Nobody's trying to take anything. We're just trying to be sure of Geraldine's future. You know if she comes with us she'll be raised by Ma who ain't got all that much money and I'm sure if what Susie told us about the insurance it would be plenty for all of us…you, Geraldine, us… "

Gerri feels like a bargaining chip for insurance money, being referred to by her mom's family like an unwanted pet to be sent to a new home. Gerri figures she'd run away rather than go live like that. She's about to explode onto the scene with her own input but before she can say anything, her dad has more to say.

"Listen to me. All of you! I have no idea what Susie actually told you and how much is just you making up stories and then repeating them in hopes that will make them true. But I'm very sure of one thing. She would never, I mean never, have left California to go back to the Ozarks. Now, Gerri and I have made you welcome to stay under this roof during this tragic time but when you get me out of bed to berate me in front of my daughter and then try to get me to barter my daughter because of something you heard, this is not something I'm going to tolerate. Do you have any feelings for anybody except your miserable selves? I just buried my wife and son? My daughter's mother? Well, the welcome mat just got rolled up."

Billy seems to be up to Stephen's challenge, "Don't get on yer high horse with us, Steve. Here's the long and the short, we said what needed to be said, and we're leavin'. We know there was a problem no matter how much you deny it. Susie did write to Ma and she was leavin you but all of that's over and done now. And by the way, I don't think we overstayed our welcome. I don't think there was any welcome from the second we drove up. Should've known when we arrive and then have to sit outside for an hour. You don't like us and I'd say we don't exactly cotton to you either, but this wasn't set out to be no pleasure visit and so no need to start another world war. We're gonna go home and I can tell you from my heart that we don't wish you no ill will. "

Before Stephen can respond, Billy grabs him and gives him a big bear hug in silence and then turns to the rest of the family standing there and looks for them to do the same.   But Grandma, Aunt June, Aunt May and Uncle Ed aren't as diplomatic as Uncle Billy. They just file past Gerri without saying another word as she stands in pajamas and mussed hair beside the sofa. Then they begin to take out their suitcases that are lined up by the front door. Within ten minutes the still muddy old car lumbers down the street and around the corner out of sight.

"Boy, oh boy! I know they're family but they are a bunch of hillbilly crooks. I'd had about as much of them as I could stand. How about you?"

"Yeah. That's for sure. I can tell you, Dad, they may be Mom's mother, brother and sister but they are no fun to be around. If Aunt May was here one more day she'd have eaten the tooth powder and soap in the bathroom. She does nothing but eat. And she never says anything halfway pleasant. She's just mean. And it will take me a month to get Grandma's horrible soap and perfume smell out of my bedroom. Yep. I'm glad they're gone and I've never heard anything before like what just happened. I'm still half asleep so I don't know how much was real and how much I dreamed. I guess I can hope what was said was a dream...a bad dream."

"Well, it's only a little after four in the morning and it's Monday. Shall we clean house today or do you want to have some breakfast a little later, leave the dishes, leave the laundry, leave the mess, get dressed and go to school today? Ya know, just to sort of get out of here for a day? It's up to you. I wouldn't mind going into school today and being a little ahead of the game this week. Then we can just make do this week, cleaning up a little at a time and then we can finish the rest of the mess over next weekend. What do you say, Gerri?"

"I don't want to go to school but I'll do anything to get out of this house, cleaning or not. I guess going back to school today isn't so bad. It's Monday. At least it's something to do. Maybe that way I can leave the window open while I'm at school and air out my room."

"Okay. Then take your time getting dressed for school and we'll just have some juice and toast for a light breakfast."

After Gerri gets ready for school, she's sitting at the cluttered kitchen table eating some cereal and she notices her dad has not eaten anything but is hurrying around and by seven he's ready to leave home. As she sees him leave, Gerri feels sort of sad for her dad because he's really showing the signs of stress. He doesn't look the same as he used to look. His shirt is wrinkled and has likely been worn more than a day or two probably because Gerri hasn't been asked to do the laundry and ironing. Yet. But with a quick goodbye and a wave, he's out the door as if he can't wait to get away from home.

Gerri's left standing alone in the quiet house and she sighs heavily and flops down on the sofa as she looks around the living room. The house never looked like this when her mother was alive. What a mess. Dishes on the table and sink. Newspaper partly on the sofa and partly on the floor. Even the sunlight coming through the window looks like it's shining through dust in the air. But Gerri's reaction is different now. People trying to take her as a way of getting money? A dad who can't show her affection or understanding? Everything dumped on her like a servant? People talking to her as if she's not a real person? Gerri just doesn't care anymore. She shrugs her shoulders, goes out the front door and closes it without locking or pulling on it to even to see if it is locked. She wonders how many ways can she can say or show she **does not** care.

"Nobody cares about me. Well, okay. Then I don't give a crap about anybody, well, except for a couple."

She slowly walks toward school but even this is different. She's not thinking about school. She shudders to think what Jake did to her so quickly and it makes her nauseated to think of what could still be devastating results. She thinks of how uncomfortable she is with Len Ferguson because there's something about him that scares her. She's thinking the only real friends she may have in the world are Paulette and Dan Penn. But she wonders if even they will stick by her if it turns out her next nightmare comes true and she's actually pregnant.

185

When school is over for the day, Gerri answers the usual shouts and goodbyes with a scowling silence. Even though it was good to be out of the house she really is tired and told Mr. Penn during sixth hour if it was okay she'd just see him on Tuesday. He seemed fine with it. So she can make the trek home and continue showing a mood of sullen anger. Seems no one can be trusted so she'll show them a different side of her. No one has ever possibly gone through the tragedy she's just endured and continues to endure. And, all alone.

Later, on the walk home she's hoping somehow the walk will last longer than it does. She gets to her street and she's relieved that her dad's car isn't in the driveway. The unlocked front door surprises her momentarily but then she recalls when she left this morning and made no effort to lock it. The house is exactly the way it was left. Dismal! What a mess! What a smell!. Of course nothing cleaned itself. She tosses her papers and books on the sofa, goes to her room and curls in a fetal position on her filthy and smelly bed. Gerri decides she's not going to clean anything at this point besides she doesn't feel very well. She just feels like lying down but suddenly there's an unmistakable feeling. Her period.

She goes to the bathroom and for sure that's what it is. She puts both hands on the sink and looks in the medicine cabinet mirror. Tears of relief run down her cheeks. She's lived alone with this fear for so long that she can't quite shake it so quickly.

"Whew. Thank God. At least that's over. I've got to forget it and never get in that position again. Too close. Way too close."

It's one less thing about which she needs to worry. She takes several deep breaths in relief and eventually returns to the living room and assumes a reclining position to rest on the sofa.

Her dad seems to be "running late" as usual. Then she hears the unmistakable sound of their car and in rapid succession the car door slams, footsteps up the porch and the front door opens. Gerri tries not to look at her dad and she's not feeling all that talkative so she's certainly not going to start a conversation.

Gerri and her dad exchange a few quiet words necessary for putting their sandwiches and milk supper together and then they eat in silence. Gerri rinses her dishes but leaves them on the sink and withdraws to her room. She knows when she leaves the dirty dishes and walks out of the kitchen her dad looks up and she's secretly hoping he'll say something so she can show him her mood. But Stephen says nothing and eventually follows suit leaving his dishes on the sink as well.

Gerri figures this must be the way life will be from now on. In her room, she lies on her bed and thinks. Her thoughts are laced with agony and anger. Maybe her father really loved her mother and now he sees Gerri as a burden for him to feed and clothe. Maybe that's what her mom wrote to Grandma. Maybe her mom knew that Stephen looks at Gerri as a burden. She wants so desperately to be held and told that her thoughts are foolish and her father loves her more than ever. She wants to be reassured that together they'll get through all this. *Together*. A year ago she thought being together as a family was reality and it would never change. Now she knows that was pure fantasy and she was the only one who was living in the dream world. Well, she's certainly awake now. Gerri's misguided perception is that the last couple of weeks have forged her into a realistic, grown woman. No more dreams and fantasy for Gerri DeMore.

CHAPTER 16
A FRIEND... INDEED

Gerri is already awake when Stephen knocks at her door.

"Morning, Gerri. You awake? Rise and shine."

"Yeah, I'm already awake. I'm fine."

She awoke earlier thinking about Mr. Penn and it sends her heart beating faster and her breathing isn't exactly panting but it's certainly quick and shallow. Now that the whole Jake episode is totally behind her she feels a renewed energy to focus on Mr. Penn. Whew! Again and again, grateful being rid of her ultimate fear and focusing on the fantasies of being with Mr. Penn send her into a near delusional state. She must decide what she'll wear to school and then later today she'll resume the daily occurrence to be with Mr. Penn after school. And of course she'll be on the lookout for him during the day for the possibility of an accidental encounter. Other than focusing on her favorite teacher, she'll not show any interest in academics today.

She begins by trying on outfit after outfit, combination after combination in hopes of looking more mature, more feminine. She tries on some of her mother's skirt and blouse combinations, and settles on a calf-length, tight pencil skirt, white blouse and black flats. She can hardly believe how well her mom's clothes fit her and how they accentuate her appearance in all the right places. She looks in the mirror, turning first one way, then the other, checking every detail.

She knows dressing like this is going to look different at school and it's a little scary to be sure. She wonders how she should react if somebody laughs because they've never seen her look this grown up. She decides she's got to be strong. Gerri knows how she looks and she'll simply ignore any comments or giggles with the sullen-angry glare. She's so happy she kept several of her mother's outfits and she's amazed at how stylish they look. Her mom really knew clothes and it's astounding to Gerri how well they fit.

As she walks to school, Gerri feels a little self-conscious at first as if everyone is staring at her but the farther she walks the better she feels. Heads used to constantly turn to look at her mom and her mom loved every second of it and now so will Gerri. It will just take a little practice feeling comfortable with her new look.

After each class, she walks slowly through the halls to her next class hoping for another one of Mr. Penn's surprise encounters. Even though it doesn't happen, she walks as tall and proud as she can.

After the fourth hour Gerri feels exhausted and wants the day finished. She heads to the fifth hour room when suddenly a firm hand takes her gently by the arm and turns her slightly.

"Oh, hi Mr. Penn. You surprised me."

"Oops. Sorry. I didn't mean to startle you but I just wanted to see if you'll have time to stay after class."

"Sure."

"Okay. Good. Gotta go. See you later, then."

Gerri is sure he found her on purpose! She makes it to class on time and she's not paying any attention about what is discussed.

Even in Mr. Penn's class she tries to look interested but all she can think about is meeting him with just the two of them together. After the final bell for the day she goes to her locker, a quick trip to the bathroom to be sure her clothes and hair look the best they can and then she returns to his room at the end of the upstairs hall.

Sure enough, she looks through the little window on the door of his room and there he sits at his desk. Gerri feels an air of excitement as she slowly opens the door and lightly knocks on the door frame.

"Mr. Penn?"

"Oh, hi Gerri. Please. Please come in." He stands at his desk and makes a sweeping gesture with one hand as an invitation. "I'm very glad to see you this afternoon. It's been one of those days and I can certainly use a pick-me-up from that pretty smile of yours. And I have

190

to tell you, the outfit you're wearing is very, very becoming . I hope me saying that doesn't embarrass you."

"Oh, no. Not at all. And I was thinking about what you said before and I can't tell you how much it would mean to me if you still want me to help you and ya know just come and talk to you …maybe sometimes…if that's okay?"

"Gerri, I wouldn't have offered if I didn't mean it. Please come sit."

And with that, he walks to a desk across from Gerri and sits down. He is silent but stares directly into her eyes, all the while displaying that big handsome smile. Gerri notices his loose tie, five o'clock shadow and tousled hair and those are enough to cause her heart and breathing to go into high gear.

"Gerri, I just thought again yesterday about an earlier conversation before your tragedy at home that maybe this would work even more now because as we discussed before, you know many people your age but maybe another friend…even a little older if that's okay… would be good. And for me, well, I seem to work all the time and I have a lot of friendly acquaintances but I also don't have many close friends so this will be really good for me, too."

"Yeah, that sounds really great. And I think I told you I don't have tons of friends, really close friends. In fact, I really don't have **any** best friends I can talk with, well except for my neighbor and she's really old, probably fifty or so.   The kids I know at school wouldn't understand what I've been through with my mom and little baby brother dying and all.   But since you're a man and a little older and stuff…well, maybe you just understand better from a different point of view. Oh, I guess that's silly, huh?"

"No Gerri. That's exactly why I offered and I'm just delighted we can be good friends."

191

"It's really been a horrible week. I used to look so forward to getting home after school. A few years ago my mother and I played the piano together and we'd sing silly, funny songs. It was so good to laugh. She was so good to me. I miss that more than I can tell you and it will never be fun like that again."

"Gosh, Gerri you are in one sense a very, very lucky young lady to have parents to treat you with such love. Well, you said it was you and your mom? And your dad?"

"Oh, he's a different story. Do you know him? He's a math teacher at Calway."

"Of course I know him. I've known him for quite a while because of combined teachers' meetings and I visited with him briefly at the funeral."

Gerri shows little interest in how Mr. Penn knows her father. "Well, you said you'd be my friend and I believe you and so I'm counting on you that I can trust you...right? There are so few people I can trust...at all."

Dan Penn holds up three fingers like the Boy Scout salute, "Of course. Whatever we talk about stays between us as friends."

"Well, at the same time my mother was having medical problems with her pregnancy...well, my dad was seeing someone on the side. I found out about it and then a day later my mother was gone. Oh, God. It's been horrible."

Gerri starts to cry and Mr. Penn stands and opens his arms. Gerri leaps across the aisle, knocking a desk askew and lands in his comforting, hugging embrace. Oh, what a relief! For so long she's needed the hugging, the loving comfort of a man's strong protective arms. This is somehow even better than when she remembers being hugged by her

192

dad. This is exciting and breathtaking. He's holding her so close and tight, right up against him and Gerri loves it, *really* loves it. She'll hold onto him as long as possible.

"Here, let me get you my handkerchief. Let's dry those pretty eyes." Mr. Penn loosens his grip and takes a half-step back.

"I'm sorry. I shouldn't have said all that and I'm sorry if I embarrassed you by hugging you."

"Gerri, it's a beautiful experience to be with a real friend and confidant. You never, ever need to apologize to me. I thank you for your trust and confidence and I have to be honest... I loved hugging you."

Mr. Penn again opens his arms for another embrace and Gerri feels even more comfortable pressing the whole length of her body against him and holding him really, really tight. She wants to show him how much this means so she lays her head on his shoulder and turns her face right into his neck. His neck has just a hint of something that smells very good.

Gerri whispers, "I've just missed having someone hold me. Since my mother died and my dad knows that I know about his cheating, he avoids me. No talking. No contact. He leaves early and comes home late. I can't tell you how lonely I've been. I thought all I needed was someone like my dad but this is so much more and it really, really feels good."

"Wow. You've really been having a tough time of it. I think a good medicine for you is talking through things and knowing I'll be here for you."

"Yes. Yes. It's what I need more than anything. I've felt so worthless and alone. During the week of the funeral my grandmother and a couple aunts and uncles were here staying at our house and they treated

193

me like dirt. They're a bunch of worthless hillbillies and on the morning they were going to leave they got into a big argument with my dad over whether I should go live with them or not."

"I'm confused. They wanted to take you with them but I thought you said they didn't treat you very well. Didn't you?"

"Didn't treat me very well? No, I said they treated me like dirt. It became clear in the argument that my mom and dad have a life insurance policy on my mom left over from the days when she was going to be in the movies. It's for five-hundred thousand dollars or maybe more so my grandma and the hillbillies said they were willing to take me with them if they got the money. My dad was more interested in proving to them they wouldn't get any money than he was about protecting his own daughter. Nope. Treated like dirt is the correct description.

Mr. Penn pulls his head back from the embrace and looks directly at Gerri and he's not smiling at the moment. "Holy smokes! That's a lot of money for an insurance policy. Maybe you misunderstood. Five-hundred thousand? "

"Yeah. I've heard it mentioned more than once. Yep. Five-Hundred thousand."

"That's huge. Well, well. At least money doesn't sound like it will be one of your future problems."

"I guess. But I don't care about any of that. I just hate feeling so lonely."

Mr. Penn takes a deep breath and resumes the embrace with vigor. She thinks he's going to kiss her but he doesn't. He's still looking directly into her eyes and in a very soft, sincere voice he continues , "Well, let's you and I put a stop to that loneliness...here and now." Another

194

little pause and then, "And now I probably should let you out of here so you can head home. I don't want to get too carried away with my close friend right here in my school room and I'm suddenly afraid that could happen. As a matter of fact I know it will happen and that might not be too good. The last thing in the world I want to do is frighten or embarrass you. Better call it an afternoon for now, don't you think?"

He takes a deep breath as if struggling with his decision to let her go, "Whew."

"Sure, Mr. Penn. I probably should go. And thank you."

As they separate Mr. Penn runs his hands down her arms and takes hold of her hands. He holds them for a moment, looks directly into her eyes, smiles at her, squeezes her hands and then hesitates before he lets go. Gerri's face feels like it's on fire.

She feels like running all the way home from school but walking slowly in the long tight skirt is going to have to do for this afternoon. For the first time in recent memory she feels good about arriving home and she doesn't care if Stephen is home or not. She can now simply be happy in the solace of her room to think about her new, very handsome, very special and trusted friend, Mr. Penn. She wonders what her reaction might have been if he had kissed her.

Once Gerri gets home she has a bit of renewed energy and she tries to begin the process to restore the house, clean up the kitchen and do the laundry. Stephen is home early and even though there's very little conversation they're both busy in different areas so the evening is going by quickly. At least Stephen is in the house and he seems to be working his tail off to help. That's more than Gerri expects and while she'll never admit it, she would give anything for a rekindling of a loving relationship with her father.

195

Around eight o'clock Stephen finds Gerri in the living room lying on the sofa reading.

"I wonder if you'll help me with one more project tonight and it's not exactly something I'm looking forward to doing but I think sorting through and cleaning out your mother's clothes and things need to be done."

He couldn't have shocked Gerri any more if he had simply poured a bucket of ice water over her.

"What? Clean out her things? What's the big hurry? I don't think I want to do that...at least not yet."

"Gerri, I'd like for you to help because I know there are things I'm sure you'll want to keep but I'm going to do this whether you feel up to it or not."

"All I said is what's the big hurry? So what is the big hurry, Dad?"

"Fine. I have to explain everything to you just to get a little help. Okay. Let me explain, Gerri.   I won't have as much time later in the week as I do right now. I know how busy I'll be the rest of this week. So If you decide to help just come on in the bedroom. Otherwise I'll be doing what I think needs to be done."

Gerri fumes in the living room for a while but eventually goes into the main bedroom. Stacks of her mother's clothes are heaped on the bed. As she begins to gently touch the clothes she can smell the unmistakable essence of her mother. It paralyzes her for an instant and then she just throws myself across the clothes hugging bunches of them and hysterically crying.

"Please, promise you won't throw these away. This is all I've got."

Stephen seems more irritated than compassionate, "Gerri. I need your help. I know you miss your mother and so do I but we've got to move on with things."

Apparently Stephen has no idea what a deep ugly wound he opens with those comments. Gerri sits up from the piles of clothes she is embracing. She stops crying and glares at him and then the volcano erupts.

"How dare you! I'm sure you *do* need the closet cleared out. Is that so Beverly Alder can hang her cheap, slutty clothes in my mother's closet? In her place? Those women were so right the other day when they said you are a two-timer, a jerk and you'll probably get fired by the school board because people have seen you and your girlfriend on school grounds, in the parking lot. It's not bad enough I found out about you but your little secret isn't so secret, is it? Seems everybody knew about it but Mom. But she must have suspected or known something for her to consider leaving you high and dry. But you sneaked around behind her back. What kind of person are you to do that?"

Stephen isn't expecting this and he's silent, mouth open as if he's searching for words.

In a calm tone of voice, "Gerri, I will not deny what you said and I cannot help what you think of me but there are a couple of things I should tell you. First of all your mother did know. When Susie first found out a few months ago she was thinking of leaving me and taking you with her back to Missouri. Your grandma wasn't wrong about getting a letter. I'm sure of it. But while we were there in the hospital and she was starting labor she called me to the bedside and said the new baby would be a new start for us all and if I was willing she'd like to try to resolve our problems and be happy again. It broke her heart when I told her that you knew about it, but Gerri, she was willing to

197

forgive me so we could have all be happy again, like old times. Now, I'd like your forgiveness as well. You and I can start fresh."

Gerri can't find words to interrupt.

"It was like a weight was lifted when your sweet, angelic mother, my Susie was willing to take me back. I promised Susie and God I'd do everything to earn her love and respect once again. I made my promise and a couple hours later she was taken from us. I just don't know which way to even turn right now. What the future holds, I don't know. So you can still believe what you want, and others can believe what they want, but now you know. And I'm going to continue here and if you feel like helping me, it's fine and if not, it's okay. I understand."

Gerri sits and stares but words do not happen and then silently, with head down, she withdraws to her room. Gerri wonders if it can be true that her mother knew about this for months. That would mean that Gerri's been living in this house with all this going on and she's the only one who didn't know until that fateful lunch hour. Shouldn't her mom have told her? Why wouldn't she tell her? Maybe they thought she wasn't grown up enough to handle it. Well, she's certainly grown up now!

Gerri spends what's left of the evening in her room trying to sort out her mental turmoil.

Growing up is excruciatingly painful.

*****

The next morning, usual preparations for school are out the window. Yesterday, the long tight skirt and today Gerri's spending a lot of time on a little hint of makeup and no ponytail. She finds a circle pin in her mom's old jewelry box so she pins it on her left blouse collar. That's supposed to mean you're not taken and not going steady-like a sign that says I'm available. Besides, she's not committed to any guy just yet. Today her long hair hangs straight down and beyond shoulder length. She surprises herself by the mirror's reflections and knows she's good looking and there's a not-so-subtle hint of provocative sexiness thrown in. She finds it stimulating to her confidence that older guys find her attractive.

As the day drags on, Gerri anticipates a surprise visit in the hall between classes and she's not disappointed. Between second and third hour classes she feels the familiar hand on her arm. At the instant of the touch her stomach feels light and fluttery. Though just a brief and innocent encounter, the touch and the smile send shockwaves through her body. Her imagination leads quickly to fantasies she's never thought of before and some of them might even make Paulette blush if she were to be told.

As Mr. Penn moves away from her, he unexpectedly takes a quick step back toward her, bends over and whispers, "Your hair looks terrific."

Gerri blushes as the surprise and compliment turn her into a temporary, happy, hallway statue.

He quickly disappears into the mass of students.

Slowly, the school day draws to a close and she can't wait to get to room 214. It seems all the more private and exciting because his room is on the second floor at the end of the hall. It's as close to being alone as possible under the circumstances and she will take whatever time she can get with *her* fabulous Mr. Penn.

She arrives, opens the door slowly and knocks lightly on the door frame. Mister Penn has his back to her and he's writing something on the blackboard but when he hears the knock he turns and smiles

199

without saying a word. She can only hope he's as happy to see her as she is to see him.

But after what he said in the hall Gerri feels very confident today. In fact, she feels brave enough that she walks directly to the front where he is standing and as she gets close to him she slightly opens her arms and he reacts immediately by stepping forward to her where they embrace very close and very, very tight. She nestles her face against his neck and he puts one of his hands behind her head and holds it tightly against him. She closes her eyes as he gently caresses the back of her head. She could stay like this forever.

He pulls slightly back from her and as she raises her face from his shoulder toward his face he stares into her eyes. His smile is a little nervous and she can feel and smell his warm rapid breath. As she closes her eyes she feels his lips lightly touch hers- brushing, teasing, pulling away, then touching again.

Then he quickly pulls away and takes a deep breath.

"Wow! As much as I'd love to continue, we really must be careful here in school."

"Of course. I'm sorry. I shouldn't have done that."

"Remember, Gerri, you never have to apologize for anything with me. But if someone were to walk in unexpectedly and see a teacher and student embracing it would be awkward and difficult to explain as the student grading papers. But I could try."

They both laugh and he takes a very long deep breath as if to regain his composure, " I was thinking earlier as next weekend approaches, I'll really miss seeing you on the weekend like we're able to see each other on school days. I'm wondering if there's any way possible we could figure out a way where I can sometimes see you over weekends."

"I'd love that."

"I hoped it might be possible but I sure don't want you to get in trouble or even have to answer any embarrassing questions at home. You do understand the chance I am…we are taking because of the age difference?   But it sure would be great if it could happen."

Gerri does not want to lose the excitement of this moment, "I understand. And you must understand and believe I am a willing participant. So, I'll find a way to get out of the house. I can do that. I will do it. Just let me figure out the details and I'll tell you tomorrow. Is that okay?"

He looks pleased, "Of course. How perfect that will be."

"So, is there anything I can help with…you know like school stuff?"

"Not really today. Don't be angry but there really isn't much of a job. I just really want to see you. Rarely will there be anything school related for you to do."

Gerri giggles, "Well, that's fine. But I guess for now I should be going, Mr. Penn. I know you probably have other things to do and I should go on home. At least I don't have to hurry, particularly tonight. My dad's got a teachers' meeting at Calway and he probably won't even get home until way after nine tonight. I …"

"Hey. Hey, I'll tell you what, Gerri. What if I leave right now, too? Let's go get a hamburger, fries and a Coke, and then I can take you on home. My treat…and we'll make sure we get you home in plenty of time before your dad gets home. Whadya' say? You and me."

For a split second Gerri has a flashback to her ride home with Jake and how it turned out. But this is way, way different and Gerri feels like she would be willing to trust and probably even do anything that Mr.

Penn asks of her. "Gosh, that would be wonderful! You'd do that? Gosh, Mr. Penn, you're wonderful! Oops. Maybe I'm not supposed to say that. "

"That's fine, Gerri. Besides, it sounds really good to have you say it. I have to tell you I really look forward to being together with you. And maybe I shouldn't say this but you make me feel very special when we're together and well I can hardly describe how I feel when I can touch you and hold you. I guess that's because we have a very real and wonderful connection. I felt it immediately when we first talked. Doesn't mean anybody has to know what we talk about or where we go. It's just the way things can be with us. This evening...now...we can go to a place, a diner I know that's a little ways away so nobody from around here sees you with an "old" teacher. Don't want to embarrass you."

"Oh, gosh, Mr. Penn. I wouldn't be embarrassed."

Gerri is in a happy, happy fog. At the moment she's not worried about anything. It's seems like a long time since she's felt this good.

At first he's nervous as they leave the school. They walk out the doors and he looks all around to see if anyone is close by. The coast is clear and they go to his car. He hurries around to the passenger side and opens the door for Gerri to hop in. He motions for her to put her head down out of sight as they leave the parking lot and drive in front of the school, then he gently touches her shoulder and raises her in the seat.

They drive from the parking lot and the farther they get from the local vicinity the more he relaxes. Even though they are going to an area of Fresno where Gerri's not familiar it seems strangely reminiscent of the route she shared with Jake and Connie. Then like a bad dream she sees the sign "BRENTWOOD'S POOL & BILLIARDS". Gerri feels a wave of shame and embarrassment and for a moment wonders if she

202

needs to duck down to avoid any chance of being seen but there doesn't appear to be anybody out on the sidewalk in front. As they pass by Gerri looks for Jake's shiny black car in the parking lot on the side and it's no surprise it's not there. Connie told her Jake is staying out of sight so it's not likely he'd park his car in a place so familiar to him.

"As she turns her attention back to Mr. Penn he's looking with a little concern, "Something wrong?"

"No. No, I was just looking around. I'm not familiar with this part of the city."

"Yeah. This is a little off the beaten track for Central High. Glad nothing's wrong. Thought maybe you were having second thoughts of being along with me. You were looking a million miles away."

"No, I'm fine." Gerri tries to give him her most affectionate smile while thinking he'd never believe all she's recently experienced.

They don't talk much more after that and in several minutes they arrive at a little diner with a neon sign on the front, "CHAPMAN'S CAFÉ". Gerri's never seen the place before because it's all the way across town from her house and the school. It's way past Brentwood's and even Brentwood's is out of her area of familiarity.

Gerri's very relaxed as they go inside. For sure no one she knows would ever be in this place. She has nothing to worry about and besides, there's nothing wrong with going for a hamburger and Coke with a teacher. Gerri is having a wonderful time and they really aren't talking about anything in particular, but they are talking and it's as if there is nothing off limits or taboo. How wonderful it is to just talk and laugh and talk some more. It's interesting and exciting to learn about things he knows, places he goes and things he does when he's not teaching. He seems to be interested in hobbies, clothing styles, trends of teenagers. The time seems to fly because Gerri loves every second of their time together.

When they get back into his car, he motions for her to scoot over next to him and she fends off Jake's ghost in the driver's seat and does as he asks. There's not much talking while they drive but just her hip touching his makes her feel like she can hardly breathe. His car slowly makes its way through the streets toward Gerri's neighborhood and her house.

Gerri imagines this is just like a real date and she thinks he really cares about her. She wonders if he suspects how she really feels about him, but surely he doesn't just suspect. Surely he knows by the way she admires everything he says and does. She's sure glad he's not a mind reader so he doesn't know some of the things she fantasizes because if he knew he'd probably run away and never come back. She wonders if this is the start of something even more. What if she's in love with him for real? She's not sure how real love is supposed to feel but right now at this instant her answer is maybe, probably, she's pretty certain, this has to be love.

Gerri   smiles and looks out the window on the passenger side of the car.

"Gerri, I need to tell you. This has really been special for me and I hope you are enjoying it."

"Oh, yes. I look forward to meeting with you every day and tonight's been wonderful. Thank you so much."

"You're very welcome and we can look forward to more times together. Sounds like we'll both enjoy that."

 "Mr. Penn, yesterday I just couldn't wait so I could see you today . I mean I really think about nothing else. And when I'm at home I really don't care anymore if my dad is home or with his girlfriend or anything. I only think about this. You. Don't laugh but I really don't care about anything except being together with you. I guess I've needed this for a long, long time."

" I'm glad because that's exactly how I feel, too but Gerri we need to be sure people don't get the …ah…wrong idea. In fact we need to be sure nobody knows anything we do outside of school or this will come to a stop real quick and I could be in a lot of serious trouble. I want to get to know you even better but we really have to be careful at school particularly and even when we aren't at school. Just always be sure our actions look like they're on the up and up."

"Of course. Nobody will guess from me. Promise."

"That's great. As long as you know when you must be home without causing a problem I can always bring you home from school and maybe we can… ya know sometimes like tonight just go somewhere for a while and talk. On the weekends, if we can arrange to meet somewhere maybe we can go over by one of the parks or take in a movie on the other side of Fresno or something. Ya know. I want to be with you…we just need to be a careful. I think as long as we avoid the areas right around the school we'll be just fine. How's that sound?"

Gerri can't believe how wonderful his plans sound to her. She's looking out the side window and blushing enough it's a wonder it's not lighting up the inside of his car. Tonight is the first time she's smiled so much since long before that terrible day when her mother died.

"Sure. That sounds fine. I don't want my dad to find out anything at all, at least not yet. He wouldn't understand, but he probably wouldn't care anyhow. He's too busy with his married girlfriend."

"Okay. There are a couple more things. At school you should continue to always call me Mr. Penn, but when we're out...ya know... like this...I guess they're sort of dates... please call me Dan."

"Okay...Dan." She's smiling so wide she thinks her face may split open.

The car turns onto Gerri's street and instead of pulling all the way to her driveway, Gerri asks Dan to let her out a bit down the street. He pulls over near the curb and turns out the headlights.

"Okay, Gerri. You're probably right and I think it's best if I drop you off here. No sense taking a chance on someone seeing us and telling your dad, huh?"

"Yeah, it's fine...Dan."

She feels Dan's hand take hold of hers and gently squeeze it. She has a floating feeling like fainting but not quite the same. This would be fainting with delight. But she's not going to faint. That's for sure.

"Okay. I'll see you tomorrow after school and we'll see how much time we have so we can maybe go someplace."

"Okay. Goodnight, Dan"

"And Gerri, one last thing to show how much I care for you."

He leans over and unexpectedly gives her a gentle, wonderful kiss. Though she's surprised she closes her eyes and presses her lips on his. This is more wonderful and exciting than before. His lips are so soft and as he opens them there's a slight flicking from him and she reciprocates.

It's over way too soon but he pulls away, "Good night, Angel. See you tomorrow,"

206

Gerri scoots away from Dan to the passenger door and opens it. She gets out of the car and bends down to look inside at him just once more. She doesn't think her feet are even touching the ground as she turns toward her house. Gerri is sure she's truly in love!

Suddenly, she snaps back to reality. Coming slowly down her street toward her is a police car and Gerri immediately suspects it might be Len Ferguson. She really doesn't want to be away from her house and encounter him. But as quickly as it frightens her it picks up speed, goes right on past and turns the corner out onto Van Ness. Gerri can't see inside the car but she's pretty sure if it was Len he would have stopped. Must have just been a patrol car driving through the neighborhood.

CHAPTER 17

ADVICE, ADVICE

Gerri's pace quickens as she walks toward her house. It's so dreary and dark.

"Gerri?"

"Paulette?" Gerri is startled and can't imagine why she'd be outside, much less since it's once again at an inopportune moment.

"Gerri, are you just getting home? I didn't see any lights at your house and I got a little concerned. It's dark dear, and you shouldn't be out walking so late."

"Oh, it's okay, Paulette. I had to stay after school for a meeting and I got a ride home. Uh...they dropped me off down by the corner. I'm fine."

"I see your dad isn't home yet so I want no arguments, young lady. You're coming to my house and I'm gonna fix you some supper that'll stick to your ribs. Come on in."

"Okay. I can come in but I'm not hungry. I just had a ...hambur..well, I got something to eat on the way home."

"Oh that's nice dear. Where'd you go?"

"Oh, just down the street by school...the Sunshine. Nothin' special."

"So the old Sunshine Diner was pretty good tonight?"

"Yeah, it was okay. The Sunshine is the Sunshine. Hard to goof up a hamburger and fries."

"Well, who was it that brought you home? "

"Oh just the mom of one of my friends."

"Well, come on in. At least if you don't want anything to eat just come talk to me for a bit. Okay?"

"Sure."

The very first step into Paulette's house and Gerri immediately notices it's clean, nothing out of place. It's the way her mother used to keep their house. Paulette and Gerri sit at the kitchen table to talk about school.

"So, for sure you've had something to eat?"

"Yeah. We got a hamburger on the way home."

"So, the Sunshine? You do mean the Sunshine Diner right down the street a couple of blocks past your school?"

"Yeah."

"Huh. That's kinda funny. I meet a couple of gals in there every couple of days or so for coffee and unfortunately it's closed this week and next for some remodeling. Maybe it was a different Sunshine Diner? That's the only one I thought there was but maybe…?"

Gerri's mouth is open and she's looking at Paulette.

"And honey, who did you say brought you home?"

Gerri has a word formed but she's not sure what it is and she decides it best to say nothing.   Silence prevails until Paulette decides she's tormented her quarry quite enough.

"Look, Gerri, I was out in the yard and I just happened to see the inside dome light of the car come on when you opened the door and it didn't look much like anybody's mom I've ever seen, unless she's a he. So, who was that? Really?"

209

Gerri's caught and she really has no reason to feel anything but innocent.

"Well, it was Mr. Penn from school. I'm sure you've seen him before and he was at the funeral and when I told you he's my language arts teacher you said he is so handsome you wanted to go back to high school again. Remember now?"

"Yes. I remember very well. He is good lookin. So, why's he bringin you home, if you don't mind me askin?"

"Well, I help him grade papers and stuff after school…just voluntary. We were just talking after school this evening and he offered to buy me a hamburger and a Coke and bring me home. Paulette, he's been so nice to me this last week. I feel very good after I've talked with him. No harm in that, is there?"

"No honey. Why should there be? I just happened to be outside when I noticed that car pull over and park down at the corner. First the lights were on, then they were off. Then I saw the passenger door open and the dome light clearly showed a man in the driver's seat and I knew it was you getting out of the car. It made me a little curious. That's all. Nothin' to be alarmed about. I'm sure…right? But when you feel like you need to tell me about having a hamburger at a diner I know is closed…well, that makes me more curious."

"Well, I'm sorry about the diner. I didn't think it was that important and I just didn't really want to have to explain something that's really no big deal."

"But more than being curious, Gerri, it hurts my feelings because I always want you to know, I'm on your side. I guess I just maybe worry too much about you. The last thing in the world you need is some nosy red-head spoilin your fun. But honey, I just want to protect you and I guess I'm not very good at it. But you don't ever have to leave

210

anything out with me. So, as you said, no harm? I suppose not. But I think sometime we ought to talk about this again. Okay?"

"Sure. We can talk. I love to talk to you, Paulette. And I feel like I can tell you everything about everything. I don't know why I acted so secretly about who I was with or how I got home or where I went to eat. It's all perfectly fine. Finally after two horrible weeks I feel so wonderful being around Dan…uh I mean Mr. Penn."

"Dan, huh? Okay, hon. And I know you've been through the grist mill for a while. And I'll bet it is good to have a few people you can open up to. Gerri, I again want to promise you I never want to pry too much or spoil your fun. I just want to be sure I can share anything with you that might keep a good time suddenly turn into a bad time. You okay with that?"

"Sure."

Well, if it's okay with you I just want to try to understand your friendship with your teacher-friend. I'm overly cautious so don't think I'm trying to embarrass you or anything. Cause I'm not. But I just want to put on my adult, woman, been-around-the-block hat and satisfy myself there's nothing that you need to be concerned with *except* havin a good time. That okay?"

"Sure, Paulette. I suppose so. What about it?"

"Alrighty then. Don't be shocked. Just play along with me. I'm gonna start with the tough stuff. Have you had any sort of touching contact with him? I know. I know. Sounds silly to you but just help me out here. I mean any kissing, hugging, holding hands, touching your face? Any of that? Don't be embarrassed. It's just me."

"Well, a little bit. Paulette, this *is* embarrassing me. I haven't done anything wrong."

211

"Sweetie, I'm not asking this to embarrass or criticize you or say you've done something wrong. I just want you to tell me. It's between you and me."

"Well, we've hugged a couple of times…at school…in his room after school. But it's been when I was talking about my mother and he just wanted to comfort me with a shoulder to cry on. That's really all."

"And?"

"And? Well, I kissed him this afternoon and Paulette it was wonderful. Nothing wrong with that is there? I mean I went to see him after school and he was at the blackboard. When he saw me he turned and he looked so handsome…and he's been so nice…so I walked up and hugged him and that led to a little kiss. I went up to him. That's all."

"Has he tried to kiss you before?"

"No but he gave me a little kiss in the car right before I got out. But, it was just him being sweet. Nothing like what you're thinking."

"Gerri, my dear, I'd bet you don't have any idea what I'm thinking and I'm also guessing you aren't real comfortable with me asking all this."

"You're right. I mean there's nothing wrong. He's just a friend and it feels good to have a friend. You're a friend. I need friends. I've hugged and kissed so many people in the last week it would be hard to count. Nothing wrong with that."

"Well, to be quite frank, I'm trying my best to determine what kind of friend your Mister Dan Penn really is. Let me ask you a question. Now play along with me 'cause I'm going somewhere with this. Why aren't all your high school teachers *your* age? Ya know… why aren't they all fifteen or sixteen years old?"

212

"Oh come on, Paulette. That's a joke. Okay. I'll try to be serious and answer your questions. First, they have to go to college so that automatically makes them older by the time they get out. And besides nobody would listen to kids their own age. Am I right?"

"Of course you're right. Teachers are hired as mature, educated adults to provide an environment at school similar to what there should be at home. Discipline, respect, rules, experience, and safety. Teachers are adults. Teenagers are children learning to grow up to be adults. It's like baby birds growing up. They grow bigger, get feathers, have wings but they need a little growing up around adult birds before they strike out on their own and get their own nest. Boy, I'm hopin this makes some sense to you."

"Yeah. I guess so."

"Okay. Next question. Would it be appropriate for a twenty year old man to date a three year old girl?"

"Oh God, Paulette. That's sick!"

"Well, there's seventeen years difference…sort of like a thirty-something year old dating a sixteen year old. Now go ahead and say it again. Tell me that's sick and I'll agree with you completely. Now am I making sense to you?"

"But it's not like that. I'm not dat…"

"Oh. It's different? How so? What you're doing is innocent and beautiful. You're a young lady experiencing all sorts of emotions for the first time. For him it's all different. He's not sixteen. He was sixteen, right where you are right now but it was many years ago. He's been through all that growing up…or so one would hope. I'm just saying he's the adult and he needs to act like one. It's not me criticizing you, Sweetie. It's Paulette criticizing him. He knows better.

213

Trust me on this one. He knows he's playin mighty close to the fire. Plain and simple. Friend? Sure. Teacher? Sure. Touchy? Unh unh! Off limits. And he knows better."

"I just don't think it's like that. I don't think you understand."

Tonight we just need to be clear about a couple of things. Do you know what it means to be vulnerable?"

"I guess."

"Think of it this way. If you get tired and run down and get a chill your body is vulnerable. Because there are nasty germs that don't care about how you feel. They are waiting and watching so when you are unable to defend, kaboom…a bad cold. They take advantage when you're vulnerable. Gerri, the last couple of weeks make you very vulnerable. You need comfort and love. Your defenses are very low so it sounds good when someone says anything sweet that makes you feel better. That's not your fault and I'm just trying to be sure your new friend isn't unfairly taking advantage by saying things he knows will play right to your heart strings. I'm hoping I'm not looking at a wolf in sheep's clothing. Your Mr. Penn is suspicious to me just from what you've said. He hardly knew or acknowledged who you were two weeks ago but all of a sudden wants to be a very special friend and everything is just speeding right along. I'm sorry to say he is likely not a nice man. Remember, where most guys do their thinkin is not up here in this brain. It's down here." Paulette grabs her crotch.

"Wow, Paulette. I don't know what to say. I just don't think he's like that at all."

"I'm sorry to burst your bubble, kiddo but if you've ever trusted anything I've told you, trust me now. Be very cautious and slow with what's been happening. As you get older you learn to trust your instincts and all the alarm signals are goin off on my instincts right

214

now. I wouldn't trust this Mr. Dan Penn any farther than I can throw him."

Knock. Knock.

"Oopsy Daisy. Who can that be?"

Paulette opens the door and there stands Stephen.

"Oh hi, Stephen. Gerri and I have been talking and I guess the time just got away from us."

"That's fine. I just got home and I'm going to fix something to…"

"Gosh, Stephen. Gerri and I ate earlier. If you need her home right away that's fine but I'd like to keep her a little longer. I just love talking to this young lady. You know we're just silly girls and we can talk about nothing and it's still funny to us. I'll see she gets home safely or walk her home in a little while if that's okay."

"Sure it's fine. It's good you're here, Paulette. Just so Gerri's home before ten. Tomorrow's a school day."

"No problem, Stephen. Goodnight."

Paulette shuts the door, turns and smiles at Gerri.

"Thanks, Paulette. I'll bet he's glad he doesn't have to dream up something to talk to me about."

"Come on. Be nice. You've been through a lot and still going through it. So has your dad. It'll all sort out for the best."

"I guess."

215

"I've said some not-so-nice things about your friend, Mr. Penn, but what do you think? Does he still seem one hundred percent innocent about his new special friendship with you?"

"I just don't know how to answer anymore. I really, really like him a lot and I just can't see him doing anything bad. He's been teaching there quite a while. I don't know…at least I've never even heard anything bad about him. I just think he really likes me…in the right way. I'm really confused. "

"Wow. I was hoping to clear up some stuff, not confuse or frustrate you."

"And he asked if I could meet him this weekend and I told him I'd figure out a way to do that. But I think right now you're saying maybe that's not such a good idea."

"Correct. My advice is cool this whole thing off. And I mean cool it off immediately. A real friend would want what's best for you-not just what he wants. And who knows, Gerri, you cool this off, don't meet him privately, or drive with him in his car, and if he's a real friend he'll understand and continue to be a good teacher and real friend...even without hugs and kisses."

"Okay. I'm not sure he's bad but I'll do what you think I should do. I don't want the trouble I may have if he's not the good , decent man I think. Thank goodness you are always watching out for me. What would I do without you?"

"I'm here for you. I love you little one."

Gerri hugs Paulette and she senses a totally different feeling in hugging Paulette and hugging Dan Penn. It's certainly not romantic but it feels safe and secure. It's what she thought she was feeling in Dan's arms but it's not the same feeling of security and trust. It feels good to hug

216

Paulette. But she's never felt anything in her whole body like when she pressed up against Dan and held him tight, hugs are definitely different and tough to know which is really the right thing.

By the time Gerri heads home she smiles at having just completed another class in Paulette's school of growing up. Gerri's head is swimming with details but she's clear on the fact that Paulette is indeed a true friend and Dan…well, she really thinks it's love on her part but what's she to do? He's good looking and wonderful but what if he is simply trying to take advantage of her vulnerability? In a way that would be just like Jake taking unfair advantage. Jake probably knew what he was going to try to do long before they got to the woods. And he got by with it and Gerri was sent into a tailspin of guilt and fear about pregnancy. Could it be that Dan is doing the exact same thing just in a slower more calculating way. Gerri recalls vividly how unpleasant the sex was with Jake and how quickly he got what he wanted but she is still left with the aftermath and it could have been absolutely disastrous. Gerri certainly has a lot of thinking to do.

Gerri has to trust Paulette and so she has to figure out how to "cool things off" as Paulette says. She'll act the same in the hall if he surprises her again. That's fun and perfectly innocent. But she needs to make up an excuse for a few days and not go to his room after classes or ride anywhere with him. Gerri feels confident she can do this for a couple of days to prove Paulette's wrong about him.

"Okay, Paulette . I'm fine with what you say. Guess I'd better go home now."

"Okay. I told Stephen I'd be glad to walk you home. You want me to?"

"Nah. It's just across the yard. I may have poor judgment about some people but I'll bet I can get home safely."

Gerri walks slowly across Paulette's driveway and as she glances toward the street she hesitates in surprise. There's a police car parked across the street from her house, lights out, just sitting there. As Gerri stops and stares, the car window rolls down and the dome light of the car turns on clearly showing Len Ferguson's face looking squarely at Gerri. For sure there's no mistake who's in the car. Gerri is frightened but she doesn't run. Nervously she gives a small wave and Len waves back, smiling broadly. He reaches up and turns off the interior car light and sits in the darkness of his car with the window down. With the little bit of light from the porch lights of the houses Gerri can see a glint of Len's face still quietly staring at her.

Gerri nervously turns toward her house and listens to be sure he's not calling out to her. He doesn't say a word and soon Gerri walks up her steps, opens the door without looking back and enters her house. She thinks it's very, very strange he'd park and act so suspicious. Gerri really doesn't like Len Ferguson, cop or not.

"Hey, Gerri, that you?"

"Yes, Dad. Its Gerri. Who did you think it would be? The boogie man? Your close friend from school?"

"I won't dignify your smart mouth with a comment. So hello and goodnight to you, too."

Gerri deflects his remark as she walks to her room. She leaves the room light off and closes the door. She goes to the window and pulls the curtains open just enough so she can see Len's car still parked across the street. Why is he doing this? Though the light is poor Gerri can see his face turned toward their house, window down, obviously just staring. Gerri carefully pinches the curtains together and hopes he didn't see her peeking but if he's watching so intently he likely knows exactly what she did.

Though Gerri is frightened she gets ready for bed in her dark room and surprisingly falls fast asleep.

✶✶✶✶✶

The next day at school she's between second and third hour hurrying to the next class when she comes face-to-face with Dan and his big handsome smile. He conveniently blocks her path and without touching her, sort of guides her over next to the wall. Gerri is aware that several students look and whisper as Dan takes Gerri aside. This is not a school secret any longer.

"Hi Gerri. Hope you had a good time last night and I know you have to get to class right now but I'll see you in class and then after school in my room this afternoon. Right?"

Her eyes dart around nervously and she isn't sure how to try Paulette's advice so her response is awkward and a little abrupt. She gently pushes away, "Well, Mr. Penn, when I missed so much school last week I got behind on some classes and I have to catch up on some stuff. Maybe tomorrow instead, if that's okay with you."

He looks disappointed and perhaps a bit irritated but he says nothing and with that Gerri walks straight away from him toward her classroom and she doesn't look back. Gerri feels a bit shaken but she did it. That's what Paulette said to do and she figures though it was awkward, she did it very well. Gerri hopes Dan isn't really angry or has his feelings hurt. Now she suddenly wishes she'd agreed to meet him today and do the homework excuse tomorrow. Gerri doesn't think she can stand looking at him in class and then not seeing him later. She has second thoughts about Paulette's advice because Gerri's intuition is that he's exactly what she thinks he is-Prince Charming. The one and only. Paulette simply cannot be right.

CHAPTER 18

IT'S ALL SO CONFUSING

Gerri's fourth period Geography class is well under way when there's a sound at the classroom door and the principal, Mr. Landers, appears. Mr. Landers pulls his glasses off and drops them to a chain so they dangle just below his neck in front. He approaches Mr. Betts and nearly in unison all heads come erect and all eyes are on the teacher and principal. Mr. Landers whispers to Mr. Betts and then they both turn toward the class. Gerri's heart sinks because it appears they are staring directly at her. What now?

With his usual severe principal look Mr. Landers quietly speaks, "Geraldine DeMore, I need to borrow you for a few minutes so please come with me."

Gerri can only think this is another bad dream. How many bad dreams can one person endure? What's the disaster awaiting her? Is she in trouble? Is she accused of something? Her mind is racing as she tries to think of anything at all that could be prompting this.

She slowly rises from her seat and starts toward the door but Mr. Landers speaks again as if he's a bit agitated, "N n no, Geraldine…bring your books in case you have to go directly onto your next class."

Gerri picks up her books and she feels like she's on fire with embarrassment. Every face in the room is looking at her, secretly glad it's anyone except them. Gerri steps into the hall. She says nothing and neither does Mr. Landers. He just motions with his head for her to follow and they begin the walk toward his office.

Gerri suddenly panics that this is about Dan. After all it was just this morning he pulled her aside and she noticed students staring as if it was great entertainment. Somehow that must have gotten back to Mr.

Landers. That must be what this is all about. Gerri tries to formulate a defense for Dan but she's panicking and can't focus her thinking. She'll just deny anything more than helping him a few afternoons and saying hi in the hall. She can't help what kids' dirty minds conjure up but for sure it's only jealous gossip.

As Gerri and Mr. Landers arrive at his office he opens a conference room door off to the side of his personal office and there at the conference table is Len Ferguson in his police uniform.

"Geraldine, Officer Ferguson is a member of the Fresno Police and please don't be alarmed. He's not here because you've done anything wrong. He's gathering information for an investigation they are doing and he thinks perhaps you may know some of the students from a little different level than I would. Okay? Go ahead and have a seat and I'll leave you two alone to talk."

Gerri's heart is about to jump out of her chest. She never imagined anything like this. Why would Len possibly want to bother her at school? She's frightened, embarrassed and her mouth is dry with a strange fear of this man.

He smiles and speaks politely for the benefit of Mr. Landers, "Yes, Geraldine. I just need to ask you a couple of questions and then get you on your way. Please…please have a seat and just relax. You're not in any sort of trouble and thank you Principal Landers. "

Len looks directly into her eyes and smiles broadly. His outward appearance is sharp, professional with altar-boy innocence but that's just a facade for what she fears is a very evil side. Gerri is uncomfortable with this and she wishes Mr. Landers would stay in the room but he makes a quick exit and closes the door behind him. Gerri sits alone in the small room with Len about three feet from her and she's facing a now arrogantly smiling but silent Officer Len Ferguson.

Gerri is not about to say anything and for a while it appears he isn't going to say anything either. He just stares at her and smiles.

Gerri is twisting nervously in her seat and thinking about claiming she feels unwell but then Len breaks the silence. He leans forward toward her and makes a low volume clicking noise with his tongue as if scolding her and then speaks quietly, "Gerri, Gerri, Gerri. It is so good to see you. Are you being a good girl? Staying away from two-bit hoodlums? Seriously, how have you been doing?"

"What do you mean?"

Gerri stares at Len's mouth. A big smile but his upper lip twitches every so often and Gerri thinks it looks a bit like an angry dog when it can't quite decide if it's time to bite or to wait. Somehow his smile looks totally phony and underneath is anger. She wonders what she's done to deserve this.

"What do I mean? I mean how have you been? Doing well in school? Staying out of trouble? Ya know? How have you been doing?"

"Okay, I guess."

"Well, that's good. That's good, Gerri. I haven't been doing all that well myself. Ya see, I've been working on this little problem in Fresno and actually right in this neighborhood. There's a hoodlum and his buddies who sell illegal drugs and commit burglaries. Now you will find this shocking and hard to even believe but these guys also have been known to give alcohol to young girls so they can schmoozle up-close and take unfair physical advantage of them. Unbelievable isn't it? Right? Right, Gerri? You' seem very quiet…if the cat has your tongue you can just shake your head up and down in agreement with me. It is polite to answer when asked a question."

Gerri feels bullied and afraid but she slightly nods, "Yeah I guess so. I don't really know."

"Hmm. Well this hoodlum and his buddies do many, many bad things-things that may shock a young lady like you. They cause me a lot of trouble and it's my job to protect the innocent public from them. So, you might say to me then why don't you just go and arrest them? Because it seems lately I'm a half-step behind. I get close and then their so-called leader disappears into a rat hole. I'm sure he's right around here somewhere close under my nose but I just haven't been able to find him. He's out of jail on bond but until his court date he's apparently decided to not be very sociable. His friends tell me he leaves town, then comes back, leaves then returns and I don't believe it. I think he's right here close all the time and what I'm trying to do is get a half-step ahead of this rat. Then I'll arrest him for some new charges and get him off the streets for so long he'll be walkin with a cane when he sees sunshine again. Make sense?"

"Not really. I don't know about any of this."

"Well, Gerri…it seems you know this guy." Len wiggles his eyebrows as if there's something crude or suggestive involved, " Ya know, Jake Waltrip. And you're also good friends with his sister, Connie Waltrip. Right?"

"Gads. This is about Jake? Of course I know who he is but I don't have anything to do with him. I haven't seen him since you did...at the cemetery. That's all. I know absolutely nothing about him."

"Right. But you're friends with his sister and I want you to find out from her where Jake hides. Just be a good friend to me and find out. Simple. That's it."

"Sure, I know Connie but I don't even see her very often at school and we aren't close friends. I can't even imagine asking her anything about Jake. She would never tell me anything."

"C'mon, Gerri. You were dating this scumbag. That's when you first met me. But oh no, you don't know them very well. Then they are at your mom's funeral but oh no, you're not friends. You and this Connie are hugging and go off into a side room. But, oh no, you don't know her very well. Then the whole gang shows up at the cemetery and stands like a bunch of clowns over to the side like they're saluting or something. But oh no, you hardly know them. So, c'mon. Don't make Lenny mad by acting like Lenny's stupid or something. That would not be wise. Maybe Jake's your boyfriend but he won't be after I find him. Just do what's right. Got it? Huh? C'mon Gerrie, answer, nod, blink your eyes…"

Gerri pauses but then shows her irritation toward Len, "My boyfriend? He's not my boyfriend. He's in his twenties and some sort of hood. He's not my boyfriend. He took me home from school once and that was it. Period. I can't help you."

"Yeah. I know. Buying you alcohol at that gang hangout, Brentwood's. How would Lenny know that? Surprising, huh? You and Jake playin licky-face and touchy-feely and hide the…never mind. Just don't give me a bunch of crap that you hardly know him. It is interesting if that's the only time you ever saw him that you were speeding right toward a touchdown on the very first time. Did you even know his name or do you just like to get, shall we say intimate when you meet somebody for the first time? Besides, you seem to like older guys. I'd say maybe older guys are your sweet-tooth from what I've seen. Like you and your professor makin' smoochie and who knows what else. You really do like older guys don't ya? So you can cut the innocent little lassie bullshit stuff like you're a first-timer."

225

"I have no idea what you're talking about" Gerri is breathing fast. She's sure he's baiting her to get angry with all the insulting things he's saying and she doesn't like this one bit. It's very uncomfortable being in this room alone with Len. What could he possibly know about Dan Penn? Maybe Len appearing outside of her house last night isn't all he's been doing. Maybe he's been spying on her constantly. He may have followed when Dan and Gerri were in the car together. The possibility of him stalking is scaring her badly.

His look and demeanor seem to change even while they are talking. One second his face looks calm and almost pleasant and the next second it's red and taught. He still has the same exaggerated smile on his face as if it's there permanently but there's no mystery about the smile being less than friendly. Suddenly there are bulging veins on his forehead in the shape of a "v" and he's leaning closer and closer to her. There is a real anger behind his words as if she's lying to him or causing a problem. Why is he so focused on capturing Jake?

"Look. I'm sorry if you thought I know more than I do but you're scaring me because I really, really don't know about any of this."

"So, I'm scaring you?" Len sits back a little and straightens up in his seat. He drops the smile. "Well, I am sorry for that. Really. I didn't mean to frighten you. It's just very important for me to find Jake Waltrip and get him locked up. I'm also sure that even though you say you can't help I'm sure you can help if you simply try."

"I keep telling you I can't help and you just sit here getting angry because you're so sure I can somehow find something out about Jake. I'm not trying to make you angry and I just can't help."

Len leans close to Gerri again, uncomfortably close to her face and his eyes are staring into hers, "Okay. Let me do this a different way and maybe you'll be more willing to help. I actually came to see you today

226

and the truth is it is more to see you than ask questions. And in your own way-too-sweet way you're forcing me… makin me say something I told myself I wouldn't do. Look, I like you a lot, Gerri and I think I could be very good for you. There you made me say it."

"Now I have no idea what you mean…"

"Look, it may seem like our ages are a bit apart but it doesn't really matter, does it? I mean if we got along really good there wouldn't be any reason we'd have to worry about the difference in our ages. Besides, I'm a cop and there are certain powers and privileges I have that most other people don't. It's called power, Gerri. I've got it. Most women think that's pretty cool."

"Wha…Now really, what do you want?"

"Okay. Draggin it out of me again, huh? I must be putty in your hands. Okay, Gerri. Draggin' it out of Lenny-boy. Momentarily you've made me powerless. What do I want? I want you to like me. I want you to like me a lot. I want you to like me the way you like Jake and your school-marm buddy and whoever else you're messin around with. I want to date you. I want to spend private time with you. And I think I can make it worth your time."

"I have to be missing something here. First you wanted me to find Jake and I have absolutely no idea how to do that and now you're completely off on something I don't understand. And in all this, I don't really know you. You brought me home one night, I saw you at my mom's funeral and at the house but I don't really know you. Then I saw you parked outside my house and that scared me. You're a policeman. You wear a wedding ring. You had a gun at the funeral. You're old enough to be my dad. I'm sure you're a nice man but that's it. I think that's enough."

227

Gerri thinks Len is nutty and she wants out of this little room. She abruptly stands up to walk away but Len quickly reaches across the table, takes her by the arm and holds her so she cannot back up.

He looks around smiling as if they are just having a jovial conversation but he slowly stands and leans menacingly close. There's no smile. His face is red and tense and he whispers so emphatically that saliva sprinkles her face, "Gonna drag it out of me again, huh? Okay. Then listen to this so you understand. There are two things you need to do…and I think you will do both of them once you understand all the facts. First, I want to date you and by date you I mean you'll only date me. Nobody else. Not some crook and not some panty-waisted, pansy-ass teacher. Now in case you wonder if you can do that allow me to help you with the answer. You can. The second thing you're going to do is find out where Jake is hiding. I 'm gonna keep looking til I get Jake once and for all. He's embarrassed me and when I get him he'll go to prison…but only after I've had a little time teachin him manners. He didn't learn much from his first lesson.

Here's why I just know you'll want to do these two things. Bein' Lenny's girl will keep me convinced to hold off arresting your crazy red-headed, nut-job neighbor who passed herself off as your mother. Can you believe it? She gave me, a policeman, a false statement and that isn't good. You don't want to see her in jail? But I can and I will. But I don't have to. See, besides the fact I'm so good looking there are other reasons for you to be my girl."

Gerri is nearly speechless but she flops heavily back into the conference room chair, "I just don't know why you're picking on me. I don't want any trouble. I never wanted any trouble."

"It also seems you sort of like that teacher guy and his problem is simple. Already certain people notice he's taken a special liking to you. He could be gone faster than a bolt of lightning if I were to insist on an

228

investigation. Teachers are handled differently. They just quietly go away to some other state. The allegation and investigation are enough to spoil a teacher's party. You wouldn't like to see that happen to your friend…soon to become a distant acquaintance status."

"I-I I don't know what to say."

"Right. Speechless, huh? So here's a little more for you. Week or so ago I got an anonymous call that said there was some funny-stuff going on at Calway High School, almost every evening, same spot in the faculty parking lot. So I go over there and go in the lot with my lights off. Guess who I found? Two teachers, a Mr. Stephen DeMore, pants off, arms and legs intertwined with another teacher, Mrs. Beverly Alder, naked as a jaybird and they are makin whoopee in the parking lot. It scared the crap outta them." Len laughs, "And you should be able to relate to getting surprised in a car, and so I made a report about the faculty escapade but I've still got it in a desk drawer. Guess I forgot to turn it in. But that name DeMore sure rang a bell. Must run in the family. Innocent little Geraldine DeMore."

"You arrested my dad?"

"Nope. But if I file that report, the prosecuting attorney will go straight to the school board and I imagine it will be quite a mess. You see, so many storms on the horizon and all I'm looking for is a little cooperation from you. Find Jake. Dump the teacher. Make Lenny feel special and Red stays home and Daddy can find a new parking spot with his pal.

Gerri doesn't say a word. She feels tears of anguish roll down her cheeks and she looks at Len hoping for sympathy. If only she could just to return to her old boring life.

"C'mon. This is something to be happy about, not cry. I know you know the score and Lenny's just lookin to score on a regular basis a

229

little of what other guys are getting. Let's make life easy and fun or it just might turn nasty real quick for innocent little Geraldine who I rescued from the woods, panties down around her ankles and that look of what just happened. Can't fool me. I'm sure what you said never happened between you and Jake had already happened so yep, you know the score. Now I suspect you're doin' the old school teacher but let's just put all this behind us. We can be special friends and at the same time you are a hundred percent insurance to protect your neighbor, your teacher-buddy and your dad. Looks like a good deal to me just for you bein Lenny's girlfriend. Sound good?"

Len gets up from the table, squeezes her shoulder and as he starts to walk past her toward the door he stops and looks down at her. He gently takes her chin in his hand and turns here face up to look at him. He's smiling, "You stay here and compose yourself. I'll get back to work and I'll tell that nice principal of yours you're going to take a minute or two by yourself in here. Enjoy school for the rest of the day and I'll be in touch real soon. Umm Hmm, I like the words you and me in touch. Close touch if you know what I mean. Has a nice ring to it."

Gerri looks at him in complete shock but doesn't say a word.

"Oh yeah. And when your friend Connie tells you where I can find Jake let me know. But c'mon, use a little common sense and be cagey. Don't tip her off why you're askin."

Len goes out the door and Gerri sits with her face in her hands. She can't imagine how all this has become so frightening and complicated.

Gerri sits for a few minutes and then slowly opens the conference room door. Mister landers secretary, Grace Stinson motions for Gerri to come to her desk.

"Hi Gerri. I hope that wasn't too bad. Police investigating things you know. Can't leave a stone unturned to get the facts I suppose. Besides he's sort of cute. Certainly too old for you but he was flirting with me hot and heavy when he first got here. Probably a good catch being a cop and all. Must be the uniform."

Gerri feels sick to her stomach hearing Miss Stinson's comments and she's probably fishing for Gerri to tell her what the policeman wanted but Gerri figures it's just as well to pass it off as being very routine, "Yeah. I really didn't even know about the people they're trying to find." She shrugs her shoulders.

" Here. Here's an excuse pass to give your teacher if you'll rejoin your class now."

"Sure, that'll be fine."

Gerri waits for Miss Stinson to tear the pass from her forms book and she happens to look over at the conference room on the other side of Mr. Lander's office. Through the door glass she can clearly see Len talking to Dan. Gerri's heart sinks. What is Len trying to do? What will he say to Dan?

Gerri takes her pass, picks up her books and walks down the hallway. She glances up at the hall clock and it's within about three minutes of the bell ringing so she veers from her path and heads to the bathroom.

Later in Dan's class Gerri senses that Dan is very nervous and hesitates to even look in her direction. Len must have threatened to get him in trouble. Gerri senses that having anything to do with Len is more frightening than anything she's ever experienced, even when she was afraid of pregnancy. She imagines there are no limits to the danger of Len.

After school and before Stephen comes home Gerri decides to take the initiative and talk to Paulette. She tries to decide how to edit the events for Paulette. But for once, Gerri has too much burden on her young

231

mind and she just wants to spill it all, or maybe just a little more than earlier come-clean sessions..

 After Paulette lights her Lucky Strike and goes through the ritual shaking out the match, tossing it in the ashtray and exhaling the first long puff, Gerri unloads more details of everything starting with the encounter with Jake, the fear of pregnancy, the blow up with the relatives over the insurance, how she found out Beverly Alder is her dad's mistress, Len stalking and his threats about Paulette, her dad and Dan Penn.

"Wow. And a few short weeks ago you complained to me that life was boring and nobody cared about you. Now you have a lot of people caring about you but some not in a good way. But ya know, it takes a lot of courage to tell me. I'm really glad you trust me."

"Everything's so goofed up right now. I don't know which way to turn without causing bigger problems. I'm so scared."

"Well, getting it off your chest is a step in the right direction. When you hold back no one can really help cause they're playing cards without a full deck.   Now you're starting to see how things work in the real world. All of it isn't pretty. We'll get through all this…notice I said we? You keep talking to me and everything will get much easier and *we'll* get it fixed."

"Well, what should I do about Len? He's scary and I believe he's dangerous."

"I think you've got a lucky break with it being Thursday. Just play it very cool tomorrow and then lay low at home over the weekend. I'm fairly certain the cop is gonna let his threats soak in this weekend and I've got to think about this. I mean messin with the cops is really some tender territory. First, is to decide a course of action to resolve this once and for all without having the world cave in on everybody. I've

232

just got to think and we'll get a plan together. But we'll get you out of all this.   Just lay low and try not to worry about it this weekend. I know, easier said than done but just try.   If you get to feeling too worried just come over and talk. But don't call on the phone except to tell me you're coming over.   That phone line has too many ears for any sort of private conversation."

"I can do that, Paulette. I know you'll help me. And believe you me, I will be talking to you this weekend. Maybe ,more than you'll want."

"So I'm a red-headed nut-job, huh? Well, maybe he at least got something right. Still wet-behind-the-ears-flatfoot. And ya know, I just happen to think … for openers, why should I be afraid of him doing anything to me?   He *assumed* I was your mom. I never gave *any* report to him at all. Just thanked him for bringin you home. Yep we'll figure out a solution for Lenny boy."

CHAPTER 19

DAN TO THE RESCUE!

Friday morning and Dan Penn or no Dan Penn, Gerri's sticking with her new, more mature, sexy look plus the resolve to follow Paulette's wisdom.

She walks toward school, thinking, walking, making slow progress. She'll see Paulette this afternoon and over the weekend . Paulette will surely figure out a way to deal with Len's threats.

"Uhhh! What the heck?"

Suddenly she sucks in all her breath and takes very small, slow steps. Her heart is pounding like a drum. Dan Penn's car is next to the sidewalk several feet up ahead. She sees his head and shoulders as he's turns in the car seat watching her approach. She looks around to see if there are any police cars. Len Ferguson causes constant paranoia. Now she must deal with the issue at hand-Dan Penn.   Should she cross the street or maybe just walk on past like she doesn't see him? Well, either of those options would be pretty stupid. She looks straight at him in the car. She sees the window is open on the passenger side next to the sidewalk. Gerri thinks the best thing is to say hello and repeat that she has to get to school and catch up on homework she missed. Gerri hopes she can do this so he doesn't see how frightened and nervous she is but she's not even sure words are going to come out in any sort of intelligible sound.

"Good morning, Sunshine."

Well, that calm voice didn't sound much like a scary old man did it? Why should it? He's never been scary or mistrustful-not like Len Ferguson or even Jake. After all, she's actually the one who's made advances at him. That voice. She loves to hear that voice. Who is she kidding? Gerri thinks she's in love with this Prince Charming.

"Oh hi, Dan."

She tosses caution aside and bends down to look inside the car and he leans across the seat toward the car window. He reaches for the door handle.

"I drove this way a little early hoping maybe I could see you before school and besides I have something for you."

Of course she's curious and it must be something she left in his car. "You have something of mine? Where'd you find it? What is it?"

"Well, it's nothing you lost. It's a little gift I got for you. Come on, hop in."

She rests her arms on the car door, peering anxiously through the open window just a couple feet from his wonderful, comforting face. "You got something for me? What is it?"

In the seat there's a little white box with a red bow. This is like the movies. Prince Charming appears from the most unusual place, then he falls for the young princess of his dreams and they live happily ever after. Paulette is wrong about him. Gerri must have made things sound worse than they are. She's so sorry she put him off yesterday but now she's certain of her instincts. This has to be real love and after all, she's more woman than girl. Besides, when she took the time to think about Paulette's little story of a twenty year old dating a three year old, it's shocking and makes sense at those ages but gets less ridiculous the older both get. If Dan's thirty when Gerri's sixteen then

235

in ten short years he'd be forty and she'd be twenty-six. What's so wrong about that? Nothing!

"Did you sleep well last night?"

"Yeah, I guess so."

Well, I have to tell you I had trouble sleeping. I have a lot on my mind but I miss seeing you just overnight. Ya know when I did fall asleep I dreamed of an angel. Now who would that angel be? " He looks at her and flashes that devilish smile.

Gerri laughs nervously and blushes.

"Dan. Don't say those things. It makes me feel funny."

"Come on. Hop in."

She's satisfied. The barriers are gone. She grabs the door handle and opens the door, tossing her books on the back floor. The little box with the ribbon sits plainly on the seat between them.

"Don't open that just yet. Wait for just a couple of minutes. I'm going to pull down the street a little bit away from being so near the school. I want to talk to you."

Dan starts the car engine, does a u-turn and drives in the opposite direction from school. He drives slowly past her street and continues driving but mostly looking over at Gerri, smiling. He reaches over and takes her hand as he drives. It's a school day and it's possible students could see them but she doesn't care and apparently he's not worried either. She scoots a little closer to him. Her tummy is tickling and feels just like it did when they kissed the other night. They drive several blocks past Gerri's street and Dan pulls the car into a dentist office parking lot. It's obviously not open yet and there are no other cars. His car glides quietly and inconspicuously to the rear of the
236

building and he parks facing some very tall hedges with the building to the rear of the car. The engine goes silent.

"Dan, how did you know of a place like this? We can't be here too long because I'll need to be at school pretty soon."

"Sure. But we've got plenty of time and still get to school before it starts. Besides, I'm good friends with Gracie Stinson and I can always be sure she'll never count you as tardy or absent. And guess what? I could always call in sick today... cough...cough so just in case you want to skip school and just spend the day…ya know…open your little gift, something to eat, maybe drive over by Riverview Park and just be together. Nobody has to be the wiser. It would be fine. You can trust me. I hope you know that. What do you say, M'lady?"

Gerri's really wrestling with Dan's surprising suggestion of skipping school and frightened at the thought if her dad found out. Skipping school? Avoiding Len? Being with Dan all day? Could she do this and get away with it?   The fear is a little too much for this day but she can't wait to see the surprise Dan has for her. Dan holds out the little box.

"Here, Gerri. A trinket for a treasure."

She slowly removes the ribbon, fingers shaking as she tries to pry open a loose corner of the box, turning it over a couple of times and finally opening it. Inside is a jewelry box and she nervously opens it to reveal a shiny cross on a gold chain necklace. The elongated cross is probably three inches long and about an inch across with very ornate red stones on each of the arrow-shaped points on the ends.

 "Oh, it's beautiful!"

"Well, here. Let me help you put it on."

Dan holds the necklace and she turns in the seat toward him, smiling in pure happiness. His hands are shaking a little as he opens the clasp and motions for her to lean forward a bit. He reaches his hands around each side of her head and gently pulls her head a little forward until their faces are within a couple inches apart. She loves his warm breath on her face and thinks she might faint from this exciting moment.

He snaps the clasp in place and lets his hands stay on the back of her neck.

" It's beautiful on you."

She shakes her head from side to side and stares at him with her most dramatic, sexy look.

Dan kisses her in a way she'd never dreamed. Whew! It's wonderful and she doesn't want to stop. It's a kiss with their lips apart and it's very intimate. She's in a trance of pure pleasure…and real love.

"C'mon, Gerri, let's cut school today and enjoy each other's company in privacy. What do you say?"

She's certain she knows what he has in mind and frankly it would be ecstasy but she can't get past the fear of repercussions. Len might be stalking, she's still fragile from the fear of pregnancy and the aftermath of assurance she's not pregnant. It's just a little too soon so she looks at Dan hoping for understanding, "I just can't. Not today. I am so nervous right now, surprised by the necklace and of course I want to be with you like you say, privately, but I wouldn't be able to enjoy it today. I have to get a little more used to the idea. Okay? I hope you're not angry."

"How could I be angry with you? Of course not. So, I guess I might as well show a little adult responsibility like you and go to work." He smiles and straightens up into the driver's seat.

238

As they leave the parking lot and head back in the direction of school he slows as they get to Gerri's street. Dan pulls to the curb approximately where he'd picked her up earlier.

"Okay, I'll let you out here. Wish I could take you on from here but it's probably best to do it this way. And I'll see you this afternoon after school because I still need to talk to you about a lot of things. Okay?"

"Sure. This afternoon. Have a wonderful day, Mister Penn…Mister Daniel Penn."

They both laugh and Gerri gets out of the car. There are a few students on both sides of the street and Gerri's very aware that some of the students, recognize Dan's car and of course they recognize Gerri. She doesn't care. One set of three girls turn toward Gerri and smile and then turn back to gossiping. Gerri is proud of her newfound bravery. She doesn't care and she's certain she'll cut classes to be with Dan in the very near future. She's sure Dan is her real Prince Charming. She just needs to think of the timeline when all this can work out. Gerri continues her interrupted and now romantic walk to school.

CHAPTER 20

THE SPEED OF ENLIGHTENMENT

It feels so good that school is finally over for the day and Gerri can spend some time with Dan. She's come to the conclusion that the next time he wants to take a day away from school to spend together she will be a willing participant. As Gerri approaches the end room of the hall she hears a very loud, distressed, woman's voice. Getting closer to Dan's room, Gerri realizes it's coming from Dan's room and it sounds like someone near hysterics. This must be one of the disadvantages of being a teacher. Someone flunking or perhaps in trouble. She's sure Dan will do the gentlemanly, right thing. There's one last outburst of anger and the classroom door violently swings open.

Gerri is shoved across the hall by a hysterical Connie Waltrip who glares at Gerri. As they lock eyes, "Better watch your step, Gerri!"

Connie runs through the hall and down the steps. Gerri stands for a minute wondering what caused the trouble and then she pokes her head around the corner of the open doorway.

"Would you like for me to wait out here or come back tomorrow?"

Dan Penn is standing near the front of the room looking at the door, trying to smile but is obviously shaken, "N-no. It's fine. Come in, please."

"Geez. I've never seen Connie like that."

Dan moves his shoulders and neck around as if loosening up. He takes a deep breath.

"Gerri, we need to talk. Come up here and sit down." He motions to a desk with one wave of his hand. Dan sits in a desk across from her and looks momentarily at the ceiling as if searching for the right words. Gerri is tingling with anticipation to find out what happened to Connie but more what he urgently wants to tell her. She's excited in a positive way. The necklace this morning, invitation to skip school, so this must be the next step that he's planned for them as a couple.

"Connie is very un-hinged right now. This will take her some time. Gerri, you more than most people understand how difficult the death of a loved one can be."

"I'm not sure…"

"I know, I know. You'd have no reason to know. I'm going to tell you what I know at the moment."

"Sure. What is it?"

"Connie's brother, Jake Waltrip, is dead."

Gerri is still recovering from the fresh wounds of death and this is like getting hit by lightning on a sunny day, "What? Jake? Are you sure? Oh my gosh. It can't be! Oh, poor Connie."

Dan's voice shakes a little, "It can't be worse for her. It was a very violent incident. Violent. It started when Jake killed a Fresno

241

policeman late last night…early this morning. As Jake was trying to escape out of Fresno, the police spotted him trying to avoid a roadblock and who knows what happened at that point. But Jake was killed by the police. Connie's lost at the moment, hysterical, absolutely distraught and she feels responsible."

Gerri's mouth falls open and she gasps audibly loud. "Oh my God! It can't be. Poor Connie. And you're sure it was her brother Jake?"

"Yes, Jake Waltrip. Sort of a small time criminal…I think, but still, Connie's brother and I know they were very close. Brother and sister."

Tears well up in Gerri's eyes as she feels deep grief for Connie and even Jake. She can't picture Jake dead.

"Oh my God! Poor Connie. But what's any of this have to do with you? Why was she here at school? Why was she yelling at you?"

"Well…no...uh…why she was here? Look, this is all very complicated but you need to hear this from me so you have the facts straight and although it may seem difficult to imagine, everything that's happened is for the good. For the good of us…Gerri, you and me."

"W-wha-what do you mean? For the good?"

Dan takes Gerri's hand and squeezes it so tight it's painful, "First, I need to hear something from you, Gerri…I'm counting on your maturity in all this but I need for you to commit one-hundred percent to me? Woman to man, promise to stick by me and trust me?"

Gerri was looking forward to seeing Dan this afternoon but this is over the top and she's not sure what Dan means. "Well, I..uh…of course I'm with you. I thought you'd know that."

"No, Gerri, that isn't the answer that will work for us. I'm asking for you to look at me and without any hesitation, I want your commitment
242

that you are one-hundred percent dedicated to me. I want to hear you promise that you love me, you'll do whatever I say…and listen to me… I want to hear you promise as a blood oath you'll be one-hundred percent loyal to me, committed to me."

"Yes. I think I already am. I haven't said it to you but I think I love you and…"

Now Dan has both of her hands and he's squeezing them as he leans forward shaking his head from side to side giving her a disappointed look that suggests she has not answered to his satisfaction.

"Okay, then I swear it, Dan." Gerri still isn't sure she knows the extent of what she just promised but she thinks he is overly concerned, probably after Len's visit to him at school. Gerri can imagine the threats Len made to Dan. She can imagine Len telling Dan that she is more interested in her policeman hero than her teacher. That's got to be the reason Dan's being so ridiculous in the way he's demanding her loyalty. He's got to be sure their relationship stays under wraps because he's a teacher and she's under age-at least for a couple more years. But she's sure she can do this. And this proves Paulette was wrong about him.

Dan releases his grip, "Gerri, I see us in the future as you graduate and turn eighteen. We can have a wonderful life and I know your dad will set you up financially and that means we can live well without worry. You'll never have to work, I can teach or not teach or do something else…just live life very well. You see why I absolutely need to know where you stand with me? I see this as quite a plan but it requires commitment and great discretion for a couple of years to pull it off. Now I've said it."

Gerri's youthful ability to hear what she wants, passes right over any hint of greed in Dan's financial plans once he can get his fingers into the DeMore life insurance. She rushes to Dan's arms and almost knocks him out of the desk. She puts her hands on each side of his face and showers him with kisses all over his forehead, lips, cheeks, and even the top of his head.

"Oh Dan, this is wonderful. I could never have dreamed."

Dan gently pushes her away and looks her in the eyes, "Now I'm going to tell you about a little darkness we have to protect. *We* have to protect."

Gerri sits back down, smiling. How could anything seem dark after what he just said?

"Around the time of your mom's funeral I got a visit from Connie Waltrip and she said that she somehow mentioned to her older brother that I showed an interest in you. I think Connie told him because of her jealousy about me but when she told her brother, Jake, he flew off the handle. He knew who you were and maybe he had a crush on you or something or maybe dated you which would seem surprising to me but nevertheless Connie was warning me about Jake and his jealousy. I told Connie *she* was the jealous one and she shouldn't be gossiping. I really didn't think too much about it.

A day later this Jake and his little band of clowns show up at my house. I saw them pull up and get out of their cars and mill around the sidewalk with their black jackets and all, and then Jake knocked on my door. He asked if I was Dan Penn and when I said yes he told me to steer clear of you and if he found out that I was even looking at you he'd see to it I got "piled up" somewhere."

"Oh my gosh. But I hardly knew…"

"Doesn't matter. So the next afternoon I stopped by the Fresno police station to tell them about this Jake Waltrip character and his friends. I

244

talked to a young cop who listened intently and actually seemed very interested. At the moment I thought he was a nice guy and sincere cop. A guy by the name of Ferguson. Len Ferguson. I think you know who he is, too."

Gerri's mouth goes dry with the names that are popping out of this. She nods her head slightly showing she at least knows Len Ferguson.

"Anyhow this young cop, Ferguson says he knows who Jake is and he'll take a close interest in my problem and Jake in particular. He said if he could take that bunch of hoodlums, the Kings or something like that, off the street it could help him get promoted. So I figured I'd get some protection. Well, far from a solution, he stirred up a hornets' nest because the cop confronts Jake and tells him I complained. So, immediately I get Jake and his guys threatening me at school, at home, and at the store. A real nightmare."

"Oh my gosh. I had no idea."

"So I went back to the cops and this time I talked to the Lieutenant over this Ferguson and told him to do something about the threats but don't do something stupid like the first time and get me in more hot water with the bunch of thugs. I mean there were some pretty nasty threats. So I guess Ferguson got embarrassed by getting called on the carpet by his bosses.

So then I got a visit at home from the cop, Ferguson and he's really red in the face angry for going to his boss and says he'll take care of it and for me not to worry. I should have known at the time this guy had problems of his own and all I did was make him mad at me. Anyhow, Ferguson starts watching every move Connie's brother was making. I know at some point, probably way earlier, he found you with Jake and wound up taking you home in his patrol car. So this cop also gets a crush on you and he starts connecting dots and then he becomes obsessed with Jake, me, and you, Gerri."

'I can't believe any…"

"So at your mom's funeral I see Connie, Jake, Ferguson at least for a moment all in the same place and I thought it was likely to be trouble. You may have noticed I spent time with your dad and barely acknowledged you. I wanted to give you a hug so badly but I didn't dare. Ferguson was looking all around and when Connie and Jake saw him they took off. I thought it better if I went home. That's why I never went to the cemetery or your house."

Breathlessly Gerri replies to the shocking story, "Just as well. The gang showed up at the cemetery and Len saw them and he had a gun. He started to go after them right there but they left too quick for him. Then he came to our house…Len did…and he tried to talk to me and I thought he was scary. You are so right. There's something wrong with him. Oh God, what a mess!"

"So, Jake got pretty quiet once Ferguson started bugging him but then I got a visit from Ferguson right here at school this week. Mr. Landers wasn't too happy about that and wanted to know what was going on. I made up something to get him off my back so Landers was no big deal. But this cop is going nuts over finding out where Jake is hiding and me staying away from you. He was sure Jake was still in town but he couldn't find him high or low. Then he gets off the subject of Jake and starts threatening me about you- even worse than Jake did. This cop belongs in a nuthouse. He is a very, very dangerous and scary guy. He's a stalker. He followed us that evening we went to the diner. Spied on us. Even knew when I dropped you down at the corner of your street. He was secretly spying on your house…you. Can you believe it? Anyhow he tells me that you are going to be his girlfriend and if I try to stay involved with you I just might disappear. I will say, Gerri, for your age you certainly have a lot of guys interested in you."

"Oh God! Oh, Dan. I had no idea about any of this. I only have ever wanted to be loved by you. Only you."

"I certainly hope so because I'm spilling everything to you. After this you know it all and it's we not I."

"Of course."

"So now I've got a crook who's planning to "pile me up somewhere" and a cop who's going to make me disappear. I was really feeling the stress. Anyhow, by the end of the week, Jake Waltrip is no more and Len Ferguson is no more, compliments of the late Mr. Waltrip."

"Oh my God! The policeman that Jake shot was Len? I should have guessed. I just never…This is too much. "

"Important for you to know what really happened."

"So why was Connie here screaming at you?"

Dan takes hold of Gerri's hands again and squeezes so tight it really is uncomfortable.

"Misunderstanding I guess. Look, I did what I had to do…for us. Connie knew Jake had threatened me about you so she thought maybe somehow I had something to do with all this mess last night. That's it. Now you know and you promised to listen to me. I'm sure people like Connie will try to make up all sorts of stories about this. It's a big deal for Fresno. So, forget Connie Waltrip. She won't be a problem and if she gives you or me a problem we'll deal with it to make it go away. Trust me. Together and committed to each other we can do anything. Then a couple of short years from now we'll be living our dreams."

Gerri pulls loose from Dan's hands and stands.

"I really should go. I love you, I'm one-hundred percent committed to you but I just have to sort through all this. My brain is spinning. People killed. Connie losing Jake. I just can hardly believe or understand what's happened... and what's still happening. I've got to think."

"Dan stands and he's not exactly smiling, "Listen to me Gerri. I just told you everything and anything else is irrelevant. That's why it's important for you to have one source you can trust and on which to rely-That will be Dan Penn. I know you like Connie but she's going through a lot right now so you must steer clear of her for a while. And honestly, I wouldn't believe anything she says at the moment. She's hysterical. She's in shock. Not in her right mind. Who knows what she might say?"

Gerri sees a look on Dan's face that is a morphed mixture of Dan, Len and Jake. How in the world did she get into this predicament when all she's ever wanted is to be loved and adored?

"No, Dan. Nothing is changed in what I said...promised. I just have to think through everything. I need to process it all through my head."

Dan relaxes slightly. "Sure. You do that and maybe I can see you over the weekend. Remember, Gerri. I'm trusting you and in turn you can't let me down. This is not to ever be discussed with anyone. You never heard any of this. Right?"

"Yeah." Gerri walks slowly out the door, down the steps, out of the school doors and she pauses on the steps. She remembers the day, not so long ago when Connie offered her a ride and Jake showed up. She recalls how excited Jake was to show her off at Brentwood's and how exciting it was to be around all the forbidden fruit of that particular day. She recalls the devil-may-care feeling of her first alcohol and what that

248

led to in the woods. She shudders to think of the fear she lived with thinking she might be pregnant. Oh how she despised the way Jake took advantage of her innocence and used her. But how could she feel anything except a soft spot in her heart the day of her mom's funeral when Jake and his guys showed up to pay his respect. And now he's dead. And he'll always be known as a cop killer.

She thinks of Len. He was scary and she should be feeling relief but surely Len had family as well. Such a waste of human life.

But Gerri keeps thinking how Dan was so strong with his statements about giving her all the facts and she should believe only him. She feels guilty for doubting him already but he never really answered why Connie would come to see him about any of this.

Gerri is confused and upset. She understands the grief and finality of death. She walks slowly on the sidewalk toward her house.

CHAPTER 21

EVENTS OF ENLIGHTENMENT

As Gerri trudges home she's aware of a car that slows behind her, inches along and then as it gets along side of her the passenger window rolls down.

"Gerri! Hey!"

A total surprise, Gerri's head turns quickly toward the car. She is surprised that the car is so close to her at the curb. Connie is looking at Gerri out of the window with a strange expression. Connie's boyfriend Rog is the driver. At first Gerri wonders if she should keep walking or even run because Connie's not smiling but she's looking at Gerri with a sense of urgency.

"Gerri. Hey, snap out of it. C'mere. I really gotta talk to you. This is life and death important."

Gerri walks over by the car in wonder of what Connie can possibly want with her. After hearing Connie in Dan's classroom and knowing she's so upset about Jake's death, Gerri is a little apprehensive about getting too close at the moment.

"Oh, Connie. I can't believe it. I just heard what happened. I don't know what to say." Gerri sobs a couple of times.

"Hop in Gerri. I really have to talk to you. C'mon. I really have to tell you some stuff you've gotta know about."

Connie opens the front door, hops out, pulls the passenger seat forward and climbs into the back seat leaving the front passenger seat for Gerri. Gerri gets in, closes the door and turns her body toward the center of the seat where she can see Connie.

"Hi Rog."

"Hey , Kid. How ya doin?"

Gerri doesn't answer Rog in anticipation of Connie's message. Rog drives slowly along the street.

"Rog is just going to drive around while we talk. It's safer this way. At least you know about Jake." Connie begins to cry, "I know he had his faults but he was my brother and I loved him so much. Oh God, Gerri. I don't know what I'm gonna do now."

"Hey. Hey, Babe. I told you I'd take care of you." Rog gives a quick look over the back seat trying to look his most caring look. But Rog is a genuine tough guy from top to bottom, front to back so looking compassionate is at best an awkward attempt. Gerri can't imagine him "taking care" of anybody in a tender sort of way. It would be as if the Frankenstein monster said the words. Gerri can only imagine what the words "taking care of" usually mean to Rog.

251

"Oh, Connie, I'm so sorry. I still can't believe it."

"So, who told you, Gerri? Penn?"

"Well, yeah. I'm supposed to help him after school and I saw you and…"

"C'mon, Gerri, cut the crap with me. Or maybe you really have no clue. I know Dan Penn and before Rog I was his little girl for helping out after school. That soon involved the afternoons, evenings and weekends that is until he started with Gracie Stinson, the attendance gal. Dropped me like a hot potato and told me if I ever mentioned it he'd see I never finished high school here or anywhere else. But I met Rog and that was good riddance to garbage as far as I'm concerned. Mr. Charmer with a very nasty side. Thought you were the first, huh? Yeah…so did I."

"You and D-Da…Mr. Penn?"

Connie laughs a little at Gerri's surprise and nearly saying the name Dan.

"Almost let the cat out of the bag, huh? Go ahead and say it…Dan. I have another name for him after what he did last night and that's what you need to know."

"God, Connie. Like what?"

"I was trying to stay out of anything between you and Jake but Jake was drivin himself, and me, crazy over you. He felt so bad he'd gone too far with…"

"So he fessed-up, huh?"

"Gerri, you've gotta understand. Jake and I were all each other had and I would have done anything for him and he for me. It was about to become that way with you but he wanted to give you plenty of space

252

because of your age and all. He knew about me and Penn last year before I became Rog's girl. Jake never liked or trusted Penn and he was all ready to beat him up when he dumped me for good old Gracie."

"How many people has he been involved with? Never mind answering that. What's the difference?"

"Anyhow the day Jake picked us up from school…who could forget. Right? Anyhow, I mentioned something about you and Penn. I didn't even think anything about it except Jake said at the time for me to be careful because of Rog bein jealous and all. Remember?"

"Yeah, I sort of recall something about that?"

"Well, Jake didn't forget it and he bugged me to find out if there was anything between you and Penn. He was furious when he found out…not at you…at Penn. Said Penn needed to find out how the cow eats the cabbage."

"The cow what?"

"Never mind. It was Jake's way of sayin' he was going to give Penn one fair warning and then who knows what might have happened? So he went to Penn's house and had a little talk with him. Ya know, basically warned him to steer clear of you. So what did Penn do? Stupid Penn goes to the cops and tells them. And he happens to get a cop who's nuts…absolutely ding dong psycho. So here's a thirty something year old teacher whining that some guy in his twenties is threatening him over his sixteen year old girlfriend. Cops must have had a great laugh about that one."

"God, Connie, I know it was Len Ferguson that he talked to."

"One and the same. So Ferguson latches onto Jake as his ticket to be a big gang-breaker cop so he could be a star. Ferguson had just busted

253

Jake for being out with you so he knew about him and decided this was his big break in the cop-hall of fame or something. You probably didn't know it but they really couldn't hold Jake without a complaint from you or your parents…they had no proof of anything, he was bonded out by the guys and none of it would ever have gone to court. But after Penn complained this Ferguson and another two cops picked Jake up and beat him pretty bad. Not in the face but his stomach and back were bruised something awful. Ferguson told Jake he was gonna get him for rape and the next time he saw him he'd figure a way to get an arrest warrant on him and witnesses that would swear to anything Ferguson needed them to say. Jake figured Ferguson would be the kinda guy to even plant a gun or something, who knows?"

Gerri is spellbound with this story.

"So, Jake's keepin an eye on you and Penn. And of course Ferguson is keepin an eye out for Jake and Penn. When Jake and I came to your mom's funeral and we saw Ferguson up front giving you a hug, Jake wanted out of there. He thought maybe you'd become friends with Ferguson and were going to press charges on him. Jake took off but that's why I stayed to ask you. And of course, there was Penn hanging around. When I told Jake what you said he really felt horrible that he'd ever doubted you. Gerri, he said he'd never been affected by anyone like you. He said he'd go back to school and become anything he could to be successful if he could spend the rest of his life with you. He was totally bonkers over you and knew you are a really cool person."

Gerri is still dumbstruck. Not a word.

"Anyhow it went downhill from there and then yesterday afternoon Penn calls me out of the blue and said he needed to see me. He'd been thinking of all the special times we'd had and all that sort of stuff. He said it was very important and he was sorry for ever complaining to the cops and it was something that would help Jake. I should have known

254

better but I agreed to meet him and he told me he'd been thinking about me and wanted to get back together with me.

True blue Penn, he added that if I didn't, he'd make a world of trouble for me with Rog and tell Rog stuff we used to do and claim it had never stopped. He really scared me. When I met with him all he wanted to know was where he could find Jake. I wasn't about to tell him but he said he wanted to go see Jake personally and square things between them. He said he felt bad about the Ferguson thing and that he could personally get to Ferguson and square that for Jake as well.

I still refused to tell him where Jake was hiding but I told him I'd set up a meeting. So I got it set for last night...well actually this morning at three in the morning behind Brentwood's. The bar closes at one and everybody's out of the entire place by two or two-thirty at the latest. So guess what Penn did? He tells Ferguson that Jake will be there by himself at three and not suspecting any trouble. Well, Jake agreed to meet Penn all right. He was there even before two-thirty and hiding by the trash bins about twenty feet from the back doorway where they were supposed to meet. About ten minutes after Jake hides he sees Ferguson and Penn talking together on the street off the parking lot and then Penn comes walking toward the back door of Brentwood's like he's by himself and Ferguson takes a hiding position behind one of the trash bins. Ferguson has no idea but he's hiding about five feet in front of Jake.   Ferguson had his gun out and at three o'clock Penn starts knocking on Brentwood's back door and looking around for Jake to answer and Ferguson's gonna shoot Jake for sure and knowing that scum Ferguson I'll bet he'd have shot Penn, too.

Well, Jake must have scared the you know what outta them both when, with his gun cocked he said 'Lookin for somebody?' Ferguson turned to fire but Jake fired first and Ferguson shot a couple of times but he was the only one hit. Killed him. I think Jake might have shot Penn at that point but Penn took off and was nowhere to be found. Jake got outta there, came by and told me all about what happened, what to tell Rog and the guys, how Penn was a lyin scum and needed to get waxed, and worst of all now that he'd shot a cop he had no choice but to get out of the state for good. Jake grabbed some of his clothes and stuff and took off. I found out later after he left our place this morning he was shot and killed by cops at a roadblock. I asked if he tried to shoot it out and the cop who came to tell me just laughed. I'm sure they murdered him cause he'd shot one of theirs but Jake didn't intend any of this. He was a hustler, not a murderer. It's all Penn's fault and he's a dangerous guy. He's got no feelings. This man will do anything, and I mean anything to be sure he comes out okay. That's why I told you to watch your step this afternoon."

"God, Connie. I just can't believe it. "

"Well, you'd better believe it. Penn is no good and you'd better watch yourself. Don't care what he says …he's an evil, dangerous man. He only takes care of himself and anybody else is a throw-away. Just watch yourself."

Connie starts to cry and so does Gerri. They grab each others' hands across the seat, each communicating a bond of sisterhood forged by complicated grief.

Rog turns to Connie, " Listen Babe, as soon as this cools down I promise I'll fix Penn. That school will be looking for his replacement."

Connie pleads, looking at Rog, "Please don't talk like that. I can't bear the thought of losing you either the way the cops got Jakie or by you getting sent off to prison. Just let this go."

Rog doesn't answer Connie but he winks at Gerri and she's certain he'll get revenge. He smiles, " Gerri, want us to drop you at home now?"

"Nah…drop me here and I'll walk. My head is swimming and I need to think. Thanks for tellin me all of it. Right now I just feel horrible. Sad, very sad. Just horrible."

CHAPTER 22

TRUE COLORS

Gerri is about three blocks past her street but she welcomes the freedom to not hear any more for right now. She needs to get to the sanctity of her house. As she walks she tries to sort out Connie's version of what got Len and Jake killed. Gerri's in a state of shock that they are both dead. Regardless of Paulette's prophetic warnings, Gerri never, ever suspected about Dan and Connie or Miss Stinson or for that matter, any others before. But she also recalls he said he thinks of her differently. Regardless of his truthfulness or what might look bad for him, she thinks it means a lot more than anyone else can understand. Connie's version of things may have been well-meaning toward Gerri but maybe it wasn't exactly factual of Dan being so insidious as to set up Jake to walk into an ambush. Walking. Thinking. Walking. Thinking.

Gerri turns the corner onto Vassar and her chaotic thoughts will once again have to go to the back burner. More complication. Dan's car is parked next to the curb. Gerri surprisingly doesn't feel the slightest bit of fear as she approaches. He probably wants to be sure she's okay with the talk they had.

Dan gets out and leans across the roof of his car, "You okay? I was worried you might be feeling a little mixed up and could use a bit of support."

"Boy. You're telling me. Ya know, I'm not surprised to see you. I think you may be the only person in this whole world that truly knows me and what I need."

"Hop in. Surely we can have a few minutes to ride around and talk. Can't we?"

"Sure we can." Gerri opens the car door and slides into the center of the front seat.

Dan smiles his approval, "That's better. Gooood girl."

His comment about good girl sounds strangely tense but he's probably just trying to get past today's stress of all that's happened.

"So, tell me what you're thinking, Gerri."

"Well. After I left school, Connie and her boyfriend, Rog, came by and…"

"Don't you listen? There are some people you need to stay away from and she's one of them. She's trouble and you can't believe a single word of that lying little bitch. I *told* you to listen to me. Hear that? Listen to me? I can see I'm going to have to teach you not to listen to every snotty-nose school kid with an ax to grind or jealous of what you've got. Do I have to spell out every syllable and word for you?"
258

Gerri is shocked at his tone. "Sorry. Didn't mean to upset you. She just wanted to tell me about her brother being killed and how he'd shot that policeman. That's all."

"Yeah. I'll bet that's all. I'm sure she has a story that makes her brother look like a saint but who knows what happened and it's best left that way for you and me."

Dan pulls the car to the curb, "Look. Sorry for getting upset but you have to understand. Everything in my...uh, our future hinges on us, you and me sticking together. Right now and for the foreseeable future you need to listen to what I say. Not anybody else. No one. Got it?""

"Fine. I never meant any trouble."

Dan pulls back out onto the street and continues to drive slowly. Up one residential street and down another with no particular destination apparently in mind. Both Gerri and Dan are silent for a couple of minutes. Gerri glances at Dan ever so often and she thinks his features are softening. Apparently his anger has subsided.

"Dan, it's almost dark. I probably should get home before too long."

"Sure. I feel better after driving around. Do you?"

"Yeah. It's nice, quiet and seems to put some of the bad stuff out of mind for a while."

As they return to her street Gerri is going to let him take her all the way home if he wants and as usual she sees her dark house next to Paulette's with her porch light on as usual. It's like Paulette's lighthouse on what has been a sort of a treacherous coastline.

"Guess it doesn't matter too much when I get home. My dad's not home yet anyhow."

259

"Good. Then let's swing in here for a while." Dan turns on the little dirt road that leads to the woods across from Gerri's house. This brings back memories that make Gerri's stomach do flip flops but she doesn't say anything. She doesn't want to displease Dan or set him off again but she can't imagine how he'd be so familiar with this road and wooded area. Obviously it's a familiar spot to a lot of people, including Dan Penn. They reach the turn around, end of the dirt road. Gerri still sees Paulette's light in the distance shining brightly. She wonders if Paulette's camped outside on the steps trying to see what troubles Gerri will drag home tonight.

Without a word, and lacking even a sliver of tenderness, Dan reaches over and pulls Gerri firmly to him in a tight embrace and kiss.

He pulls away from the kiss, still so close she can feel his rapid breath, and he stares at her. His eyes are wide open and his lips apart, nostrils open wide with each of his quick and near- panting breaths . Dan takes one of her hands in his and brings it around to his lips and he kisses it. Gerri thinks this is more like what she's missing with Dan. She licks her lips and tosses her hair a bit and she feels one of Dan's hands behind her neck and in a more firm, directive way he pulls her forward. Their lips meet again. He pulls her tightly against him and she knows Dan is head over heels in love with her , not any of the others who perhaps are only fictitious, jealous lies. Nothing could be better than this instant and she allows herself to be lost in passion and love.

As they separate from the kiss again Dan's near expressionless face is staring at her and again she feels him firmly pulling her face toward him. He stares at her keeping one hand behind her neck and reaches slowly toward her with his other hand. His fingers toy with the necklace and he pulls it to the outside of her blouse. He runs his fingers from the necklace down the outside front of her blouse. She looks down and doesn't want to resist at all. He starts to unbutton her

260

top blouse button but she reaches up and puts her hand over his. Gerri's struggling to stay in the moment of passion but she's having flashbacks of this spot with Jake, the feelings of passion, how quickly things got loosened and pants pulled down, and how quickly she was pulled over on him and then everything else that quickly happened,
Over-thinking the past and present has the effect of cold water poured on the flames of passion. Any other time she would be a willing participant for what he wanted but tonight she just can't.

"Don't, Dan. Please don't. Not now. I just can't right now. Just hold me."

Dan does not take his hands off of her and his voice is harsh, "Can't? Or maybe you mean won't. Remember your promise? You do what Dan wants, when Dan wants. School must not be out for the day because it seems you still have a lessons to learn."

"What? What do you mean?"

That did not sound kind, loving or anything of the sort. From behind her neck she feels his firm pressure pulling her forward again-likely for another kiss, which is fine. But the pressure is pulling her face forward and down. Gerri pulls back, resisting his effort but he's stronger and he pulls her forward with more force. This is not good at all and it isn't gentle. Gerri pulls back much harder in protest and fear of something she can't handle. Now he's rough and pulling her head forcefully over toward him and down toward the seat or his lap. He applies enough force that her hair falls over the front of her face but even through her tousled hair she sees he's sitting straight up in the car seat and the entire front of his pants are open.

"It's okay, Gerri. More than any promises you make, this shows Dan that you'll do as Dan says like a good girl. "

Gerri is in full panic mode now. He's hurting her and she's never heard the tone he just used. He's holding one of her hands with one of his and pulling with his other hand on her neck so hard it hurts. She's got to get out of here!

"Stop! AWWWW! Stop! What are you doing?"

He pulls more and she pulls back against his force twisting her head from his grip, jerking her hand away from his and grabbing the door handle.

"AHHHHH! Don't touch me!"

She opens the door and rolls out of the car, by luck landing in an upright position. Gerri stumbles a couple steps into the dark, trying to keep her footing in the ruts of the dirt road and without so much as a look back she starts running toward the beacon of hope, Paulette's porch light. The skirt is pulled above her knees and she holds it with her left hand as she runs. Completely panicked she leaves the road and makes a straight line through the field of tall weeds, the quickest route to safety. She has a couple hundred yards to get to Paulette's. She's got to get away from him. Gerri glances back to be sure he's not running after her and he's not but she hears his car start and sees the headlights quickly turn around and bounce wildly up and down as he speeds along the rough dirt road to leave the woods. As Gerri clears the edge of the weeds she races across the street without looking either way. She has one goal and only one goal. She's got to get to Paulette's. As she races into Paulette's yard she glances back and she sees Dan's car is off the dirt road and coming up the street in her direction. He's now just a couple hundred feet from Gerri. The car engine is racing.

It's a miracle! Paulette's front door opens and she comes outside whistling carrying a broom probably to sweep her front stoop for the fifteenth time today. It's a miracle!

Ten feet from Paulette's steps, totally out of breath and scared out of her mind Gerri manages to get out a weak sounding, "Paulette."

Paulette jumps in fright and puts her hand over her heart, totally unaware of the rapidly unfolding crisis and Gerri's encounter in the woods across the street.   She simply hears her name and quickly turns to see Gerri totally out of breath standing at the base of her steps.

Paulette pays no mind to the car as it now slows and cruises past on the street. "So let me guess.   Up too late last night, forgot your homework at school or you went to the Sunshine Diner or…?"

"Oh God, Paulette. Help me! He's after me in his car."

"*What*? What are you talking about? *Who*?"

"Paulette, he's after me. You've got to help me!"

Paulette is taken totally by surprise but she drops her broom, comes flying off the steps to Gerri and wraps her arms around her.

"What's happened to you? You look like you've seen a ghost."

With that Paulette turns Gerri's shoulders toward her porch and they hurry up the steps. As they reach the door Gerri stops, turns and looks up and down the street. Paulette instinctively cranes her neck to see around Gerri and looks the same directions without knowing what she's supposed to see.

Then, almost at the same time they both spot the black car sitting about a hundred yards up the street partially blocked from view by a hedge. As if waiting in ambush, Gerri knows it's Dan's car.

263

"Oh my God. He's back! Don't let him get me! "

Paulette quickly pushes Gerri inside her house and as she draws the door closed she barks orders like a drill sergeant, "Stay inside. Don't come out. Stay! I'll be right back."

Gerri pulls back the curtain just enough so she sees Paulette grab the broom by her front door, dash down her steps and run in the direction of Dan's car all the while flailing her arms and the broom in the air and screaming, "Goddamn son-of-a-bitch! You want trouble? I'm comin with a shit storm like…"

The car pulls quickly away from the curb and speeds down the street before Paulette gets close enough to make broom contact. Paulette alters her course and runs into the middle of the street still waving the broom and screaming obscenities as the tail lights disappear in the distance.

CHAPTER 23

RISKY RESOLVE

Even after the car is gone Paulette remains in the middle of the street for a moment, hands on hips as if she'd singlehandedly vanquished the villain. Actually that's exactly what she's done and Gerri can already feel the safety net of Paulette and her home.

Paulette returns to her house, broom in hand, climbs the steps and as she enters the house she's audibly gasping for breath, the result of her angry, victorious sprint.

"Oh, dear. I need a Lucky, " and she goes straight to the coffee table and picks up her cigarettes.

Gerri doesn't say anything at first. She watches the ritual of Paulette methodically shaking one cigarette from the pack, nonchalantly packing it on her thumbnail and placing the cigarette on the edge of her lips. It must take practice because the cigarette seems to magically stick to her bottom lip right where Paulette places it. The cigarette is ceremoniously lit and the first inhale of smoke seems to be extra-long. It's followed by an equally long exhale of more smoke than Gerri can imagine being in Paulette's junior-sized lungs. Paulette pinches what must have been a bit of tobacco on her lip and makes a little quiet spitting sound before finally speaking.

"Okay. It's gonna… take… me a… minute to… catch my breath… but it's not me who needs to be talkin, so… you go ahead and start. What the *hell* is going on, Gerri? Was that the teacher? What's he doin chasin you?"

Gerri's mouth is opening to tell the frightening tale when Paulette steps right in front of her.

"Hold it a second. First things first. Are you hurt? Tell me if you are. You've got to tell me if you've been hurt."

"No, I'm just scared out of my mind. I was…well…he…"

"C'mon with me. I'm getting a cuppa joe and I'll just bet you could use one, too. Cream and sugar. Right?"

"Yeah. Sure. Okay."

Gerri follows Paulette into the kitchen watching her in amazement. Paulette is still struggling to catch her breath but putting out volumes of smoke clouds in rapid succession. Gerri can't tell if she's angry, just struggling for a breath or maybe she's scared, too.

"Sit right here while I'm getting the coffee and tell me everything. The last few minutes went way too fast for me to make any sense. I just happened to hear my name and there you were looking like it was life or death. I guess as it turns out it was a 'Lucky Strike' I was close by."

Paulette holds up her cigarette pack as she makes her little joke and her raspy little laugh would normally make Gerri smile but today a smile isn't anywhere on the horizon.

"I had no idea at first that anything was wrong. I never noticed any car when you first came up.   But as I said a second ago I'm guessing that was that teacher's car facing this way up by that hedge. Right?"

"Yeah. Dan Penn...Dan Penn's car."

"Listen to you.   Dan Penn.   He's a teacher for God sakes!   He's probably old enough to be your father. Well anyhow this isn't a lecture so I'm going to shut my trap.   I want you to tell me what happened. And listen to me, little one, please don't leave anything out of your story this time. I think it's high time we hear it all and put all this to rest…whatever it takes. Somehow I thought we were past this guy but obviously not. You look scared and I don't want you to gloss over anything 'cause I need to know exactly with all the little accurate details… so, let's hear it. What's going on?"

Coffee in hand, Paulette sits down at one end of the kitchen table and Gerri sits up a little straighter in her chair, holding her coffee cup with both hands. The warm coffee mug feels good and Gerri takes a small sip of the hot coffee. It tastes good.

"I really messed up, Paulette. I made a horrible mistake! Everything just got so out of control and he was so awful! He got them killed. He

266

planned it. They're dead. Jake Waltrip and the cop Len Ferguson. Dead!"

Gerri drops her gaze after blurting out the recent events and Paulette's mouth drops open. She stands up, steps forward, puts her cigarette in the ashtray, lays both her hands over Gerri's and gently presses.

"Whoa! People are dead and somehow you're mixed up in it? This can't be possible. You just take your time. Okay? Start at the beginning. I'm already lost. People are dead? I have no idea how you're involved in all this but take a deep breath and look at me. This will be okay, little one."

Paulette's face is drawn, her eyes squinting in concentration so Gerri begins, trying carefully to remember exactly what happened starting with agreeing to meet Dan in his room again after school.

"I knew I shouldn't but he was so sweet giving me this necklace this morning and so then I agreed to meet him."

"So you saw him earlier today and he gave you a necklace?"

"Yeah, this one." Gerri pulls the elongated cross from inside her blouse and holds it between her fingers.

Gerri goes on to tell of her arrival at Dan's classroom and being shoved to the side by a hysterical Connie Waltrip. She describes Dan's shocking news about Jake being killed. And how Dan insisted Gerri was the only girl for him and demanded she promise to be loyal to him. Gerri tells Paulette she thought Dan's insistence on her commitment sounded strange but probably the results of the confrontation with Connie and the news about Jake's death.

Gerri also thought it was strange that Dan never mentioned specifically that the policeman killed by Jake was none other than Len Ferguson

267

until he sort of worked the name into another strange statement that implied the two deaths were a good result for Gerri and Dan. Finally, Dan never did directly answer the question to about why Connie would confront him about her brother's death.

Gerri relates how she left school heading for home, very confused and trying to reconcile all the loose ends from her talk with Dan. It was along the walk home she met up with Connie and Rog. What Connie told Gerri filled in a lot of the missing pieces around Dan's vague details if they are all to be believed.

Connie accused Dan of basically trying to rekindle the fling that Connie says she and Dan had last year. Once he convinced Connie to go out with him he threatened and coerced Connie until she set up a middle of the night meeting between Jake and Dan. Dan told her he just wanted to make things right with Jake. But according to Connie, Jake didn't trust Dan so he got to the meeting point early and hid out of sight. A while before the meeting was to take place Jake saw Dan and Len together close by and figured Dan was setting Jake up for a takedown by Len.

Apparently Len hid within just a few feet of Jake and never realized Jake was right beside him. When it was time for the appointment and Dan was knocking on the back door of Brentwood's, Jake surprised Len and in the confrontation Jake shot and killed Len.

Jake went by Connie's as he was escaping from town and told her all this. Then before Jake could make good on his escape he got shot by police. Gerri tells Paulette about how Connie and Miss Stinson had previously been Dan's girlfriends so Gerri thinks maybe some of Connie's story may be tinted with jealousy.

"It's just all so complicated and confusing, Paulette. I don't know who to believe and I've gotten to where I really don't trust anybody one-hundred percent…except you of course."

"Holy jumpin shit! You couldn't make this stuff up if you tried. And of course it warms my heart that somehow I just feel I'm jumpin right in the middle of a deep cesspool with no life preserver. No more edited and sanitized versions of what's happening. It's no game and we have to do something. Have to. We'll sort it all out."

Gerri continues her story that soon after Gerri got out of Rog and Connie's car there was Dan waiting for her. Since it was nearly dark she didn't resist going across to the woods but very quickly Dan had become a totally different person. He scared her with his demands, referring to her as a good girl and then he tried to force her to have oral sex. Gerri was correct when she said to Paulette it wasn't anything about love or passion. He looked evil and was simply demanding she do it almost like he wanted to prove to her he owned her, and that's when she ran from his car.

"Paulette, I didn't imagine what he was doing when he first began pulling my head toward him. I guess I thought he was going to kiss me but when I realized what he was doing I was scared and it was sickening. For a second I thought it was too late and I just wanted out of that car and away from him. Oh, God Paulette. I didn't even see when he opened his pants. Maybe he was already like that when I got in the car. That's so sick. He's sick."

Paulette sits back, takes a deep breath and lights another cigarette, attending to all the little packing and lighting rituals.

"So you're sure hon, he kissed you, touched your hand and the back of your neck? He never tried to touch you anywhere else? Up here…Or down here?" Paulette's hand gestures toward her own body are plenty descriptive.

"No... Well, that's not quite true...he did take hold of the necklace as if he was admiring it ...but ...well...he ended up trying to unbutton my blouse but I put my hand up and said no and I think that's what triggered the next thing. I think he was going to make me do it just to show me he could make me do anything."

"I believe you and understand how you were not in the mood for any of the smoochie stuff tonight but *he* certainly didn't care about you at that point. I think you're right. He was going to make you do something to show you how powerful and in control he is and that's what makes creeps like him so dangerous to a young girl like you. He catches you off guard, unsuspecting and before you know it you're being hurt...badly. I just want to be sure about the touching thing. That was it? Right?"

"Yeah, cross my heart. That was it. But that was scary, Paulette. That's awful!"

"I know it is, honey but I've gotta tell you I was worried when you came in here that it may have been way more than that. Yes, it's bad enough but Gerri, my dear, it could have been a whole lot worse. Believe me. The first thing that crossed my mind is that you'd been forced to have sex. Ya know, raped. I was so scared and what little mind I have was racing trying to figure the next hundred things to do starting with your dad, the police, the hospital and all of the horrible after effects. I know it's bad but again, Gerri, it could have gone a lot worse. Well, let's see. We have killings, we have a pervert teacher tryin to lure a girl and then chasin her up and down the street. Whew!"

Paulette grinds out her cigarette in the half-full ashtray. She pushes and twists the mixture of tobacco and paper between her fingers into the

270

ashtray until it's unrecognizable bits of tobacco shreds and scraps of lipstick covered shards of paper. It's obvious to Gerri that her cigarette just paid the price of her anger.

"So, I guess the next thing to figure out is where we go from here. Today, tomorrow, day after, next week."

"Well, I can't go to school Monday. That's for sure. I'm afraid to go anywhere right now. Please can I just stay with you?"

"Of course you can stay here for now. You just need to stay right here with me until you're feelin better and your dad comes home."

"Oh, don't tell my dad, Paulette. Please don't tell him. I don't know what he'll do."

"Well, that's part of what we'll figure out. And remember I said we. But this has to stop once and for all."

"Just don't tell my dad."

"Now stop giving me a hard time already. We haven't even had time to unravel all of this."

Paulette folds her arms and gives a poster-child look of determination.

"I don't think there's anything more that's gonna complicate things tonight or even over the weekend. I suspect your Mr. Dan is by now in a dark little hole somewhere with wet pants trying to figure out how he's going to get out of all this without getting in trouble with the school and maybe the law, too. Hey, anything else you forgot to tell me?"

"No. I'm pretty sure that's all.

"One day at a time. I don't think I've ever told you but when I was just a kid in Oklahoma my daddy used to take me out to shoot guns. He wasn't much of a hunter but liked to target shoot. The one thing he would shoot was coyotes. He hated them because he said they weren't like the rest of animals. He said other animals hunt to eat and survive or defend themselves or their homes but coyotes sneak around whether they're hungry or not, looking for smaller animals that are hurt or defenseless. He said some folks are like coyotes, just harder to recognize. But I think we saw one today, didn't we?"

"You're not going to shoot him are you, Paulette?" Gerri's half standing from her seat.

"Oh, heavens. We haven't even figured all this out just yet. C'mon for heaven's' sakes. Maybe what he deserves but no, dear, no shootin today. I just meant there are other Dan Penn's in this world, the coyote types and you need to get better at spotting them. I'm not an I-told-you-so kind of person but I seem to recall my warnings were pretty clear. So I never really expected anything like this to happen...and for sure not just one day after we talked."

"Paulette, I swear I was on my way to school thinking how proud I was that I was going to put him in his place and be done with it. Honestly I was thinking it all was my fault for telling you things about him and maybe you were wrong and maybe he was okay and then, Paulette he was parked right there. He was so nice and I just knew everything was okay. Boy, I sure messed up. He seemed so nice and I thought you misunderstood. I'm so sorry. If I'd have listened to you and not doubted a bit of what you said, none of this would have happened. I'm so sorry."

"You don't need to apologize to me. You're innocent and pretty darn defenseless after just one Paulette talk. We'll get better at this. And by the way, not every time you're around a boy will it be bad. You just

272

have to be able to choose the good ones from the critters. And I guess I'd say the older the critter the worse cause they've had more practice and escaped a few times."

"Paulette, would you mind if I just lay down on your sofa for a few minutes?"

"Oh, honey. What's wrong? Don't you feel well?"

"No. I'm okay, just a little tired from all this and worrying about what's yet to come. I just need a few minutes to recoup."

"Sure. That's fine and in fact it will give me a chance to think. You just take your time. You don't need to worry. Everything's gonna be just fine."

Gerri lies down on the sofa and closes her eyes. She can already feel her heart isn't pounding quite as hard but she's still frightened out of her wits. She cannot imagine how she'll be able to go back to school with Dan being there. If only she never had to see Dan Penn again. But even Paulette can't fix that.

"It feels good just to lie down for a minute, Paulette. Must be the stress."

"That's good. You just relax as best you can. I know you've heard and seen a lot today. While you're resting here's what I'm thinking. If I...er... or we go to the police they'll have to question everybody including your dad, the school folks, you and Dan Penn. Of course he'll deny everything. It could get complicated. I don't know how much to trust those school people or the police. They all seem like a bunch of politicians sometimes and ya know, try to take care of their own. It would not serve any purpose if the results turn into sort of a he-said, she-said argument. And I also have to tell you, while I love your dad and I certainly loved your mom I've always been surprised at how your folks dealt with problems.

I don't know if you even remember when your dad parked on the street a while back and somebody came along and sideswiped his car. Luckily the guy stopped but it was almost as if Stephen felt like his parked car had jumped out and hit the other car. He was so nervous and I kept thinking why are you so nervous cause it was the other guy who hit your car. He kept laughing and apologizing for his car being on the street. I know the guy who hit your car was bumfuzzled by Stephen's display and he wanted to make it right with money but I listened to your dad tell him the damage wasn't bad and just forget it. I couldn't believe what I was hearing. So I'm just telling you this because I don't want to get the hornets' nest stirred up and find out your dad's going to laugh it off or act like he's afraid to wade into this with both feet. 'Cause, Gerri, this *isn't* okay and whatever we decide to do I *am* gonna be sure this stops real quick... once and for all. I'm steppin way over my bounds here but I'm in this till it's done."

"So what can be done?"

"I think maybe Monday I need to personally pay Mr. Danny Boy a visit and explain things like Paulette knows how. Just maybe I can nip this in the bud and take care of it. If it goes the way I think, then you won't ever have to worry about meeting Penn in the hallway or anywhere else. By the way, gimme that necklace and cross. I'm gonna return it to him. You okay with me doing this?"

Gerri unfastens the necklace and hands it to Paulette. "Well, how can talking to him solve anything? He'll just deny everything. What can you possibly say to him?"

"Gerri, a good magician never shows how the tricks are done. I just need to know you trust me to take care of it. If it doesn't work then we

274

can go to the school, your dad or even the police. But the more I think about it the more I'm feelin fired up about this and see no reason why I can't get it resolved. What do you say? Shall I try?" She strikes a strongman pose and flexes her biceps as if to make big muscles.

Paulette says she'll call the school first thing Monday and ask for a conference with Mr. Penn. She'll make no hint of anything wrong, more like a thank you session. Gerri knows his free period and he doesn't have a second period class from nine-fifty until ten-fifty in the mornings so if Paulette's lucky she'll suggest perhaps she can meet Mr. Penn at ten o'clock. Paulette knows enough about the school procedure that she'll check in at the office and ask if she can meet Mr. Penn privately in the teachers' lounge since she smokes. If it all comes together like Paulette thinks, she and Dan Penn will be face-to face Monday morning.

Gerri finds herself feeling uneasy and beginning to squirm as Paulette repeats her vague plan.

"Maybe we should forget this and maybe if I just make up an excuse for my dad and stay home next week and then go back week after next and maybe everything will have blown over. I can just avoid going near his classroom and..."

Paulette jumps straight up from her sitting position.

"Gerri! You've got to stop this! This is exactly what I'm talking about when dealing with a predator. You stay away from school to avoid him and he's the one who's done wrong. You sneak around your own school. You run to school because you're afraid of seeing him. You remain the injured, defenseless one and the critter feels more powerful because nobody's gonna call his hand on it."

"I guess you're right but I don't see how you can…"

Gerri, after I divorced my husband I dated another guy and it looked like we might get married but there was something I just didn't trust. Down deep I figured he just wanted the money from my dad's farm and when I stood eye to eye and confronted him with that, he didn't even argue. I told him he had no balls or maybe they'd just shrunk to peanut size from lack of use. He didn't like that a whole lot but he left rather than even argue. No balls, Gerri. Here's the interesting part. Sometimes us gals gotta have balls, too. Well geez... I hope ya know what I mean. You have to stand up and show your fangs and be ready to fight for what's right. Not everything turns out rosy, but ya have to try. And right now, little girl, you're the most important thing in Paulette's life and I'm takin some big balls to the playground Monday."

As she talks Paulette waves both arms and with her legs spread apart sways her hips as if she's dangling something. The more she talks, the more she means serious business.

Gerri's laughing through tears at Paulette's tirade, still frightened but safe and feeling like she has a true champion in her corner.

"Okay, Paulette. I trust you. Just tell me what you want me to do and I'll do it. I won't let my end of it down."

"Young lady, that's a girl. That's balls! Big brass bowling balls."

Once again, Paulette has an entertaining way of getting Gerri to a confident state of mind. Maybe part of it's from the stress or nervous energy but Gerri can't remember when she's laughed this hard. Why is it so easy to find things to laugh about with Paulette even when things have been so unhappy? She recalls laughing with her mom and dad but that seems like a distant memory. So very much has happened. Gerri wonders if her life will ever be where she can laugh like this every day. Many times every day.

CHAPTER 24
ONCE AND FOR ALL

"Oops. Your dad just drove in. I hope ten minutes made you feel better."

"Oh gosh. He's home? But yeah. I'm fine. I'm not going to say a word to him about any of this.

Gerri goes home but never mentions the day's events to Stephen and he isn't inquisitive. Out of Paulette's presence Gerri feels guilty for not telling Stephen everything but she's afraid Paulette's plan will be sent topsy-turvy if her dad gets involved. A few casual comments and each of them turn in for the night.

The weekend is uneventful. Gerri spends the weekend studying and reading, anticipating Monday when everything may come to a head. Stephen seems pleased to spend a quiet weekend at home and he only leaves the house once to stop by the grocery store.

Finally Monday arrives and it could have been a clue to Stephen this morning but he misses it entirely. In Gerri's most innocent and loving voice she asks her dad to drop her at school. Even though she knows it's totally out of character from her rotten, rebellious attitude of late, he doesn't question it except that it will be a little early for her to get to school. Gerri tells him that's fine because she needs to study until school starts. She feels like such a phony! Paulette is obviously right about going to school a little early because as Gerri and Stephen pass the school parking lot, Gerri doesn't recognize the three cars in the lot but she's sure of one thing, none of them are Dan's.

She waves goodbye to Stephen and goes into the school. The corridors are dark, cold and a sudden rush of fear washes over Gerri. What if she

277

comes face-to-face with Dan Penn? What will she do? She tells herself she's got to stop thinking like this. Gerri takes a deep breath and remembers Paulette's wisdom. It's very unlikely that Dan Penn ever gets to school early and even if he does, he isn't likely to be roaming the halls. He's probably in his room or the teachers' lounge so Gerri's to stay as far away from those two areas as possible. He might even be parked up the street waiting for her to walk past. Walking close to the wall of lockers, she passes through the hallway toward where her first class will be and luckily on the way another classroom's door is open and the lights are on. Mrs. Dugger is at her desk and looks like she is having a cup of coffee and grading papers. Gerri figures she was good at being phony with her dad so she might as well continue her skills with Mrs. Dugger. She lightly knocks on the door facing and stands there at the door with a pleasant smile.

"Hi Mrs. Dugger. I'm sorry to bother you but is it okay if I just sit at one of the desks and study until some other kids start arriving?"

"Of course, Gerri. Just sit anywhere you like. I'm just doing a few papers I didn't get finished last night."

Within about 30 minutes Gerri hears a trickle of students, then a steady flow of students and the recognizable voices of some of her first period classmates trudging through the hall. So thus far, the day is successful.

Once in class, she forces herself to get into the swing of the school day. She's such a phony but has to admit when she participates in some of the discussions and pays attention the class goes much faster. Pretty soon the bell rings ending the first period. Gerri gathers her books and goes into the hall thinking about her second hour class. Suddenly, there's Dan Penn coming down the hall directly toward her. Her mouth goes dry and her pounding heart nearly jumps out of her chest. She gives an audible gasp, squeezing her books to her chest like a parachute pack, awkwardly turning into the next doorway and stepping to the side of the room so she won't be visible from the hallway. She's relieved that Miss Winters is in the classroom and she's writing on the blackboard so she hasn't noticed Gerri pressed against the wall trying to be invisible but breathing like she'd just completed a marathon. Surely he's gone past the room by now and maybe he didn't even see her so she takes a breath and inches her way along the wall toward the door. Simultaneously Miss Winters turns and gives a surprised look as Dan Penn's head suddenly juts through the open door.

"Good morning, Julie."

Then he turns his head directly toward Gerri and looks directly at her but doesn't say anything. His face is not kind nor handsome. It's evil looking and his eyes glare at Gerri as if to gloat about scaring her.

Miss Winters is surprised to see both of them, "Oh, hi, Dan. I didn't hear you at the door. How are things going for you today? And… oh my, Gerri, I'm sorry I didn't even hear you come in or know you were standing there."

Dan mumbles something, laughs out loud at his private joke and then his head disappears as quickly as it had appeared.

Gerri is plastered against the wall in terror.

"Gerri, did you need to see me about something? I didn't even know you were there. I'm sorry."

"No, Miss Winters. I just stepped in here out of the hall for a second to make sure I hadn't left one of my books in my last class."

Gerri edges slowly toward the door thinking what if he's right outside the door waiting?

"Okay. Did you find it?"

279

"Yes. I'm fine now."

Gerri looks into the hall and sees Dan going toward the teachers' lounge. That may be why he was in this hall or maybe he was looking for Gerri just to scare her. She hates being afraid but Paulette's a hundred percent right. The coyote's getting stronger and bolder to make her afraid, circling to toy with the prey. She feels physically sick as she sits in second period class, a sort of queasy-sick, not like throw-up sick. When the bell rings she's very careful to look up and down the halls as far as she can see just to make sure the coast is clear.

Third hour passes quickly and now that it's lunchtime, she has a nagging fear about seeing him and knowing that will happen sixth hour no matter what. Hopefully there will be strength in numbers and she'll just be phony one more time today and play like nothing is bothering her. She will avoid eye contact. She's not worried about him saying anything to her in class and then as soon as the bell sounds she'll get out of the room in the first wave of students that leave even if he calls her name or tries to get to the door first. Gerri also considers simply skipping sixth hour and see how the dust settles at day's end.

But down the hall Gerri sees a familiar person by the front doors, the unmistakable and heroic Paulette Guthrie pushing the outside doors open as she's leaving the school building. Now Gerri's really afraid of seeing Dan later in class because she has no idea of the outcome of Paulette's visit.

Even with Paulette's assurances from yesterday, Gerri's scared out her wits. As she passes a doorway or intersecting corridor she walks in the center of the hallway giving wide berth to be sure there's plenty of room to avoid a surprise encounter.

She can't imagine what Paulette said to him. What if it didn't go well and it made him more determined than ever to do something evil. It's easy enough for Gerri to imagine how Dan would be reluctant to involve the police since his going to the police about Jake backfired so badly. But her fears this day are for naught. For the remainder of today there's never a hallway passing and though she plans to go to his class when the time comes Gerri cuts class and hides out in the girls' bathroom. She'll worry about getting an excuse tomorrow.

When school is over, Gerri cautiously comes out the doors and looks carefully in the teachers' parking lot to see if Dan's car is there. It's not there. Maybe he's waiting for her. It will take a few minutes to get home and Gerri's plan is to go directly to Paulette's. She's wondering the results of Paulette's visit. Paulette said her intention is to put a stop to him bothering Gerri once and for all. But how can she do that?

"Goin' my way, Sailor?" Gerri jumps from the surprise but oh my gosh it's certainly a welcome voice.

"Paulette, what are you doing here? I didn't even see you."

"Didn't I tell you yesterday to trust me and I figure that includes a second walk to this school today and the exercise will do me good. Well, I'm not so sure that walking in these shoes is good for anybody and I'm certain they're not the most comfortable way to make the trip but it's fine. So how was your day?"

"Fine. Well, you know, as good as it could be I guess. Watching out for him every time I was out in the halls. I was a little scared at first but this afternoon I got better as the day went on. But I chickened out when it came time for his class. I didn't go. I hid in the bathroom."

"Aww. Tell me ya didn't. Oh well, if you thought it was best, then it was for the best." Paulette smiles and the bright sun shows the nicotine stains on her teeth but Gerri loves everything about Paulette. It's as if she's eight feet tall, bullet-proof and indestructible.

281

"C'mon, Paulette. I'm dying to know what you said to Dan."

"Who? You know I'd rather you'd refer him some other way other than if he's a friend. He's no friend. How about calling him Slimeball or Jerkoff. Oh, forget it. Call him whatever you want. I don't think you have to worry about him."

"Tell me what happened. I'm dying to know."

"Well, you're just gonna have to wait a little longer until we get to my house. Right now it's all I can do to walk in these slippers on this concrete and force that nasty fresh air into my lungs. Ugh! But when we get to my house, I'll kick these off, have a Lucky and a cup of coffee and tell you all about it. I hope the suspense is killin' ya. Want a cuppa joe when we get home?"

"A cup of what?"

"Oh, never you mind, honey. That's just what GI's call coffee. Ya know cuppa joe as in GI Joe, cuppa mud…"

"What's a GI? Mud?"

"Oh, Dearie, you and I have a lot to cover. What a sheltered little bubble you 've been living in. Maybe good, maybe not so good but Paulette's gonna get you out of any bubbles and into real life. Honey this is the fifties and things are a happenin'! You hear about this rock and roll thing? Elvis?"

Gerri laughs, "Of course. I think it's all really cooool, Daddy-o."

They laugh and slowly walk. Gerri's not even thinking about black cars or slimy guys. She feels so good to be with this little dynamo, this little woman beside her, several inches shorter but mighty in strength. Big balls. Paulette's rattling on about something and Gerri's silently laughing. It's a wonderful, pleasant respite.

282

They reach Paulette's house and Gerri drops her books inside the door and automatically goes directly to the kitchen table. She knows the routine and Paulette's kitchen table is where business is conducted in the Guthrie house. The cigarette and coffee ritual is familiar and somehow seems like a comforting prelude to an entertaining story that Gerri's dying to hear. Finally she can't wait any longer for the story to begin.

"C'mon Paulette. You're just doing this on purpose. Tell me what happened."

 "Oh, honey. You'll be bored by the details. Let's just say…just us girls… that Mr. Daniel Penn is convinced I'm serious and he sincerely is sorry for the error of his ways. I just bet at this moment he realizes he's in the wrong line of work, in the wrong city, in the wrong state."

Gerri leans forward on the edge of her seat. "Stop, Paulette. I want to know what you really said and did."

"Well, honey okay. You told me his free hour was from ten minutes till ten until ten to eleven and since I called it was all set that he'd be in the teachers' lounge to meet me at that time. So I got to the school a little after nine-thirty. That Miss Stinson took me from the office to the teachers' lounge and she said even though I was a little early I could just wait and she even had a little sign she hung on the door that said the lounge was in use for a private conference. Perfect! Miss Stinson said that after I met with Mr. Penn I could just leave by the front door at the end of that hallway. By the way, that Miss Stinson seems to be a real nice young lady. I hope she's not too much of a good friend anymore to Danny-Boy, if you know what I mean.

Well, I walked into the lounge with Miss Stinson and met another couple of teachers who were just finishing their break. When the bell rang they left and in came Mr. Danny-Boy. We did all the sweet little

283

introductions but he clearly was puzzled. He didn't remember me from the funeral and he didn't recognize me from running at his car Friday night and I could tell he didn't know who I was or why I was there. He didn't recognize my name of course. So he was on his best behavior, best handsome smile and very polite...just like a snake in the grass."

"Oh this is gonna be good."

"Yeah, it gets a bit better. By the way, I'm gonna have another ciggie. Want one?"

"Paulette! I don't smoke. I want to know what happened."

"Okay. Okay. When I saw he was alone, I thought I'd play it up a little..ya know…kinda tough. Paulette style.”

" I know Paulette, balls at the playground." Both of them start laughing at this.

"Ya know. I thought and thought about this in great detail. Some of it we talked about Friday but I had to be sure if I was gonna do this right… well, I had to be sure I solved this problem as I said before, once and for all. I suppose the right thing would have been to go to your dad and let him handle it. You are his daughter. But I just didn't think your dad would handle it right. And I'm willin to take any consequences from this that come my way. I mean I'm not even a member of your family but I just want to get it wrapped up. I thought through going to the police myself…”

"C'mon, Paulette."

" So I began to think what might be the way to have him *want* to be far away from here. Now that's something I thought I could handle. So we were all smiley from shakin hands and as we stood there I told him I found something of his that I needed to return. I batted my eyes and smiled as sexy as I could. I was so cute. I had your little cross necklace in my fist so he couldn't see what it was. Well, he smiled and in fact I think he was sort of excited about what I'd found of his. So, I blinked my eyes at him and asked him to hold out his hand and when he held out his hand, palm up, I drove the tip of that cross right into the palm of his hand. I don't think it went all the way through but on second thought it might have, cause it was buried up to the cross bar." Paulette makes a powerful overhand swing like she's stabbing something. "Just like that. Drove it home! Right in the Son-of-a-bitch's palm!"

Gerri gasps but doesn't say anything. She puts one hand across her mouth.

"He stumbled a step back, his eyes got huge, he grunted and groaned out loud and twisted his face like he was going to faint or scream, but he didn't. He grabbed and pulled at the necklace. It took him about three times of pulling to get it out. Then he knew why I was there. He's sure a lot bigger than I am but he wasn't going to do anything. He was in shock. I tossed a handkerchief across the front of his face and when he reached up for it his face was bright red and a big old vein in his forehead was bulging out...a pretty telltale sign of both his pain and rage, and spraying me with a mist of spit while mumbling something about having me arrested."

"Oh my God!"

"Okay, okay. Here's how it went. Now he's been jabbed by a crazy woman, his hand is hurtin' real bad and he has out my cute little hankie for a bandage. He's wonderin what's next? So then I said to Danny-Boy..."

Paulette puts her hands on her hips and sways them as she is really enjoying her own story.

"Whoa there, Cowboy. Take a deep breath and shut your Goddamn mouth. You look carefully at what I've got and you listen *real* careful to me. "

Paulette opens her handbag on the kitchen table and pulls a small revolver out, laying it on the table. "Let me introduce you to Revlon."

"Oh my God, Paulette!"

" Ya see, Gerri this morning I took Revlon in my handbag, wrapped it in a hankie and so when I tossed the hankie in his face I already had pulled Revlon out. I poked it really hard right on the forehead of his milky white face. I pushed on it so hard it pushed him backwards another step and he fell or sat real hard into one of those big old chairs in that lounge. His eyes were about the size of dinner plates and he was sitting spraddle-legged with me standing now in between his legs."

"Is that a real gun?"

" Revlon is *very* real. So anyhow he's trying to put his hands up, hold the handkerchief on his hand and not get shot by this crazy woman and all the while Revlon is cocked and denting his forehead. I think it's safe to say I'd gotten his attention so now's the time to make my point and then get the hell outta there. Anyhow, I was gonna grab his tie with my left hand and pull his face toward me but instead I was so close I reached forward real quick with my left hand and grabbed him …well, a little South of his tie while he was sittin there... like this."

Gerri's mouth is gawking , wide open.

Paulette continues her demonstration, right hand as if she's holding the pistol on Dan Penn's forehead and with her left hand she swings her left hand like she's pitching a softball underhand. It ends by grabbing in a cupped-hand and then she makes a squeezing motion like squeezing a lemon.

" At this point I had Danny-Boy well in hand."

Paulette playfully acts like she's elbowing Gerri and Gerri's laughing hysterically.

"Paulette! You're making this up. You can't just walk into school and do this, stab him in the hand, pull a gun on him and grab his …you know whats."

Paulette laughs, "The hell you say! Can. Did. Know something? Funny you put it like that 'cause that's almost exactly what Danny-Boy whispered with his crossed eyes staring at what he could see of my pistol on his forehead and my hand squeezing his 'you know whats' as you call them. So I told him to shut his weasel mouth and listen to me. I told him I didn't originally come there to shoot him but after meeting him face to face I was seriously considering it. I told him if he ever even thought of looking at my Godchild, Gerri DeMore again we might as well get it over right now by twistin off his little package and leavin a small powder burn on the bridge of his nose- right at this minute. He was very silent and I told him it's his choice. Or, I said he can go screaming down the hall when I leave and call the cops and then we'll see who goes to jail the longest-him or me. And eventually I'd get out and find him and at that point finish it. He was in pain but he got the message.

Of course Gerri, I used a couple of extra words that you won't find in the Sunday crossword puzzle. Words that I think he needs for his education and understanding. Mr. Daniel Penn. I will say just between you and me, he really looked relieved when I finished talking, loosened my grip on him and put Revlon back in my purse. He never said a word and I actually thought he was gonna wet his britches or faint. So I walked out, came home and hid Revlon for a while in case he was really stupid and called the cops. Well, by this afternoon I knew he'd absorbed our little chat and so when I came to meet you I was feelin' pretty brave so I brought Revlon along just in case. Made me feel good. Made me feel like *we* won. But Revlon's gotta go back out of sight again. I hadn't even had it out since my divorce when I first started living alone.

Gerri's shaking her head in disbelief and laughing so hard she can't stop.

Paulette takes out a Lucky Strike, starts through her routine and finally it's lit. She pauses for a second and then offers the lit cigarette to Gerri.

"Gerri. I know you don't smoke but this has been a hell of a day for us both and you can try it if you want. Or you can just put it out in the ashtray. Or you can just hold it. It's just one of those things that when you and I talk, it's different. It's you and me. We are just what we are. I swear on my life little woman that I'll never be nothing' more…and certainly nothin' less. I love you like my own daughter…if I had any kids. I want you to know I'm here for you and I'm there with you…in other words. You need me for *anything* and I'm your gal. Hell or high water. Deal?"

"Oh, that's a deal? Can I tell you something, Paulette?"

"Of course you can. You can ask me anything, anytime and I'll answer. If I don't know an answer, we'll figure it out. No…that's not quite the way it ought to be. If I don't know, you and I will go to lunch, then we'll go shopping and *then* we'll figure it out together."

Gerri's struggling to talk, tears streaming down her cheeks. Happy tears.

288

"Oh, Paulette I have done so many things wrong . I just didn't know as much as I thought I did. I've been trying to live a fairy-tale. I know my mom and dad love me and probably did the best they knew how but it wasn't reality. I just wanted to hurry and grow up. But it was a fairy-tale just the same. When my mother died, I truly felt like I was orphaned. Not like I was sent to live somewhere else, but as if I was suddenly separated from everything that was familiar to my life. I know that was never intended but it happened and last week I came to the conclusion I had to make my own way in life- orphan or not. I felt so lonely and I was sure I was going to live the rest of my life like that. Then Dan Penn gave me a better feeling about myself and just everything in general. You know, it's funny, I think I knew down deep it was artificial. I knew he was too old. But Paulette, I was so miserable I just wanted somebody to care. And I guess I may have felt more about Dan Penn because I wanted my dad to show me some love and attention. I guess down deep I thought I was getting that from Dan. Boy, am I ever nuts!"

"No, honey. That's not crazy. Not crazy at all. You make an awful lot of sense."

"But being here with you, Paulette, I feel excited about going to school and doing fun things. Things I can always tell you about."

Paulette and Gerri hug and Gerri senses something very new to her. She's hugged her mom, she's hugged her dad, She's hugged Dan Penn, she's hugged relatives and she's hugged perfect strangers at the funeral; but hugging Paulette at this moment she feels Paulette's energy and trust pass to her as they embrace and a bond is forged.

"I'll always have scars from Mom's death and my dad will probably never change but I think the open wounds will eventually heal as long as I have you. I'll always think of you as my mom from now on, if that's okay with you.   I 'm done being an orphan and I want to learn how to be a good mom, like you, when I have kids of my own."

"Sure, kid. But be careful what you wish for. Ya' know you're gonna have to get some gold shoes...and promise me the only Revlon you'll ever use is lipstick."

They laugh together as only a mom and daughter can laugh.

Suddenly they both become silent at the knocking on the front door. Paulette motions for Gerri to stay where she is sitting. From the look on Paulette's face Gerri thinks Paulette believes it might be the police to take her away.   Even with all the bravado and stories it's apparent that both are petrified.   Paulette slowly opens the door and there stands Stephen.

Paulette gives an audible sigh of relief. "Hi Stephen. I'll bet you're looking for Gerri and I'm the guilty culprit. I've had her here entirely too long. Come on in."

Stephen smiles politely and steps inside the door.

 "Oh, it's fine that she's here and maybe it's good that you're both here together. I need to say some things and it's appropriate for you both to hear."

Here we go again. Gerri's stomach tumbles like she's falling off a cliff. What more can she possibly endure than what she's been through the last two weeks? Is this where he says he's going to run away and marry Betsy's mom and truly abandon her?

"I know for the past weeks Gerri's been closer to you, Paulette, than anyone. With her mother not doing well and then the worst possible happening, I've been the most irresponsible father, husband and friend in the world. I was feeling sorry for myself and allowed myself to be

290

open to anything that gave me some comfort. Gerri, I'm not sure it's even fair to ask for you to forgive me but I'm asking anyhow. Right here in front of Paulette. I was not fair with your mother. She knew what I was doing but our way of dealing with it was to act like everything was okay. It wasn't. She was hurting and worried. I've been totally selfish and self-centered. I've been in total denial about life, problems, my relationship with your mom, my relationship with you, Gerri…just everything. Susie was always so concerned about you, Gerri and she didn't want you or anyone else around here to know about our marriage troubles. And so, between the two of us we did absolutely nothing to talk about or resolve our problems. I was concerned in words only. I see that so clearly. You are at an age when you need very close confidants and I just left you hanging on the clothesline in the wind. That's not fair. I'm so very sorry. And I ask you to forgive me."

"Oh, it's..."

"No, just let me finish. I will not see Beverly Alder again. I will apply for the job of being the best father I can be to you. Paulette, I don't know what would have happened to this young lady if you hadn't stepped in. There are all sorts of unsavory people in this world who might try to take advantage of a young girl if given the chance and..."

"Really, Stephen? There are people Gerri might run into that she wouldn't be able to trust?" Gerri and Paulette break out laughing.

Stephen stands looking surprised and puzzled by their laughter. " I really didn't mean it to be a joke..."

"No, you didn't. And it's not a joke but we've had a little thing that's near and dear to us that rings a bell with what you just said. Shall we tell your dad, Gerri?"

291

"Yeah, it's kinda embarrassing cause I was so stupid but I think he needs to know."

Paulette and Gerri give Stephen the whole Dan Penn saga and Stephen ranges from rage like Gerri's never seen to holding his face in his hands and openly weeping. Real live emotions. Her father! Of course he couldn't get through the teachers' lounge part of the story without laughing in disbelief.

"I'm going to the principal and the school board president tomorrow and I'll be sure he's gone. Gone from teaching in the state of California and my guess is he will never be allowed to show up at any school again."

"Oh, Dad, I think it will be okay now. Maybe it's better if we just get back to normal."

"Gerri, what I just told you when I apologized was that I intend to change in every way. That's not going to be easy for me but if the very first opportunity I have to stand up, well if I muff this, then it's all hot air. Look, your best friend, Paulette took the bull by the horns or however you'd like to rephrase that," and he made an underhand grabbing motion to illustrate his point.

They all laugh. Stephen hasn't missed a single detail and he's not backing away.

"I *will* see the principal and I *will* see the school board president. And even though I think it may be a little soon, Gerri, I want to talk to you and *we* can decide about *our* future together. Just the two of us. You know me all too well, particularly my worst side. I was thinking it might be healthy for us to plan how to adjust to life for the two of us. I know how to play the piano and sing all those corny songs we used to sing and I'll teach math or not teach, whatever seems to be the best for us."

292

Gerri stands up and her dad holds his arms wide apart. She runs to him and so does Paulette so the three of them laugh and hug. Paulette has tears streaming down her face.

" I hope the two of you will have a little time for Paulette once in awhile and that I can even come over to your house once in awhile to check up on the both of you. Ya know, just to be sure you're eating properly and keeping the house reasonably clean."

"Paulette, you're family and you'll always be. You'll have your own key...and even a place in our house in case you ever want to stay over or even if you just need some extra storage...ya know like for glittery shoes or exotic cosmetics… particularly Revlon. Never know when someone might need a little *pointed and colorful* discussion."

www.ingramcontent.com/pod-product-compliance
Lightning Source LLC
Chambersburg PA
CBHW060856250626
47159CB00008B/2768